The Boi of Feather and Steel

The Metamorphosis duology

The Girl of Hawthorn and Glass
The Boi of Feather and Steel

The Boi of Feather and Steel

ADAN
JERREAT-POOLE

Publisher: Scott Fraser | Acquiring editor: Rachel Spence | Editor: Shannon Whibbs
Cover design and illustration: Sophie Paas-Lang
Printer: Marquis Book Printing Inc.

Library and Archives Canada Cataloguing in Publication

Title: The boi of feather and steel / Adan Jerreat-Poole.
Names: Jerreat-Poole, Adan, 1990- author.
Series: Jerreat-Poole, Adan, 1990- Metamorphosis duology ; 2.
Description: Series statement: The metamorphosis duology ; 2
Identifiers: Canadiana (print) 2021011004X | Canadiana (ebook) 20210110058 | ISBN 9781459746848 (softcover) | ISBN 9781459746855 (PDF) | ISBN 9781459746862 (EPUB)
Classification: LCC PS8619.E768 B65 2021 | DDC jC813/.6—dc23

We acknowledge the support of the Canada Council for the Arts and the Ontario Arts Council for our publishing program. We also acknowledge the financial support of the Government of Ontario, through the Ontario Book Publishing Tax Credit and Ontario Creates, and the Government of Canada.

Printed and bound in Canada.

Dundurn Press
1382 Queen Street East
Toronto, Ontario, Canada M4L 1C9
dundurn.com, @dundurnpress

For monstrous feminists, queer witches,
and magical enbies everywhere

Part One:
Exile

One

TAV

Tav was dreaming.

The river was frozen over with thick black ice. When they knelt down, they could see blue-and-white flames trapped under the surface. They placed a palm over the ice, feeling the cold burn like fire. The flames flickered wildly, trying to reach their hand.

A hairline crack snaked its way between their feet. Tav stepped back, uneasy. As they watched in horror, the river tore itself in two, ice and water and earth splitting apart. Tav stumbled and fell, narrowly avoiding the spears of ice stabbing the air like a fractured bone puncturing skin.

A great chasm stretched across the frozen river. Tav found themselves on one side of the fierce water, which gushed through a cracked mirror of black ice.

A boy climbed out of the depths of a world splintered by frost and starlight.

Cam. Eyes like stone, hard and cold. Blue veins glistening on exposed skin.

Cradled in his arms lay the crumpled body of a girl, a sprig of hawthorn growing from her chest.

She was dying.

"I brought your Heart," he said, stepping onto Tav's side of the river. The curve of his smile was a fish hook. He stopped an arm's length from where Tav crouched, their fingernails etching lines into the crystalline landscape. He waited.

Tav rose slowly, unsteady on their feet. Sweat dripped down their neck. They could smell rot.

Pain surged through their shoulder blades. They cried out as great feathered wings burst from their back. The wings were black as ink, with an oily lustre of gold and purple and green. As the pain began to subside like a waning crescent moon, Tav found Cam's eyes and forced the breath from their lungs into the shape of a single command.

"Give her to me."

"You've left me no choice," he said. His fingers curled around the hawthorn, twisting brutally. The girl whimpered.

"Let her go!" Tav beat their wings and white flames burned through the ice at their feet. The ice floe was unstable, and one wrong move could lead to hypothermia and drowning. The stars glittered overhead, their lights reflected in the dark mirror. The universe was burning.

The branch snapped, and the girl screamed, a body made of bone and glass crying out in agony.

Tav lunged, nails like talons curving around Cam's throat.

When it was over, Tav was on all fours, frost licking their knees. Blood everywhere. Body parts were scattered across the ice. Tav wetted their lips and looked down, catching a glimpse of their reflection —

the face of a witch.

Tav woke suddenly and found themselves back in their apartment, the sheets soaked through with sweat. In the dim room lit only by distant streetlights, the shadows looked like blood. Tav fumbled for the bedside lamp. When the yellow pool of light showed no evidence of a crime scene, the anxiety curling its claws around their wrists and ankles released its hold. It was just a dream; already it was fading. Tav listened to the sound of their pounding heart, waiting for the rhythm to slow. Proof that they were human.

Tav closed their eyes against the pain of sudden brightness, but it was too late. Already a headache was spreading through their temples and pushing into the corded muscles of their neck.

They switched off the light and lay back down, opening their eyes to the dark. In the distance sirens sang out, the clear, sharp pitch breaking through the dull roar of engines that never ceased. Threaded through the darkness was the magic of the Heart, which wound its way through walls and doors and flesh and bone. Tav fought the urge to reach out and grab it, to make themselves strong, to heal their pain, to take that power all for themselves and use it.

Use *her*.

Eli was sleeping on the couch with only a wall between them. The thought sent a shiver of excitement through Tav's body, but of a different kind. They kicked off the lounge pants they'd fallen asleep in and lay back in their boxers. Eli's hair would be messy, her body tangled in the blanket. Tav remembered her body; they had followed the path of her collarbone with their mouth, traced the curve of her waist with their hand …

Tav rolled their face into the pillow to stifle a moan. They lost themselves to fantasy before sleep finally returned for them.

In the morning they had forgotten about the dream.

THE HEART

Eli was sitting cross-legged on the roof. It was early, and the moon still hung behind a shred of cloud even as the sun began its ascent into the sky. Eli wanted to bear witness to the funerary procession of the dead rock as it travelled around the Earth. She wanted to remind herself what was at stake.

She had woken from a nightmare and had been unable to fall back asleep. The dream returned suddenly — the sound of a thousand wasps, the sharp edge of a blade, and the eyes of a girl who had been trained to kill without mercy. Eli shook her head, sending the shadows of distressed dreams back into the corners of her mind. There was no daughter with hornet blades, and no one who could craft such an exquisite murderer save for Circinae, and Eli's mother was gone. Eli had conjured this threat with her own fears. Or perhaps the Heart remembered a daughter long dead. Eli was struggling to keep her memories separate from those of the Heart that possessed her — they flowed together like mercury.

Eli watched the moon fade from the sky. There would be no justice for the moon or the remnants of its people, the ghosts that Eli had once hunted through the streets below. It was too late for that world, but not for this one. The Earth could still be saved. There was still time. Time to learn how to live in this body, how to be the Heart, how to harness the new power running through her veins.

Only a few days had passed since the confrontation in the Coven, and Eli was still learning the shape of her new body. She loved it; it was hers, and hers alone, and it was free. But sometimes it flickered in and out of existence, and now she could see magic everywhere, the world bursting into colours and light unexpectedly — not just when she switched to her magical pure black eyes.

Eli had grown up in a world of magic, but being able to see its threads, tendrils, shoots, leaves, feathers all at once — this was something else entirely. The constant movement and colour gave her migraines. Being in the human world, in the place the witches called the City of Ghosts, made it a bit easier. She couldn't control these new abilities; they seemed to come and go at random.

Sometimes it felt like this body was a garden and someone else was planting gardenias and calla lilies and bleeding hearts and turning the earth over with a blunt spade, cutting through roots and weeds, disturbing the worms underneath.

The clamour of the street rose from somewhere below her, and Eli closed her eyes and sighed. Time was running out. She knew that Cam and Tav had given her these few days to heal, but the Coven wasn't resting, and every day they lingered, the Earth was dying. Even Clytemnestra's fierce warrior-children, fighting desperately to wrest control of the City of Eyes, couldn't suture the wounds that had been made in the planet.

Only Eli and Tav could.

Tomorrow, Eli decided, eyes opening like a pair of morning glories. She rested her hands unconsciously on a belt of blades strapped to her hips. When her fingers brushed a hilt of bone, the knife rang out with a melody that only she could hear. *Tomorrow we start.*

The moon was fading from view.

Eli faded with it.

KITE

"I bring a message for the Heir Dormant."

An underling appeared, a witch acolyte adorned in frail streamers of fabric, gauzy and pale, almost like smoke moving through the room. Low magic. A nobody. Kite was surprised they had been able to find her. Most were too afraid of the tomes in the library, the ancient books swollen with malice.

Kite looked up, blinking, an opalescent tear sliding down her nose and onto the book before her. Her hair was piled like a waterfall on her head.

"The Witch Lord has requested an audience."

Kite bowed her head, causing tentacles of hair to fall over her face, unrolling across the floor. When had her hair grown so long? She had no concept of time.

"Thank you for telling me." Her voice was musical, the lilting song of a harp. Dangerously gentle.

The Coven knew she spent most of her time in the library, poring over ancient histories and forgotten magic. The Witch Lord hoped to use her knowledge to increase the Coven's power.

She had something else in mind.

The acolyte left. Kite stared at the lettering underneath her hands. Quickly, Kite ripped the page from its spine, shoved it into her mouth, and chewed, letting the ink run down her tongue. The words would confuse anyone who wanted to know what she had been thinking. Living in the library had its advantages. A sea of words, and she could put them together however she wanted.

Kite swallowed. When she smiled her teeth were stained black.

Then she rose and went to see her mother.

The room she was summoned to was dark, but Kite could smell the Beast. She sunk onto her knees and bowed her head. She could feel the Beast sniffing her out, testing her mind strength, tasting her aura. Then the smell faded, and a small whimper echoed through the chamber.

Kite suddenly felt weak. Looking down, she could see her material body peeling away, revealing her magical essence, the aquamarine light of her being; her true shape. Her most powerful — and vulnerable — body.

No one came hidden in skins to an audience with the Witch Lord.

Taking a deep, calming breath, Kite closed her eyes a moment before she dematerialized, and let herself fall into her true state of being. Naked, she drifted, a furious ball of light in a small prison, before the invisible eyes of the Witch Lord.

And then the moment passed, and Kite was in her body once again, hair slick as seaweed against her face. Pain rocked her body, and she curled up on the floor like a child, waiting for it to pass.

A show of strength, then. A reminder of what the Witch Lord could do. Unravel her in a moment, steal her skin, reabsorb her power.

"Welcome, essence-daughter," said the Witch Lord.

"Lord Mother," whispered Kite.

"Are you ready to take your rightful place in the Coven?"

Kite scrambled to her knees and bowed again, pressing her forehead into the earth. Her mouth watered at the scent of delicious dirt.

"It is time, daughter, to declare you Heir Rising."

Excitement bubbled up in Kite, water dribbling from the corners of her lips.

She had been the Heir Dormant for so long that she had stopped believing the Witch Lord would ever allow her to use her full powers.

"You have shown loyalty by rejecting the human-touched girl, but there are some on the first ring who still have their doubts. You will dispel their doubts, command their faith and their bodies, and take your place as my right hand in the war against the children-abominations who even now rise up against us in acts of treason."

Eli. Of course. Kite should have known that her attachment to the made-girl had not gone unnoticed. No true witch would befriend an object. And the Heir Rising was more than a witch, more even than a symbol of the Witch Lord's rule: they were the right hand of the Coven. She shared a modicum of the Witch Lord's power. She might even rule distant planets in her mother's stead.

"It is my honour to serve you, Lord," said Kite.

"Bring back the Heart."

"It will be done, Lord."

"Swear with your essence, and prove your loyalty to me, who was and am the source of your magic. Magic above material."

"Magic above material," Kite repeated.

Again, she found herself stripped of her body. But this time she was not alone. Another essence, glowing white but rainbowed, gleaming different hues and shades of brilliance, so beautiful it hurt, reached out a tendril of light and

touched.

Kite screamed with no mouth, a soundless prayer of obliteration.

When the pain passed, Kite's bluegreen essence bled with shades of pink and gold. Kite felt a rush of power burn through her body. And knowledge, sweet and crisp as pear on her tongue.

Kite now understood how to steal magic.

"Bring back the Heart, and I will give you more power than you can imagine."

Then the Witch Lord was gone. The air lightened; the dark lessened, retreating. The whimpering stopped. Kite lay on her back, panting in the dirt, pain pulsing through her entire body. She rolled over and vomited ink. The Beast shuffled forward and lapped it up.

Kite smiled.

She had done it. She had become the Heir Rising.

TAV

Then —

The bus had been late.

The bus stop was abandoned. The shelter was covered in posters for suicide hotlines and band stickers and blocky marker lettering spelling out catchy phrases like LIVE LIKE NO ONE IS WATCHING and DANIELLE IS A SLUT.

People really sucked sometimes.

It was November, and frost was beginning to paint itself up the sides of the Plexiglass shelter in floral bouquets. Tav was shivering under the threadbare peacoat they'd thrifted from Value Village last year.

It had been a shitty day.

Sure, they'd gotten ten out of ten on their biology quiz, but their teacher had deadnamed them again, and then someone had written slurs on the locker of the only other Black kid in Tav's year (no, they're not related). To top it all off, the vice-principal had just announced that the GSA was being cancelled due to lack of funding — as if the kids didn't know it had everything to do with the provincial government and anti-LGBTQI legislation being put in place. Teachers acted like all teenagers were stuck in the 1950s with only a crappy radio or smudged black-and-white newspapers to learn about the world. Tav had been on social media since they were a kid — and damn, the kinds of information they had been able to access.

Not that they needed to read the news to know how Black queer people were treated in Canada. Tav's classmates liked to say that Canada was better than the U.S., that Ontario was better than Quebec, that a city like Grace didn't have "those problems." But they were liars.

Something in Tav was changing, a seed of knowledge that was beginning to grow. The world was damaged, and it needed to be fixed. The sad adults they saw every day had given up on hope and change, had resigned themselves to the everyday grind of life and fear and hiding. You could tell when you looked into their tired eyes, the light leaking out like a broken egg yolk: they didn't believe.

But Tav did. And days like today reminded them how much needed to change. If no one else was going to do it, then they would. The anger was hot and fierce and it warmed their body even as their fingernails turned blue and the bus still did not come.

Someone joined them. Or maybe — something? The person (were they a person?) was wearing a wool scarf that covered their face and a bulky parka. They looked a bit like a mirage, not quite real. When Tav stared directly at them, they could see through the body — but when they blinked, the body was solid again.

Tav and the ghost waited for the bus in companionable silence.

Laughter cut through the quiet like a knife. It was the kind of laughter that made the last few autumn leaves turn brown and fall from the trees, that caught the breath in your lungs and pulled it out through your mouth until you were left gasping in fear.

Tav knew that laughter. They knew the boys — not by name but by reputation, by their handwriting on lockers and the ugly worlds they spat from mouths twisted by hate. It was their parents' fault, Tav's father told them, year after year. They teach their kids to hate. They don't know any better.

"How heavy it must be, to live with so much hate," said Tav's mother. Tav had guiltily stashed away their own hate and anger, wondering if it would ever be useful. Wondering when they would be allowed to use it.

The voices snapped in the air like a wet towel on skin. Tav shoved their hands in their pockets and rooted themselves to the ground. They looked right ahead of them.

Tav wasn't afraid. Tav was angry.

"Look who it is. The lesbo. Where's your brother? Heard he didn't like our artwork today. We want to talk to him."

Tav ignored them.

"Come on." One of the boys leaned forward, eyes shining like frozen tears. "You can tell us where he is. We don't bite." He snapped his jaw, and they both laughed.

Tav's hand tightened around the knife in their pocket.

"Aww, come on, don't be like that," said the other boy. "We're just being friendly —" He reached a hand out. To touch their shoulder. To grab their sleeve. To — what? Tav didn't know. They just acted.

Tav twisted away and pulled the blade free, ready to scare them off. Ready to draw blood.

The ghost moved.

Flickered.

One moment it was beside Tav and the next it was in front of the boys, its mouth opening wider than any human's possibly could. Swallowing the hand that had reached for Tav. Swallowing the arm.

Tav closed their eyes. A scream was cut short — was it theirs? No. Someone else's. A human noise.

They opened their eyes again, throat tight, hand shaking.

All that was left were a pair of earbuds and a wool scarf lying discarded on the sidewalk.

The seed broke open. Tav's heart pounded. As they left the bus stop — walking, running, flying over the pavement, needing to move, driven by adrenalin that blocked out the cold, the fear, the fury — a new thought burned itself across their brain.

Magic was real.

Magic would be their revolution.

Now —

"He's back," said Eli, peering out the window.

"Mm."

"Does he come here a lot?"

Tav tried for a noncommittal shrug, fiddling with one of many zippers on their motorcycle jacket — also thrifted, and a couple sizes too big.

"Why does he follow you around?"

"Let it go, all right?" Tav banged on Cam's door. "Let's get this over with."

"I don't like it." Eli pressed her forehead against the glass. "I don't like that he's here. The Coven —"

"You're being paranoid."

The exposed skin on the back of Eli's hands lit up, tiny lights crawling just under the surface like insects. "You have no idea what they're capable of."

Tav didn't know if Eli meant the ghost or the Coven. They didn't ask.

"We have to go." Tav banged again.

"Coming!" yelled Cam.

"He's dangerous."

"Eli." Their voice was a warning.

"He's killed people."

"So have you."

Eli opened her mouth to protest, but instead vanished.

Tav waited a few seconds for her to reappear, and when she didn't, turned and walked to the door. Grabbed the keys. So that was how it was going to be. Fine. She'd better show up when they needed her.

Cam emerged from his room, tousling his hair. Tav could see through the glamour to the stone-studded body underneath — flecks of granite and limestone and mica roughening his smooth skin. He had made a bargain with the sentient stone of an alien planet, the Labyrinth that shimmered over the witches' city, often invisible to those who did not know how to feel, but always watching. The walls that had sunk their teeth deep into the foundation of the world.

They had all been changed by their time in the City of Eyes.

The thought of using Cam as their shield, of watching him put his body between them and the witches' blades, made Tav's heart twinge.

"I'm ready," he said, then frowned. "Where's Eli?"

"She'll meet us there." Guilt blurred the edges of their vision. It wasn't fair to keep throwing the dead human in Eli's face, but that isn't what they'd meant when they'd compared her to the ghost. Tav had come to an understanding that everything and everyone was dangerous — and that didn't mean they deserved to be dead. Tav slept easy knowing the ghost was out there, wandering the streets, watching over them. It always felt like a homecoming when the ghost stopped outside their door or made its way to The Sun. Not quite a friend, not an enemy. Another misfit, maybe. A memory. The moment that changed their life forever.

Eli felt differently. And now she was AWOL.

You can't rely on anyone, thought Tav. Something their mom used to say.

Cam was watching them warily. "Tav —"

Tav hated the gentleness in his voice. "It's fine, Cam. She'll be there."

Cam nodded, grabbed his jacket, and walked out. Tav paused at the door and turned back to look at the apartment — Oreo crumbs and coffee stains, a single puzzle piece in a cocoon of dust. A marked absence of framed photographs and schoolbooks.

Magic everywhere, like dirt.

THE HEIR

Kite folded the page into the shape of a hummingbird and spat on it. With a tiny pop, the bird vanished, winging its way to the Labyrinth. Full witches were forbidden from knowing the passages of the sentient stone walls that thrived on secrets and mischief.

But Kite was not like any of the other Coven members.

Kite had been named.

The name Eli had tasted in her blood was a different kind of magic, the kind of bond that only children can make. The name had been a gift. Kite had not stolen it.

When Kite crossed over to the human realm in her coming-of-age ceremony, she pretended to bring back the name she had already been given. Without a name, the small passageway between the City of Eyes and the

City of Ghosts closed behind her. She had never left her mark, never completed the ritual, never fully left the childhood world of dreams and selfishness. She wasn't an adult, and she wasn't bound by adult law.

It was the only law she wasn't bound by.

She remembered the first time she told Eli she was the Heir — it was years ago, on their island, when Eli was just as imprisoned as Kite. They had both been tied by bloodlines and expectations and the stories told about their bodies. They were like balloons tethered to the land by pretty ribbons.

But Eli had escaped, as Kite had always known she would.

"You could do great things," Eli had whispered, her human sweat intoxicatingly sweet to the young witch. They had been lying close — they had always been close, then — limbs entwined, hair knotted into one tangled nest, faces pressed together so no one else could taste their secrets. "When you are the Witch Lord, you could change everything."

"The first thing I'll do is make you Witch Lord with me," she whispered, nuzzling Eli's neck. When she drew back, a line of salt crystals had glittered on Eli's skin.

But Kite would never rule the City of Eyes. She had been made by a conqueror with a hunger for empire, a ruler who would need puppets on the new worlds she discovered and digested. If Kite was very good, she would one day be given the Earth — or what was left of it.

As Heir Rising, she was only a step away from being named the regent of Earth. If that day came, she would lead her own army through the human world, taking and twisting and playing with death. Kite wondered if her mother had intended to keep the Earth alive, but had been too greedy to stop herself from draining its life source. Maybe Kite would be promised a new planet, a new solar system, a new galaxy. But she would only ever be a vessel for her mother's power. She was also an extra body, another shell for the same essence, and she knew that if she caused any trouble the Witch Lord would take that body for her own and create a more obedient child.

She was an extension of the Witch Lord's power, not a threat to it.

But other threats had bloomed in the shadow of the Coven, and now the Heart of the world had been stolen. The Witch Lord was weak, and Eli was no longer within reach of the Coven.

Kite pressed a damp hand against the wall. Ink bled from her palm to the stone as she asked the ancient structure for passage. The stone shuddered, and then tore itself open. Fossilized pages pressed into shale marked Kite's journey from the invisible passage in the library to the Labyrinth.

When she emerged from the passageway, she was pleased to see that she had ended up exactly where she wanted to be. Desire and wishes were powerful in the City of Eyes. Especially the wishes of children.

"Oooh, the Heir, come to grace us with her presence." Clytemnestra sat on a miniature throne made from popsicle sticks and glitter. She lowered her chin and peered up at Kite through long, fluttering lashes. "To what do We owe the honour?"

"I know what you're doing," said Kite. "I want to help."

TAV

It made sense to start here.

This was the place that had first taken them between worlds. This small seam, the one the Hedge-Witch had made years ago. So here they were at 5:00 a.m. in a back alley, eyes crusted from sleep. The first cut. The first healing.

Hopefully.

Tav's body felt itchy, and they could sense how easy it would be to clear their mind, reach out, and nudge the tear open.

It was a dangerous impulse. Taking all three of them back to the City of Eyes could be deadly.

"Do you have it?" Eli had been waiting for them. Tav didn't want to admit how much of a relief it had been to see her in the flesh. They couldn't do this without her.

Tav nodded, holding up the potted plant. "It was a gift from the Hedge-Witch, so it should work." They hesitated, and then added, "I think she would help us."

Eli frowned. "She wants the Heart, Tav. She wants power. I don't trust her."

"She taught me everything I know about magic," Tav said quietly.

"She's a witch."

"So?"

"So she won't help us without a bargain. And negotiating with witches is dangerous."

Tav snorted. "I know how you negotiate. Knives out, right?"

Eli shrugged. "Gets the job done."

Tav shook their head. "We need —"

"No, we *don't*," Eli interrupted, her eyes flashing.

"You disappeared —"

"Not on purpose!"

Tav's knuckles tightened. "So learn —"

"That's enough," said Cam wearily. He hadn't been sleeping. Tav heard him tossing and turning each night, talking to himself. They wondered what would happen when the glamour Clytemnestra had cast started to wear off.

"Can you two stop?" he asked. "Let's get this over with."

Eli flicked her magical eyes into place and stared at Cam for a long moment.

"Is that a yes?" he said, attempting a smile. "It's rude to stare, you know. I know it's hard to remember, the less human you become."

"I'll take that as a compliment." Eli kept staring.

Tav knew what she was seeing, because they had seen it, too. The magic in Cam's body was changing. It used to slide along the surface of his skin like a coat. Now it was deeper, as if merging with his very cells. Eli wasn't the only one who was becoming less human.

"He's right," said Tav. "We may as well try this. It's small, so it should be easier."

Eli rolled both sets of eyes. "It's always about size with you humans. I thought Clytemnestra taught you something about that."

"Is 'human' an insult now?" Tav arched an eyebrow. "Good thing we're all hybrids, I guess." They tried to keep the bitterness out of their voice and failed.

"It won't be easy," said Eli bluntly. "It's relatively new, so it's not used to being touched by humans and witches, not used to being tampered with. Get into position. Let's start." She let her hands run along the hilts of her blades for a moment. "You have yours?"

Tav nodded. The obsidian blade, gifted by Eli, would tie them together. Hopefully, they would be able to use the power of the Heart to change the wound into a door.

As they handed Eli the potted plant, the wiring in their brain lit up with panic.

They had no idea what the fuck they were doing.

Their eyes roamed to the rooftops, and Tav realized they were looking for the ghost. He hadn't followed them this time. He hadn't come. Their heart sank. They thought he would be here to guard them. Had Eli scared him away, or hurt him? No. She wouldn't do that to Tav.

Feeling uneasy, Tav turned back to Eli. The three of them would have to be enough.

THE HEART

Eli held the plant in the air and focused on the seam. The aloe plant slowly stretched itself up into the heavens, growing larger and thicker, spines bursting from its base, which had become a trunk; leaves uncurling, flowers budding, blossoming, and then dying. White petals rained down from the tree onto the three bodies underneath.

Eli closed her eyes and felt the brush of a petal on her eyelid. She smelled wet earth and rain, and the burnt-coffee-and-metal scent of home-brewed magic. She took the petal from her eyelid, opened her mouth, and laid it on her tongue. It tasted of apple and summer.

The petal dissolved onto her tongue.

The vine breached the sky.

Eli flinched, sweat beading on her forehead.

"What is it?" asked Tav. "Eli, what's happening? Why isn't —"

Eli couldn't hear them. See them. Feel them. All she could feel was the pain in the world, the agony of a planet being devoured by witches. The seam was a bloody wound in time and space. Tied by magic and flesh, by the sense of kinship Eli felt with the entire universe, Eli *was* the wound. The Heart ached with the dying world.

Something had gone wrong. It wasn't supposed to hurt this much.

Eli was the sky being ripped open. Eli was the body being drained of life. The pain seared through her body and mind.

Eli moaned, and her eyes rolled up into the back of her head.

THE HEIR

Kite burned a brilliant greenblue as she walked through the long hallway of the Coven. She was flame, and ice, and sky. She was the northern lights that danced across the human world. She was power incarnate.

She was the Heir Rising.

Today she was leaving the Coven. She had been blessed by the Witch Lord herself to travel to the City of Ghosts, to the very stars if need be, to recover the Heart. Today she began her journey, and the entire City would hold its breath for their Heir.

The animals were still. The plants unfurled their leaves and petals, the woods groaned a lament of farewell. The sky was still and unchanging. The world honoured her.

For years, Kite had studied ancient tomes in the archives, trying to find a way to set Eli free, to change her fate. But Eli had escaped without Kite's help. Kite had never been prouder of her friend than when Clytemnestra had told her. Eli had broken the cycle.

Now Kite would break the world.

Sometimes dead brush needed to burn to create new life.

"*When you are the Witch Lord, you can change everything.*" But Kite had never wanted to be the Witch Lord. Kite longed for her books, for her writing; she cared for forgotten magics and ones that had not yet been created. She cared for the walls and the children and the flora and fauna lost in the wastelands. She wanted to listen. She wanted to create. She had never wanted to rule. If she played the game well, she wouldn't have to.

And Kite was good at games.

She appeared before one of the Coven guards, the bodiless shadows that stalked the keep and spoke in mellifluous tongues.

"Heir." The shadow bowed low, a mark of respect.

Kite reached out and touched the shadow's face. "Rise," she commanded. "And witness this day: for when I return, you will have two Witch Lords."

Murmurs flowed down the hallway. Shadows flittered across stone. A full vanguard stood at attention.

Kite walked slowly, carefully, her bare feet leaving damp prints. She turned to each shadow and met their eyes. As she walked, she shed pieces of clothing like strands of hair. The bruises and scars that marked her skin would be heralded as portents of change. She had earned this moment with her flesh and blood, with bone and magic and essence.

Whispers danced across her naked shoulders as she left her past behind, bringing only herself into the angry light of a hungry and desperate world. Her world. A world that was ending.

When I return, you will have two Witch Lords.

The Coven itself heard these words, and felt their power, as if carved into the foundation.

A thousand eyes watched as Kite summoned the Vortex, the pathway between worlds. Assassins who were made from human and magic and frost and stone could move easily between worlds, but witches were pure magic. Their essences were vulnerable in the cold nothingness of the void, and were often rejected by the portal, refused entry into a world so alien to their nature. That was why crossing the threshold was the rite of passage from childhood to adulthood. Many witches died in the Vortex.

Kite closed her eyes and felt for the seam between worlds, the one that had been used so many times that it almost opened on its own; some nights, if you stood on the roof of the Coven to stargaze, you could see a small tear in time and space, and through that hole, the glittering lights of the human city.

The seam opened easily, and Kite stepped inside.

It was dry. This was always the strangest, most unnatural sensation for Kite. The lack of water ached in every part of her body, and she found herself gasping for breath like a dying fish. Like the fish she coaxed out of the river to sacrifice themselves for her nourishment. She felt small.

Her skin was stripped away, like tearing the bark off an old tree. Her fragile essence was exposed to the darkness, to the empty nothingness.

The only thing you brought into the Vortex was yourself.

It was so easy for Eli, who was overflowing with life, who was a patchwork of lives. Kite had only ever been one lonely thing. And the Vortex knew it.

Kite concentrated on the connections that drew her to the human world: Eli's hair in her mouth, saliva sinking into her bloodstream when Eli bit her too hard.

There. The City of Ghosts appeared in her vision, and all Kite had to do was hold on for a few more moments.

Instead, she threw herself recklessly out of the Vortex.

She fell for days.

When she emerged, flame extinguished in the gentle wetness of her own body, she was comforted by the smooth stone under her palms.

"Took you long enough," said Clytemnestra, sitting on a new throne made of daisy chains and bicycle spokes. She was alone. She inclined her head slightly, the closest to respect that the outlaw leader of the children would grant.

Adopting a dilettante drawl, Clytemnestra continued. "I have a task for you, after all." She lowered her chin bashfully and pulled out three eyelashes. "You're going to build me an army."

TAV

Eli's body was shaking, her eyes rolling wildly. Tav flinched toward her, but caught themselves and drew back.

"Do something!" Cam was trembling, the stones on his arms and torso ringing out as they brushed against one another.

"Not yet."

Above them the sky had been torn open, and through the gaping hole in the world they could see flashes of colour, glittering geometric shapes, and glimpses of faraway galaxies. A storm, dark and crackling with electricity, circled the emptiness.

"If we leave it open too long —"

"I said *not yet*."

The moans died and left behind a void of silence. The rip in the sky was widening, like the mouth of a monster.

No one moved.

Not yet.

The Heart flared bright with righteous fury.

Now. Tav exhaled.

"She's *glowing*," whispered Cam, the sound of the stones dissonant and out of tune. "Something's wrong."

"And we're going to make it right." Tav turned to their friend. "If anyone tries to stop us —"

"I can handle it. Go do your magic zipper thing." He smiled. It wavered on his face and then collapsed.

Tav nodded once, and then wrapped their arms around the tree, around Eli, around the pulsing, glowing, angry magic. The obsidian blade was held firmly in their hand. Gently, so gently, Tav pressed the knife against their palm.

It shouldn't have surprised them that it cut, but it did — not skin, but something else that lived in Tav's body. Dark purple steam rose from the cut. Quickly, Tav did the same to the back of Eli's hand.

Tav pressed their wound over Eli's. They closed their eyes. *Open.*

Are you here? Eli was the wound, the tree, the pavement, the boi, the ghost, the human, the past, the present, the world. She was lost in all she was and how much hurt she carried.

I'm here. Tav had opened a door between them — and now Tav, too, was the wound, the Heart, the tree.

We don't have time —

I know —

If I lose control, the storm will destroy everything it can —

We won't lose control —

Tav was the tree, the Heart, the door — and more than that. The maker of doors. They had their own magic, and a strong sense of who they were. They would not lose themselves in this union. And they wouldn't let Eli lose herself, either.

Tav stretched out the obsidian blade and plunged it deep into the trunk.

The tree bled tears.

Tav stabbed again. (Cam, watching, saw how both bodies, intertwined with the tree, were glowing like a sun, painfully bright. He had to look away.)

Tav stabbed again. The tears running down the trunk crystallized into pieces of salt.

Breaking apart the old door was more exhausting than the pure physical action; every movement took magic and intention. Tav found themselves shaking with weakness. Then a hand gripped theirs, fingers threading through theirs.

My turn.

Eli lifted Tav's hand holding the blade and directed it into the tree, peeling off great sheets of bark that crumbled to the ground and transformed into red petals.

In her other hand, Eli raised the pearl blade that would tear the unnatural magic from the natural world.

Both blades fought against the brutal witch-crafted magic that had torn open the galaxy.

The leaves started to wither and fall from the trunk. The vines started to retreat, and some of the pain, the hurt, the poison, was leeched out with them.

The wound was healing.

Soon, Eli was holding a small clay pot filled with dirt, salt, and red petals.

Tav let go of her and stumbled back, wiping sweat from their forehead. Wisps of purple smoke still curled from the cut on their palm. The storm was fading, leaving flecks of electricity like glitter in the sky.

"That wasn't so bad," they gasped.

"Good — that was the easy part," said Eli, grasping their shoulder. Tav could see veins of stone under her face, could see spots of blood where thorn had grown through skin. This had been hard on her body, too.

Eli took a deep breath, her fingers digging into Tav's shoulder. "Ready?"

"Or not." Tav placed their hand over Eli's, and the jolt of electricity that passed between them had nothing to do with magic, just skin on skin, the meeting of two bodies.

THE HEART

They feel like feathers, thought Eli, grateful that their minds were no longer merged.

They had closed the wound. Now they needed to reopen it — but as a door that worked both ways, that allowed the two worlds to live in harmony. A symbiotic relationship, instead of the predatory assault the witches had been making for years on the soft blue planet. A door that would return the lifeforce to Earth. This part was just Tav, and Eli was the power source. Like a battery.

"This is when they'll come," Eli told Cam. "The Coven will have felt what we did." She gave him the stone blade, the defender.

He wrapped his hand around the rough hilt and winked at her. "I'll be careful — this is like, an arm for you, or something, right?"

Eli smiled, making sure to show her set of crocodile teeth. "Would you rather borrow something else?"

"Nope, this just great, thanks. Besides, you never know when you might need to chew your way out of something."

"They have been very useful," she teased, smiling wider.

"I'm not sure I want to hear it."

"*I* do, but maybe later?" Tav was still shaky.

Eli squeezed their hand. "Don't die," she told Cam.

"Haven't yet."

Eli could feel the sutures she and Tav had clumsily sewed between worlds, the magic they had used to heal the tear.

Eli's part in this was done; she had formed a connection between herself and Tav. They could now draw on Eli's power without touching. They were tied together with blood. Together they had mended the wound. Now it was up to Tav to turn that scab into a door, to resuscitate the human world. To give it new life.

Eli had many powers, but not this one.

This one gift had been granted to a human. A boi with eyes like embers and neon purple hair.

Eli could still feel the warmth from Tav's arms around her. The weight of their body, the rhythm of their human heartbeat, their breath on Eli's neck –

"Okay, let's do this," she interrupted her own thoughts, afraid of where they might lead.

"Thanks for your permission." Tav was breathing heavily, their delicate body made of cartilage and keratin struggling under the weight of so much alien power. They were still clutching the obsidian blade, which was and would always be a part of Eli. And now they had shared blood. There was no telling what that would mean.

Tav became a little less human every day. Eli had noticed it in flickers and glances, in the way Tav's shadow sometimes lagged or their reflection trembled and stuttered in glass windows. Eli wondered if Tav knew. They hadn't said anything. For better or for worse, there was no going back to their old life.

Tav was glowing with the same light that flowed through Eli. The power of the Heart.

Tav returned the blade to the strap on their left arm. Now was not the time for cutting out the rot. It was time to open a door between worlds, a door that let magic and light and love and hurt flow between celestial bodies.

They closed their eyes and raised their arms. The wind whipped up, ruffling their hair. They didn't move, even when a strong gust pushed Cam and Eli backward.

Tav entered a trance.

That's when Eli heard the first cries.

"Vultures," she said to Cam.

"Birds?"

"Scavengers."

"I don't understand."

"You will."

She grabbed the thorn blade and stabbed it into concrete. She drew a jagged, uneven circle around Tav for protection. Then Eli knelt down and pressed her still-bloody palm against the scar in the pavement. The circle darkened to the colour of dirty blood for a moment and then vanished.

"I hope that holds." She didn't say, *I wasn't trained to protect, to heal, to help. I was trained to kill.* She no longer needed to switch eyes to see the magic she had used. The spell she had cast was clumsy, like the gaping stitches in a beginner's embroidery. But it was all she had. Hopefully, when something crossed the threshold that didn't share her blood, the thorns would strike.

The stones on Cam's body fell silent.

The vultures were here.

Eli looked up in time to see three great winged beasts bear down on them. She jumped back, drawing pearl and bone.

The first one, scaled and taloned, with a face like an arrow, crashed into the protective barrier and was immediately ensnared by vicious briars. An unearthly wail pierced her ears. She smiled grimly. The barrier had held.

"Cover me!" Eli leapt with superhuman grace and speed onto the back of the wounded vulture. A dozen invisible spines pierced her skin — but her bones were made of granite, and she would not break.

She stabbed the bone blade into the soft spot on the back of the creature's neck, in between metal spikes and scaled armour. Clear, sticky blood oozed from the wound, smelling of lilac and decomposing leaves. The blood covered her fingers and burned them, leaving her hands covered in boils. *Fuck.*

Behind her, she heard the scraping sound of metal on rock, and knew that Cam was shielding her from the other two. She hoped the stone blade would work for him. It had been willingly given, but her knives had minds of their own. They were, after all, alive.

But Cam was part stone now, too.

Eli threw herself off the dying creature and spun around. Her hands ached. Vaulting over Cam, she let out a challenging scream and threw her bone blade at one of the remaining vultures. The vulture reared up, extending its wings to their full length — seven or eight feet — casting shadows over all of them. The blade glanced off the metal scales on its belly.

Eli wasn't done. Without stopping, she flung herself on the outstretched wing, opening her mouth wide and letting crocodile teeth overflow her human jaw. Biting down, she began tearing through the wing. The vulture crowed in rage and pain, and tried to stab her with its face. The arrow-face pierced her shoulder and went clean through, impaling the vulture's own wing. Furious, the vulture tried to shake her off, but Eli's teeth were deeply embedded in its wing.

Eli ripped the wing from the vulture.

Screaming, the vulture stumbled back and collapsed, the life bleeding out of it. Eli had slain it.

"Finish it!" she yelled at Cam, who had been keeping the third vulture at bay using both his body and the dagger as shields.

Blood poured from Eli's shoulder, and her hands were on fire. As her teeth retreated into her mouth, jaw aching from the strain, she reached for the thorn blade, the ensnarer. She would tear all the vultures apart. Fingers fumbled for the hilt.

It was like holding a live ember.

Eli dropped it. As it clattered to the ground, the blade glowed white-hot for a moment, and then was a tangle of thorns again. Eli stared at it in horror.

Eli stood, frozen in shock, the magical glow seeping out of her body. She swayed slightly, her head growing foggy. Out of the corner of her eye she saw the half-dead vulture rise again, powered by hatred and desperation. Cam had not killed it.

She felt weakness sweep through her body. She sank to her knees and looked up. The sky was like a mirror, glittering with light and colour. For a moment she could see her own reflection in the sky, and then something shifted, and it went dark. Through the darkness she could see the greygreen clouds of an alien world. She could smell salt and cinnamon. Why was she still alive? Even granite can be ground into sediment.

Then she understood: Tav had opened a door.

Tav had sent the vultures back across worlds.

Tav had saved them.

Could the Heart die? Eli watched her blood make patterns on the pavement. With her last fragment of willpower, she stretched out a ruined hand and drew a design in the blood, trying to tether her physical body to the world.

Darkness. A void.

Nothing.

THE HEIR

Kite felt an unfamiliar buzz of excitement when she heard Clytemnestra's plans.

"You can move between the Coven and the Labyrinth," mused Clytemnestra. "We'll use that to our advantage. The Witch Lord will never suspect her own daughter." She blew Kite a kiss.

"And if I'm caught?"

"I'll mourn your death with a funeral worthy of a child," said Clytemnestra solemnly. "A seven-layered cake and arson."

"I'm honoured."

Clytemnestra crawled closer to Kite, giggling. The Beast growled softly. "How soon can you do it? Can we do it now? I'm bored!"

"No."

"What about now?" she whined.

"I need to time to prepare, sweetie. The spell I'm thinking of is old — I don't want to make any mistakes."

"What about *now*?"

Kite felt the newfound power slither through her body, ready to reach out and snatch a piece of the child's essence. It would be so easy to silence the brat, to grow strong on stolen magic. The feeling of power in her veins was intoxicating.

Kite drew back. "We'll do it soon," she promised.

She didn't tell Clytemnestra about the Witch Lord's secret, how she had grown so powerful by devouring her own. Stealing another witch's essence was a travesty, taboo — sacrilege. She had no way of knowing if Clytemnestra would trust her if she knew what Kite was now capable of.

Children love to keep secrets.

Clytemnestra started doing somersaults on the stone floor, singing half rhymes to herself. Kite watched her.

Clytemnestra led the children in games of jump rope and ritual murder. She taught them to play and she taught them to listen.

She told us we could be something else, something other than what the Coven wanted.

Clytemnestra had been to Earth, had stolen many things, little things, little broken hearts. She had seen the damage in the City of Ghosts and the City of Eyes. Had felt it. Children see things differently than adults. The children lived for wildness and loved one another until it hurt. The children didn't want the worlds to die. The children didn't want to live in the Labyrinth forever or submit to the will of the Coven. And Clytemnestra had showed them that they didn't have to submit.

"When this is over, you won't be the Witch Lord," Clytemnestra said suddenly. "We won't bow to you."

"I have never wanted to be the Witch Lord," said Kite honestly. "And you know that isn't why I was created. It was never what I was meant for."

"And what are you meant for now?" Clytemnestra climbed back on her throne and started eating it, which explained why she had a new one every time Kite saw her.

"I want to save Eli," said Kite.

Clytemnestra chewed on a pink plastic handlebar for a minute and then spat it out. She stared at Kite. "You are the strangest witch I've ever met."

It sounded like a compliment.

Clytemnestra was an oddity, an outcast among witches, tolerated only in the underbelly of the city, and only as long as she kept to the walls and left the Coven alone. An abomination like her would never be welcomed into the Coven. But Kite would. Kite, who had pretended to grow up, who was the Heir to the Coven's power, a witch who dared to love a human thing.

A revolution needs more than bodies, more than a charismatic leader with razor-sharp nails. It needs information. It needs connections.

Clytemnestra needed her, and they both knew it. So even as Kite bowed and smiled and promised to follow orders, they knew that this alliance was between equals.

Kite was sure that Clytemnestra hated it.

"I will do what you asked of me. A show of power. A spectacle. And I will help you eliminate the Coven. But Eli lives."

"I will not slay her," said Clytemnestra. "I can't speak for the world." She suddenly burst out laughing. "We will burn the Coven down! We will dance on their bones!"

With an indulgent smile, Kite picked up the discarded handlebar and started chewing.

Nine

TAV

Sweat glistened on their forehead and their muscles ached, but Tav was wide awake. The taste of euphoria and the smell of blood and grass flooded their senses. They had done it. They had opened a door between worlds. Not a wound, but a channel. They could feel in their shoulder blades the magic of the City of Eyes touching the human world, casting warmth and light over them. They could feel the tumultuous mix of human emotions reaching out to the witches' realm of magic and chaos.

Is this how symbiosis worked? Is this how worlds kept one another alive?

Tav had done it. Tav, with the "bad attitude" and straight As that would never pay for college, a part-time job at the gas station and fistfights in dive bars.

The euphoria faded and Tav looked away from the door and back down to the dirt: round silver glasses in a pool of blood. *Eli.*

Cam was already there, stones trembling, hands fluttering over Eli's body. "I can't find the wound," he said. "I can't see it. But there's blood everywhere. So much blood. She doesn't have a pulse."

"Maybe that's normal now," said Tav. "She's not human."

"She's part human! There has to be a way to stop the bleeding."

Tav wasn't so sure. Tav had started to think that Eli was invincible. They had never seen the assassin fail. And now, Eli was not only made of hawthorn and red blood cells, but memories and planets and the magical essence of a world. But they had been wrong. Worlds can die.

Everything dies.

Fuck that.

Tav unsheathed the obsidian blade and pressed it against Eli's forehead. *This is you, I'm holding you, and you can't die while I'm holding you.*

"Give me the shield," said Tav, and Cam handed the stone knife over. Now Tav held two knives, two parts of a person. Tav could see the different magics that kept Eli alive sparking and flickering like a dying flame. With one motion, Tav stabbed both blades into the magic, the essence, the dark.

Heal.

The blood vanished. Eli started breathing with little wet gasps. Tav dropped the knives and pulled Eli into their arms.

"You're okay," they murmured. "You're going to be okay. You have to be okay."

"They'll send others," said Eli, struggling to get the words out. "Leave. We need to leave."

"Soon."

Tav noticed a curious design painted on the asphalt. Dark and wet. It hadn't vanished with the rest of the blood. Their heart sank. Eli was resorting to using her blood. Why? What was happening to her? They were sick of Eli's secrets. How do you get close to someone who can't tell the difference between a lie and a truth?

How do you hold someone who is always disappearing? Already Eli was flickering in and out of existence again. There was no one in the universe like her. Sometimes Tav loved that about her, and other times — like now — they hated it.

Eli coughed out a word. "Thorns."

"I have it." Cam stepped forward, holding out the blade. Eli recoiled.

"Keep it. I mean, for now. Later. I'll take it later."

Tav helped her stand. "Cam — you take the car; I'll take her on the bike."

Cam nodded. "If something happens —"

"We'll see you soon." Tav cut him off and turned back to Eli, leading her to the bike. Cam watched for a few long seconds, something like hurt flashing in the corner of his eyes, and then quietly did as he was told.

"You healed me," said Eli. "With door magic. How?"

"Who cares? You're alive, aren't you?"

"Because of you. Magic boi. The Healer."

"Fuck that!" cried Tav. "That's a terrible nickname. I don't ever want to hear that again."

They revved the engine and the motorbike took off down the street, leaving behind only a few black feathers, a handful of salt, and a prayer written in blood.

The nickname stuck.

THE HEIR

Kite couldn't remember a time before the library. The smell of ink and sour lemon, the tall bookcases that stretched into the air. She remembered climbing up and up and up, until the gold thread on the spines of ancient fortune volumes were obscured by clouds. Once, she had pulled a book from a shelf, somewhere near the top, and it had fallen apart into a pile of loose pages that had drifted down, strewn across the shelves on the floor.

She was still piecing that book together. Recently, she had found the first page lodged behind a trunk full of ghost stories. The trunk was usually invisible, which made it difficult to find. Fortunately, Kite had been looking for a bobby pin that a paper crane had snatched away while she was reading, and she stumbled over it. She hadn't found the bobby pin — now, as a strand of hair slipped into her eyes, she wished she had — but she had come across page one.

Kite wondered if she would ever get to finish restoring the volume. It was her favourite project, and she had spent so many days carefully smoothing out the lost pages that the paper now smelled of sea salt and rotting fish.

She turned the page. Her candle had burned itself out, spluttering and dying in a puddle of white wax. Smoke curled up through the dark as Kite breathed in the familiar and comforting smell of home.

"This one is from before the moon," she said.

She thought about lighting more candles, but decided against it. The last thing she needed was to be caught back in the Coven, after her dramatic exit. The thrill of breaking the rules washed over her like seafoam.

A glowing ball of light hovered nearby, bobbing near a bookshelf that was painted red and gold, with pages spilling out of its open mouth like flames.

"If you come over here I can read better," said Kite. Clytemnestra's essence ignored her.

Kite had never reached the top of the bookshelves, and besides, the library was always rearranging itself; sometimes a forest of books; sometimes an underground den, with pages buried in earth. She had used a chisel and hammer to break partial histories out of rock; had smoothed the covers with a fine brush, used her breath to clear the fine particles of dust; had caught paper birds in flight and unfolded their pages feather by feather, stitching them together painstakingly as the bird squawked in panic.

Kite was always going to be unusual, even for a witch. She was the only daughter of the Witch Lord, made from a fragment of her mother's essence. Having children like this was rare, not only because witches couldn't die from old age (they could be killed, of course), but because a witch's essence didn't regenerate. It was much safer to fashion an obedient daughter from animal skulls and bottle caps and scraps of faded velvet than risk birthing a witch.

But the Witch Lord needed an Heir to secure her position, to prove her power, to expand her empire.

So she made Kite.

Kite had learned from an early age that "the Coven" meant many things. There were the rings of the Coven, the system of power in the witch world. The lower rings were unimportant. The first ring — they were the mysterious, shrouded figures who did the Witch Lord's bidding, who claimed control of the world. But the building that housed them was older than her mother, older than the petty squabbles of witches, older than the legacy of death that Kite had been born to inherit. Kite usually referred to this Coven, this sentient building, with its sense of humour, ability to hold grudges, and playful tendency to turn doors into walls and windows into chambers of light, as the library. A palace of knowledge.

It had been long neglected. Malicious intent had twisted the tunnels into spiteful creatures, had turned the Heart into a hungry mouth that devoured the unwanted, had caused the building to fold away its bright histories and poetry and rituals in drawers locked with no keys; in towers guarded by smoke snakes, buried in coffins wrapped in curses.

Until Kite.

Until the child who dripped seawater over old pages and left salt incantations on the clothbound covers. The child who gave her own blood to restore the faded ink, who fed sacrifices of insects and fish bones to the living words.

Witch children are not raised, not taught in schools, not coddled by their parents. They are not, and then they are. They are children until they cross over to the human world and steal a name. Before they have a name they are no one, nothing. The Witch Lord had ignored Kite for much of her life. And so Kite had been given the freedom to fall in love with the library, and, even worse, to fall in love with a made-thing.

I'm bored, the glowing ball of light told her as Kite smoothed a hand over a page of long-forgotten incantations for communing with the stars. *How is this helping?*

"We could speak to the stars," said Kite dreamily. "Can you imagine?"

If she catches you, she will kill you. And more importantly — she'll kill me.

"I know." Kite turned the page. "Do we have any taxidermied wings lying around?"

To speak with the stars? Only if they'll sing me a lullaby. The ball of light whirled around Kite once and then hovered over her left shoulder, illuminating the page. A crown of light flickered over Kite's head.

"No," she said, closing the book regretfully. "To burn magic stone."

A creature of smoke and lightning, with a face that looked a little like a fox and many legs — some hoofed, some with paws, and at least one lizard claw — snapped at the ball of light, which darted out of reach.

Do you have to keep that thing *around?* the light complained.

"Oh, he won't do any harm, will you, precious?" Kite offered the dead candle to the Beast, who ate it, and then started chewing on her hair.

The light-essence flickered. *Burn*, Clytemnestra's voice whispered excitedly in Kite's head. *Burn, burn, burn.*

Kite carefully tore the page out of the book. "I have what you need," she said. "We can go now."

Two witches — one flesh, one pure light — travelled through the forgotten pathways of the library, crossing the shadow door back to the Labyrinth, back to the Children's Lair, back to the army and the promise of vengeance.

The children love burning things. Clytemnestra's glee shimmered in Kite's skull. *It's time to teach the Coven fear.*

Kite wondered if she would regret giving this knowledge to the rebellion. But if it saved Eli, it was worth it.

She would do anything to keep Eli alive.

Eleven

THE HEART

Eli was back on the roof of the building. A scattering of stars shone overhead like a handful of costume jewelry had been flung into the sky. It was the only place she could breathe. The only place she could escape from Tav and Cam's worried looks and unasked questions. Escape from their *doubt*.

Eli had almost died today.

She waited for that knowledge to scare her, to spark a reaction in the flora of her limbs. She had been created with a strong sense of self-preservation. She should never have been able to put herself in that kind of danger.

But death didn't scare her half as much as being rejected by her blade. Her blades were a part of her body. Cam had brought the thorn blade back to her — it hadn't hurt him. It hadn't rejected him. Eli had wrapped it in a silk scarf from Cam's drag collection rather than touch it with her bare hands. Now it hung dormant at her waist. But Eli could no longer trust it, and the pain of that knowledge ached.

The persistent thud of a human heartbeat — *Now. Now. Now.* Eli let her eyelids shut as she leaned back and fell into the rhythm of her body.

She could still feel the obsidian blade tenderly pressed against Tav's forearm. A shiver tremored through her body, and it had nothing to do with the cool summer night air.

She let her hands run along the hilts of her other blades — frost, thorn, pearl, stone. A sound like a chime echoed in her skull when her fingers brushed each material, resonating in the capillaries and bronchioles and joints of her patchwork body.

"Why didn't you help us?" she asked.

The ghost said nothing, just stood there, wavering slightly as if unsteady on his feet. Watching her.

She tried again. "Where were you?"

Nothing.

Eli sighed. "If you want your revenge, we can help you find it." She shifted slightly, the pain of sitting in one position for too long arching up her spine.

The ghost was flickering badly.

"Stop that."

A spark of light in the corner of her eye. Eli looked down and saw through her skin a constellation of granite and hawthorn and pearl under the surface. Blink. Her arm faded to light, to nothingness. Blink, and she was solid again.

The ghost opened his mouth in a sucking *O*, or maybe a question, or a cry for help. Then he vanished.

Eli wrapped her arms around her knees and prayed to be left behind. But she vanished, anyway.

What happened, when a girl turned to light, taken over by the magic of a distant world?

What did it feel like?

Flashes of memory — golden trees, rocks like giant teeth. No sense of time. No sense of being one. She was everything and nothing.

Where did she go?

She didn't know that, either.

All she knew was waking up — but that wasn't the right word, because she was never asleep, never more aware of the taste of sunlight and the scent of shadow than when she was her true self, the Heart freed from the prison of matter.

One moment she was on the roof and the next she was in a field of flowers stained indigo. Then she was in Tav's bedroom, staring at the rumpled sheets they never bothered to make, stray purple hairs on the pillow. Then in the attic apartment with wine stains and dust bunnies. Cam and Tav, deep in conversation, fell silent and stared at her. She placed a shaky hand on the counter for support and tried a smile.

"Miss me?"

"Can't you use the fire escape like a normal person?" complained Cam. "You know that scares the shit out of me."

"What's the point in being the Heart if I can't enjoy it?" she said.

Cam had several heartsick, heartbreak, and heart-attack puns ready.

Eli let herself exhale and fell into a mantra that was half truth and half wish. *I'm here. I'm here. I'm here.*

THE HEALER

Tav watched Eli for signs of pain, fatigue, or weakness. There had been a moment, after the battle, when Eli had been pressed against them on the bike, and Tav thought she was finally opening, finally letting them in.

But that door had slammed shut, and not even Tav's magic could open it again.

"How are you feeling?" Tav winced at the sound of their own voice, so careful and tentative.

"I said I'm fine." Eli's nails tapped on the wooden arm of the sofa. "We're losing time and momentum. We need to do the main seam. The Vortex."

"Closing the Hedge-Witch's seam was hard," said Tav. "Eli —"

"Don't say my name like that." Pure-black eyes snapped to meet Tav's. "I'm fine. We have to do this."

"We will." Tav took a shaky breath. "But we need to make sure we're ready —"

"I'm ready." Her voice was clear and strong, but Tav could hear the chords of uncertainty underneath. "This mission matters more than anything."

"That sounds like the old you," said Cam quietly. "Your purpose —"

"Do you want to let the world die?" Eli snapped. "We have to do this. *Alone*."

Tav nodded. They looked away, unable to meet Eli's gaze.

"Tonight," said Eli firmly. She was starting to fade, her body slipping into the Heart. Losing herself in it.

What would happen if she didn't come back this time?

Tav had already decided. They needed the Hedge-Witch.

"Early morning," they said. "We have to set the wards, keep humans out. We don't want collateral damage."

Eli's body had disappeared, but her face was still visible, and her eyes were sad. "I think it's a little late for that, don't you?"

When she was gone, Tav sank back against the old sofa and closed their eyes. Maybe Eli wasn't the only one who was coming apart. "We need help, Cam."

"I'll go," said Cam. "I'll bring the message to the Hedge-Witch. You need to rest."

"No." The word felt like gravel scraping their throat as they regurgitated it. "It has to be me."

"Why? I don't —"

"Let it go, Cam. Just — I'll go. Wait here."

"I'm always waiting here." His voice was soft, but with an edge of tension. "Look, I can help."

"You do help. You saved us back there, remember? We need you. And I don't know that we should trust the Hedge-Witch." Tav felt the truth behind their words as soon as they spoke them, and it chilled their blood. The Hedge-Witch had welcomed them into their home, had birthed them into the world of magic. Tav felt the new distance between them like a cut. Eli's mistrust was contagious.

"I've worked with her, too, you know. You're not the only one."

"Did you give Eli the blade back?" Tav changed the subject. They didn't want to talk about the Hedge-Witch with him. He didn't understand. He had never been close to her the way Tav had been.

"Yes." Cam's brow was furrowed. "She seemed afraid of it."

"Did she say anything to you?"

"No."

Tav put their head in their hands. Another complication. An assassin who wouldn't use her knives. A girl who kept disappearing. An unstable Heart.

"Well, keep an eye on her."

"I was planning to."

Shaking their head, Tav stood. "If — *when* — Eli rematerializes, tell her ..." Their voice trailed off.

"Tell her what?" Cam handed Tav their jacket, worry in his eyes. Tav didn't want to see it, so they looked away.

"Nothing. Don't tell her anything."

Cam's reproachful stare followed them out the door, down the stairs, and into the night.

THE HEART

Eli reappeared in front of the ghost, mouth full of the taste of honey, light pouring out of her body. Hands went to her blades, slipping — still — over the empty sheath, falling on stone and pearl. She bared her teeth.

He turned to face her.

The cold wind whipped her hair around her face. Her bangs were getting too long — they caught in her glasses and eyelashes. The wind ruffled the collar of his coat and the ends of his tartan scarf.

They stared at one another, girl-Heart and ghost, hunter and prey. Two misplaced magics on a rock slowly turning on its axis in a dark universe. Two beings drawn to a boi with silver earrings and a smile like a bullet.

He was old, Eli knew that. He had been haunting this city for a long time. He looked like a human. He even moved like a human, the right amount of grace and clumsiness.

But Eli knew he wasn't one. She could smell the decay and sadness like sour milk on him.

She raised the pearl blade in front of her.

"If you hurt them, I will kill you," she told him. *It.*

He stepped forward.

Eli's hand tightened on the blade as she narrowed her eyes. "Leave us alone."

Another step.

An image flashed across her eyes. The Heart's pain surging to the forefront. Memories that wounded. The forest was burning. Smoke burned her eyes. So much pain. So much destruction. Her children were screaming in agony —

Blink. Back to here, now, this body, this threat.

Step.

Another memory — young witches, their teeth sticky with sap and blood, offering strands of hair to her. Feeding her fire, dancing in her soil. Watering the land with tears of joy and loss.

A cold wind cut through the image, and the chill seeped into her human bones. Eli shivered, and the blade in her hand trembled. Her grip relaxed.

The ghost was in front of her now, his dead eyes boring into hers. Her grip on the blade was unsteady, her heartbeat wild and erratic.

The ghost touched her wrist.

Light flowed from her body to his, and for a moment Eli could see the outline of the person he had once been. Before the witches. Before death. When his magic was pure and strong like hers.

He had a name, once.

Many names.

Many sisters, with clever hands and shadow wings, and on his name-day they had carried him up into the sky to look over the blue-and-white planet that danced below them.

They were all gone now.

No one knew why some survived — if you could call this new form *survival* — but he had stayed while his sisters had died. They were dust now, reflecting the sun back on the Earth, sleeping in the dead craters of the husk of their world. And he was here, feeding his emptiness with hate, growing sluggish with revenge and regret.

Not all killers are made out of hawthorn and glass, but all killers are made.

Eli pulled back, gasping for breath, the ghost's memories and feelings still swimming in her veins.

Then the light extinguished, and she was just a girl again, with asthmatic lungs and a weak heart. Her hand fell to her side.

She tucked her hair behind one ear and turned away. "You want to come along? Fine. Just don't get in my way, understand? I won't end up like you. I won't."

The sound of the motorcycle revving. Disappointment heavy in her stomach, Eli went after them.

Eli didn't look behind her, but she knew the ghost was following.

Her hand was still shaking.

THE HEIR

The main square of the City of Eyes glowed white, a light that was brutal and painful to behold. It was also very beautiful, like a polished star. Beauty that could kill — like her mother, thought Kite. Like every magic in the world, every gold- and silver-touched thread of power. Every tooth and blade and bone.

Unbidden, Kite's mind conjured up an image of a teenage girl with yellow eyes and crocodile teeth, the reptilian girl's knuckles white and lined with dark veins as her fingers tightened around glittering blades.

Perhaps the danger was what made them beautiful.

"I shouldn't be here," said Kite. "If I'm seen —"

"You won't be seen." Clytemnestra threw a handful of glitter confetti at the Heir Rising. Kite's tongue snaked out and caught one of the silver flakes before darting back into her mouth.

They were standing at the entrance of a shadow door, one of the many ways between the invisible Labyrinth and the city underneath it.

"I could be researching —"

"No." The word fell like a fragment of stone, heavy and sharp. Clytemnestra twisted her head and neck to face the other witch. "No. You watch."

"You don't trust me not to warn them?" Kite's hair writhed, the strands twisting over one another.

Clytemnestra giggled. "Of course I don't trust you."

Kite's hair stilled. A single wave rippled down the long bluegreen waterfall that stretched nearly to her ankles. She understood. "This is a test."

"Anyone can see your power," said the child. "You are more than a child, Heir. You've never been one of us. And trust is earned."

Kite closed her eyes briefly and called up the memory of prismatic light bonding to her essence. Felt the thrum of power, the taste of a dead and drained witch strengthening her body. Shuddered at the slick feeling of it, like gasoline on her tongue.

Craved it.

Needed it.

Just a taste more —

Kite's eyes opened to slits, and through the narrow field of vision she could see the whitegold light quivering under Clytemnestra's skin. Could almost taste the honey and whiskey fire of the Warlord's fierce magic.

What she could do with that magic, how much stronger she would be —

The Beast nipped at her heels.

Kite's eyes widened, and the potent scent of witch essence faded. "Shhh now, that's a good Beast," she purred, reaching down to run a hand over the motley feather, fur, and scales. The Beast rubbed against her legs, trembling slightly.

Clytemnestra went up on her tiptoes, excitement visible in her entire body. "Almost time now. The children followed your instructions. All it needs is the trigger."

Kite frowned. "What's the trigger?"

Clytemnestra clapped her hands together. "It's you, of course."

She reached out and plucked a single hair from Kite's head.

The pain was slight, but all the other hairs rose up in protest, slapping at Clytemnestra's hands, whipping around Kite's face like a tornado.

The Witch Lord reached out and touched her essence. Pain blocked out all other senses, memories, feelings ...

When Kite's consciousness resurfaced, she was huddled on the floor, arms wrapped around her body, heart pounding. She was still in the shadow door, but Clytemnestra was gone. The witch leader had crossed into the main square.

From her hiding place, Kite could hear her voice, magnified by magic.

"I bring a message from the children," Clytemnestra announced, floating up into the air.

The sound waves were so strong that Kite felt them rattle across her essence. The other creatures felt them, too. Carriages screeched to a halt. Witches froze on their way to or from the Coven, arranged on the steps like statues. They turned to watch the abomination, who was crackling with energy, with electricity, eyes glowing like flames. She looked like a demon-angel, a baby monster. Her voice was strong and could not be ignored.

Kite knew Clytemnestra had been working on the spell for a long time. This message would be heard throughout the world.

Every witch would know what happened here today.

"The rule of the Coven is ending. The children have risen, and we bring chaos, freedom, and anarchy. When the Witch Lord is ready to meet our demands, she can find me in the Labyrinth. We are not afraid," she went on, "and we are no longer in hiding. Welcome to the end of the world — and the beginning of a new one."

A glint of bluegreen in Clytemnestra's hand began to sizzle, the strand of hair going up in the smoke. The trigger.

The main square exploded.

THE HEALER

The bike was waiting for them. Tav let their hands run over the leather seat, inhaling the scent of gasoline and lavender. Their Kawasaki Vulcan 900 was their most prized possession. Tav's cruiser was reliable, loyal, and it got them where they wanted to go. It was black and chrome, with an aquamarine mermaid spray-painted on the fender. Cam liked to make fun of the design and had taken to calling the bike "your girlfriend," "Starbucks," and "Ariel." "Ariel" was Cam's favourite. Tav liked to think it was a reference to Shakespeare's imprisoned spirit in *The Tempest*, but Cam insisted that was an affront to both Hans Christian Andersen and, more importantly, to Disney.

To Tav, the sea monster was a masthead, and a symbol of their freedom. Their bike was their ship, and it turned the city into an ocean. It opened up the world to them, offered the freedom and adventure that Tav imagined explorers used to have when they risked their lives sailing the seas to discover faraway shores.

But while those fifteenth-century voyagers had carried genocide and slavery with them, Tav would carry vengeance and justice.

A sliver of guilt cut through the pleasure that riding always gave them. They had left Cam behind, again. They knew he hated that. Tav didn't want Cam anywhere near the Hedge-Witch's manipulations or machinations. But they had another reason for leaving him at the apartment — they wanted to be alone tonight. The apartment was crowded with bodies and magic and feelings, and Tav needed time to breathe before the next attack.

It felt like a very long time had passed since they had last gone for a midnight ride with their thoughts. Sometimes when they were anxious, it helped to talk it out with Cam over a beer or an espresso. But not even Cam could help Tav with the burden they now carried.

The bike purred to life, and Tav sped off into the night, following the familiar pathway to The Sun, letting nostalgia mingle with heartache. The moon was slipping into a waxing gibbous, shadow and light coming together on the surface of the dead rock. It was beautiful.

Flashes of memory burst through the solitude.

Eli's waist under their hands, her skin soft and warm.

The made-girl's breath in their ear, whispering their name.

Foreheads pressed together, yellow eyes burning with intensity.

Tav's knees tightened around the bike, a shiver wracking their body. Tav had dated around and was well known in the queer scene. They'd had crushes on dozens of girls, taken them on dates and kissed them in the back seats of their moms' minivans, got lipstick stains on collared shirts. It was fun, and exciting, and Tav had spent their fair share of nights thinking about ripped jeans and a sharp collarbone. But nothing had lasted long, had ever meant much. Tav slipped in and out of relationships like jackets — a new one each season.

They had never felt this way about anyone before.

Maybe it was the weight of growing up different, of growing up sharp as a needle, but Tav never let anyone get too close. Tav learned to smile and laugh while their nails cut half moons into their palms; learned how to flirt and tease and buy shots for pretty girls. Learned to shrug it off when the girls left with their white boyfriends or girlfriends. And since the ghost, since discovering magic was real, they'd stopped showing up at the gay bar, stopped going to drag shows, and cheering on their exes at roller derby. The only people they saw were Cam and the Hedge-Witch. They'd even started avoiding their parents, not wanting to deal with the disappointed looks and tense hugs.

With Eli they could be themselves. They could be angry, sad, flawed. They were allowed to want impossible things. They were allowed to *do* impossible things. And the way Eli looked at them when they used their magic — like they were special, like they were someone Eli wanted to touch, or maybe taste.

That look kept Tav up at night.

A few bats fluttered overhead. Tav liked the company of other nocturnal animals. They had never been very good at sleeping, had often gone for walks at 3:00 a.m. It was the safest time to go walking alone.

Eli wanted Tav. But maybe it wasn't them at all. Maybe it was just the magic she wanted to fuck. Maybe when the wounds between worlds had been healed, Eli would go back to the City of Eyes and leave Tav behind. Maybe when she met someone who had more power, she would follow that source of magic instead, and would taste someone else.

But she wanted you before she knew you had magic, Tav thought, their stomach twisting with anxiety.

Maybe she's lying to you.

The Sun appeared too soon, framed by the half-light of the moon. Tav flashed their lights a few times and then waited. After a long moment, the lights inside the café flickered on.

The Hedge-Witch was waiting.

THE HEIR

Fanged horses screamed, sweat and blood leaking from their nostrils as they climbed into the sky to escape the trauma. Carriages were ripped apart, spiked wheels tossed across the square. Witch bodies were torn from their essences. Smoke and flames rose from the ruin. The steps leading to the Coven were demolished, a pile of burning white rubble.

Proof that the Coven was no longer untouchable.

The rumours would start here — that the Coven was weak, the Witch Lord fallible, that the centre of power could be destroyed. That the Heart of the world was failing, or perhaps, even, that it had been stolen. The stories would circulate throughout the world.

Thousands of eyes watched the bloodbath, and tongues whispered of fear and failure and disobedient children.

Above it all, golden curls bouncing, face smudged with soot, Clytemnestra was resplendent — her essence glowing through her skin, her smile benevolent and gentle.

She was a queen crowned on a throne of mayhem.

A tiny worm of fear slithered behind Kite's eyeballs. She had done this, piecing together forbidden magics in the library and using that knowledge to destroy. She had brought the spell work to Clytemnestra, and she herself had whispered the words. The Beast whined against her skirts.

"It's okay," whispered Kite. "This is what we wanted."

But her voice trembled.

Acolytes rushed from the mouth of the Coven to quell the flames. Jade steeds lay on the ruined marble, wounded and shrieking, blood flowing like ink.

Clytemnestra was giggling.

"They will come for the children," said Kite.

"They can't enter the Children's Lair. They can run through the entire Labyrinth and will never find us!" The Warlord clapped her hands together. "We will play a game of hide and seek."

The flames were already extinguished, members of the higher rings of power emerging to cast protective wards and heal the wounded. Smoke fluttered above the Coven, stretching upward toward the sky. The Coven itself was unharmed; it was an impenetrable fortress, a living creature of stone and earth and magic. But the message had been delivered — the announcement of a coup, the proclamation of a rival lord. And the challenge had been written in gunpowder on the very steps of power.

The children had come out of hiding.

A few bloodthirsty children pushed past Clytemnestra and Kite, casting flashes of light to spook any animals that were uninjured and tossing hexes at the Coven witches before vanishing back into the Labyrinth. A boy in a tutu lay on his back and made ash angels, sweeping the soot with his arms and legs. One naughty girl in pigtails set off fireworks, the gold-and-red glitter mixing with smoke.

"They can never resist a demolition," said Clytemnestra fondly.

"Even if you hide, they will find you. They will hunt you."

"They won't have to find us." The Warlord yawned, her pink tongue sticking out of her mouth like a kitten's. "We'll come to them. The children are ready to fight — and you won't take too long to find us some new recruits, will you, my little matricidal Heir? Besides, people will be lining up to join us once they hear about our magnificent performance!"

Kite stared at the smoking street that would soon be polished over again in marble and magic. But the stone would remember being broken. There was no going back.

Clytemnestra's eyes were shining as she turned to Kite, capturing the Heir's gaze as easily as she stuck insects with hat pins. Her voice was reverent as she whispered, "The revolution has begun."

THE HEALER

Then —

They had been picking up milk from the corner store when they first saw it — a glimmering light in their peripheral vision. When Tav tried to focus on the light it disappeared, playing in and out of their line of sight. The carton hung from one hand, the other stuffed into their coat pocket. Flakes of snow drifted past, gently brushing their shoulders and forehead.

A few months earlier they would have turned away from the strange glimmer. Made a box of KD with cut-up hotdogs. Binged reruns of *Friends* (they had a crush on Charlie, the highlight of season ten).

But that was before the ghost.

This was after.

The light was a different kind of magic from the ghost, but it crackled with the same electricity. Smell of burnt sugar. Aftertaste of rotten fruit and mouthwash. Sickly sweet. Tav's mouth watered, saliva pooling in the corners of their lips.

Their cell rang.

"Hey, Mom. Working late again?"

"Don't make Kraft Dinner, okay? You can't live off that shit."

"I won't."

"You home yet? What's that noise in the background?"

Tav glanced up, and a flash of greenblack burst into their vision, lights flickering down an invisible chain before vanishing into the distance. They were leading east.

"Yeah, I'm home."

Tav hung up, opened the carton, took a swig of milk, and started walking. They weren't reckless — most of the time — and their guidance counsellor insisted they were smart. So Tav didn't follow the thread of promise and power. At least, not on foot.

They stole their mom's bike.

It was early December and the bike hadn't been stored away yet. It had been an unusually warm fall, and this was the first snow. At least the roads weren't icy. Tav buckled the helmet and pulled on their mom's leather gloves, feeling braver and stronger than they had yesterday. Finally, after weeks of waiting, and wondering, and looking everywhere for magic — *finally*, they had a lead. And they weren't going to lose it.

Tav turned the key in the ignition and grinned as the bike roared to life. They took off into the city. The thread of light wound its way through Grace, through the busy downtown heart of the city crowded with buses and traffic lights and neon signs. Past the city limits with the faded, kitschy welcome sign.

Tav had been out on the bike before, arms locked around their mom's waist, wind in their ears. But this was different. This time, the bike responded to their touch. As the road fell away under their wheels, Tav felt the bike becoming an extension of their body, a new way of moving through time and space. A feeling grew in their chest and then burst across their body, thrumming in their shoulders and heels. *Escape*. The throaty roar of the engine and the whine of the wind that couldn't keep up — *this* was what power felt like. *This* was the sound of freedom.

The magic thread ended at a small building that looked like a fairy-tale cottage, with round windows and a tiny brick chimney with a curlicue of smoke hanging above it. Tav shivered with anticipation. A sign outside the cottage read THE SUN. Another hipster café pop-up — not unusual in the city, but definitely out of place this far from the bustling streets and customers desperate for another hit of caffeine.

This café was the source of the magic. Tav was sure of it.

Tav dismounted, kicking the stand into place. They unbuckled their helmet and tucked it under one arm, staring into the round windows. Taking a breath, Tav stepped forward and opened the door. Chimes tinkled faintly, and a sense of calm washed over them.

The woman behind the counter had dark red hair and eyes that — Tav blinked, and then looked again.

The woman's eyes were milky white with a thin, jagged pupil like a cut across the white. Tav tried not to flinch as those eyes crawled over their body.

"What can I get you, love?"

Tav walked forward and tapped their fingers on the counter. The magic hummed in their bones and made every shape and shadow come to life. They could taste the cedar in the air. They could smell the limestone bed under the soil.

Tav met the woman's gaze. "Just coffee. Black." They hesitated, and then forced the words out. "Do you believe in ghosts?"

The cactus on the counter began quivering, its single red blossom opening and closing in an undulating rhythm. The spines grew longer, twisting wildly. Tav stared at the plant and pulled their hand away.

"Oh, you *are* interesting," said the woman, a smile unstitching across her face like it belonged to a rag doll. "I think I'll have a coffee with you." She leaned across the counter, until her alien eyes were only a few inches from Tav's. "Of course I believe in ghosts, Tav — I believe in everything that's real."

Now —

"I believe in everything that's real."

Tav hoped that was still true.

The sign was rotting, the paint chipped and faded. They could barely make out the words *The Sun*, and the red paint, once cheery and reminiscent of child-drawn hearts and wrapping paper, now looked like dried blood.

Tav lingered outside for a moment longer, fidgeting with their keys, flooded by memories, feelings, and the overwhelming magic that radiated from the building.

It had been more than a year ago when they had first set foot in this space. The Hedge-Witch had taken them under her wing, had shown them magic, had promised an end to the violence that broke the city. Their time at The Sun had changed their life.

But all of their plans had hinged on Tav retrieving the Heart. What would the Hedge-Witch do when they returned empty-handed?

Tav breathed in the smell of freshly ground coffee and diluted magic. They had always been able to sense the magic in this space, and it had pulled them away from the small house on Church Street and the promises of a normal teenage life.

But Tav had never been normal. Finding the Hedge-Witch had been, in a small way, like coming home. The Hedge-Witch had welcomed them into their family of misfits and rebels, and for a while, Tav had felt like they belonged. Among humans and a witch and sometimes a ghost, those bodies who lived on the edges of society; the outcasts from different worlds, coming together to build a better future.

That goal had spoken to Tav. Tav was Black, non-binary, and queer, in a city of white men in business suits who bulldozed the poorer parts of town any chance they got and used their power and influence to destroy anyone who was not like them. Tav had been born into injustice, and they knew — had always known — that they would never be able to live in the corners left for them by those in power.

They would have to remake the world.

The Hedge-Witch had promised change. For over a year, Tav had run errands and delivered messages, tracking witches and assassins and ghosts, recruiting, following orders, listening, nodding, learning. Being told to trust no one, not even Cam. Told to speak to no one, listen to no one, except the Hedge-Witch.

The Hedge-Witch, with her plant children and her human lover. Tav had adored her. Trusted her. Choked down the doubts that filled their mouth whenever the witch told them to wait; that it wasn't time yet; that humans couldn't learn magic; that magic would destroy Tav. Had never let themselves question the Hedge-Witch's intentions.

Until they met Eli. Until they discovered the magic within themselves that lay dormant, waiting. The magic that let them see ghosts and the essences of witches. Until they realized that not only could they see magic, they could touch it. Use it. They had opened doors between worlds. They had met creatures who were neither witch nor human nor object. They had fought monsters and fallen in love with monsters and come to understand that the universe was a much more complicated and dangerous and beautiful place than they had ever imagined.

Tav was not the same person who had stepped through these doors many months ago.

Could they treat with the Hedge-Witch as an equal?

And what if the Hedge-Witch refused to help? Would they find themselves on different sides now, of what looked like a many-sided war, a struggle for power, for recognition, for survival?

Tav wanted to believe the Hedge-Witch would join them. Would help them. But they weren't so sure anymore. The doubts that had drifted like pieces of sand in their bloodstream now flowed thick and dark through their arteries and veins. Was the Hedge-Witch, with her single-minded pursuit of the Heart, all that different from the Coven?

Shoving one hand in their pocket, Tav made a fist with the other and knocked once on the door.

The door swung open. The tinkling of chimes broke the silence. Tav ran a hand through their purple hair (wishing they had time for a haircut) and crossed the threshold.

Immediately the weight of the magic pressed on their lungs; like dust, it clung to every surface and hung in the air, thick and cloying as perfume. The

Hedge-Witch must have increased security measures; either that, or she had been casting some complicated enchantments recently.

"Can I help you?" A young woman with gleaming white teeth stood behind the bar. Otherwise the room was empty.

Tav could see through the glamour as easily as looking through a window.

"Did you miss me?" Tav grinned and spun their keys around their pointer finger, flashes of silver playing over the walls. "I've had quite the adventure." They walked over to the nearest table and sank into a thin wicker chair, throwing one leg up on the table, hands behind their head.

The face of the cheerful but bland woman melted away to show the sharp eyebrows and wide mouth of the Hedge-Witch. "You've been gone longer than expected."

"I have," Tav agreed. "And there's no homecoming party to welcome me back. I'm disappointed."

"But surely not surprised. Will you submit to an examination? To ensure you didn't come back with some nasty Coven spell behind your eyelids or under your liver?"

"Sounds painful, so I'll pass."

"I thought you might." The Hedge-Witch suddenly appeared in front of Tav. Tav managed not to flinch, even when the witch's shadow leaned over and handed them a mug of hot coffee.

"Cute trick." Tav swung their leg off the table, accepted the coffee, and took a sip. It burned their tongue. "Tasty." They smiled. "Thank you."

"Etiquette should always be observed, even in these uncivilized times. The Sun, as you know, has always been a sanctuary."

"For whom?"

"For us, and our allies." The Hedge-Witch sat across from Tav. "You've come into your powers, then."

"You knew?"

"I suspected." The Hedge-Witch sipped her espresso. Tav felt a surge of anger play across their cheekbones.

"Why didn't you tell me?"

The Hedge-Witch arched an eyebrow coolly. "I didn't know for sure. You had to discover it on your own."

Tav tightened their grip on the mug, feeling like a child being reprimanded. Had the Hedge-Witch always been this cool, this calculating?

Isn't that why you admired her?

"There's news." Tav took another sip of the bitter drink. "The Coven is destroying the Earth. They're devouring it, drinking its essence." They paused, fumbling over the words and their terrible meanings. "I have a method of healing the damage. I think."

"You think."

"We could use your network."

"To save the world?" The mocking tone slipped under Tav's rib cage.

"To save both worlds, actually." The plants that lined the room were stretching out tentacles of magic. Tav pretended they couldn't sense them drawing closer. They had seen first-hand how deadly the Hedge-Witch's children could be. Their heart began to race. It would be so easy to open a door, to disappear …

To break the promise they had made to Cam and Eli. Not to use their power. Not to attract attention. Not to show the full extent of their power.

Not yet.

Tav took a sip of coffee and forced themselves to breathe.

"A conspiracy theory?" The Hedge-Witch shook her head sadly. "The real battle is here. Will you let your city get overtaken by the alt-right as you chase after a fantasy? I left that world for this one. I'm not interested in hearing about the Coven's squabbles. All we need is their power. Not their politics. Not their problems. We have our own, Tav." She finished her espresso and leaned forward, elbows on the table. Her eyes latched on to Tav's, her pupils expanding and contracting like oil flowing across water. Soothed magic hummed around the Hedge-Witch's body like an aura.

"Did you get it?" she whispered. Her eyes were hypnotic.

Would it be so bad if I gave it to her? If we turned the Heart over to the Hedge-Witch now, and let her lead us? She has power and experience.

And then it wouldn't be me. It wouldn't be our problem anymore. Would it be so terrible to let someone else carry the burden?

Just tell her where the Heart is.

But the Heart was a person, and Tav had made a promise. (They were losing track of their promises: the ones they had made, the ones they had broken, and the ones that would ruin them.)

Tav wrenched their eyes away, their human heart racing. Words fluttered into their mind, a memory — the first conversation they ever had with the Hedge-Witch.

"The Coven has something we could use to end the struggle. You could do it — Tav. I've seen *it."*

"But the ghost —"

"The ghost was a sign. It brought you to me."

Tav shook their head, snapping back to the present. "We failed."

The Hedge-Witch drew back, the plants lining the window ledges wilting. Her lips thinned. "That's disappointing."

Tav exhaled. "It's not too late —"

"It's disappointing that you felt the need to lie to me," the Hedge-Witch interrupted. "You know I've only ever wanted to help you. To see you succeed. To see your people thrive. I thought we had the same goals."

"I thought you wanted the Heart."

"Of course. I need the power of the Heart to help you. To bring justice. To create a new order."

"And who would lead it?"

"We would, of course. You and I."

"Not the others?" Tav remembered the private lessons, the secrecy, the insistence that they were special. No one else was given the morsels of knowledge that Tav was offered, handed out like a handler training a dog.

"They can't handle the responsibility. But we can, Tav. We can bear the burden. You just need to share the Heart's power with me, and everything will change."

Justice. Change. Power. Those words had once been irresistible to Tav, but now, spoken with such hunger, Tav heard them differently. Why did the Hedge-Witch care about the treatment of queer people, people of colour, poor people? The truth settled like sediment in their stomach: she had never meant to share power with Tav. She had only meant to use them to gain control of the city. Perhaps even to build her own Coven on the blue planet. Eli had been right, after all — the Hedge-Witch couldn't be trusted.

But she could still be useful.

Tav leaned forward. "We still have the same goals. But I have to do this first. You need to trust me." They forced the next words from their mouth. "If you help me with this, I will give you the Heart."

"Pretty words from a human. You've already broken one promise."

Tav took a switchblade out of their pocket and pressed its thirsty tip against their palm. Three drops of blood fell into the dregs of their coffee. They pushed the cup across the table. "I swear it on my blood."

Outside, a car was waiting. Jazz music danced through the open windows.

The Hedge-Witch raised the mug to her lips and purred. "I will help you." She drank deeply, and Tav's sense of foreboding grew with every swallow.

Outside, a car waited for them. The driver of the dirty black Hyundai wore a pair of aviator sunglasses and was playing with his moustache.

With trembling hands, Tav opened the door and climbed in.

"I told you not to come."

"I thought you might need backup."

"You were right." They shuddered violently, their body shaking off the stray threads of the Hedge-Witch's magic that clung to their clothes and hair.

"What about the bike?" he asked.

"I don't think I can drive. We'll come back for it later."

A few bars of trumpet played between them.

"Does she know?" he asked finally, face creased in worry.

Tav shook their head, heart pounding. "No."

As they took off down the city streets, raindrops starting to fall forlornly on the asphalt, Tav realized Cam had probably meant the Hedge-Witch.

THE HEART

A girl and a ghost watched Tav get into the car and drive away. To Eli's surprise, Tav's prized motorcycle was left behind, looking lonely and sad.

"What do you think?" she asked the ghost.

The ghost said nothing.

"I think it's trouble." She sighed, playing with her blades. The obsidian knife called to her from where it rested against Tav's skin. She could follow Tav anywhere. They were a burning arrow in the night.

"Should we check it out?" She nodded at the café, the pulse of magic sending off alarm signals in her fingertips. But hey, she was the Heart — what could go wrong?

The ghost turned around and started walking away.

"You're probably right. It isn't the right time."

She went to retrieve the bike. It was a good thing she'd had Cam make copies of the keys. She could kill the Hedge-Witch later.

It was the only way Tav could be free.

THE HEIR

"You have proven yourself a traitor to the throne. We should celebrate!" Clytemnestra appeared while Kite was trying to read, having set up a makeshift desk and bookshelf in one of the stone chambers in the Children's Lair. Every so often the walls would shake violently, dirt sprinkling over her page. The Coven had sent patrols into the Labyrinth, and their magic was upsetting the living, breathing walls.

Kite had been thinking about Eli.

Kite looked up. "Have you heard from her? I think I found a way to restore her shattered blade. I found it in this manuscript under —"

"Can we do that after we burn down the Coven and let a few fire creatures loose and make bets on who lasts the longest?"

"We're not burning down the library!" Kite's hair floated around her head, poised like coiled serpents.

"You're no fun." Clytemnestra stuck her tongue out. "And neither is that broken thing you insist on keeping. I want a *new* doll."

"You love old, broken things." Kite smiled, her hair swirling in lazy loops. "New things all taste the same."

"I want a new doll."

"I'll get you one."

"I want one *now*."

Kite's hair snapped down like a whip, leaving red welts on her bluegreen skin. "Be patient, little one."

"Oh, I'm very patient, *young* one." Clytemnestra reached out and stroked Kite's hair. "But the children are not. I've promised them some fun, and you know how babes get when you ruin their game."

"That's your problem, not mine, Warlord."

"It's our problem now, traitor."

"You forget yourself. I'm still the Heir."

The two witches stared each other down, glowing bluegreen orbs meeting the painted eyes of a china doll. And then Clytemnestra flew up into the air, her skirts flowing around her.

"Your Majesty." Clytemnestra performed an upside-down bow mid-air, twisting like a circus performer. Her voice dripped with sarcasm. "I am your loyal subject. I only request, as your humble servant, that you —"

"I said I'll get you one. Soon."

Clytemnestra smiled widely. "That's a good girl. You're one of us now." She vanished with a *pop*.

Kite looked down at the book and sighed. With all the commotion, she had lost her place on the page.

THE HEALER

The morning broke like a dinner plate, jagged and precious. Pale yellowpink light poured through the attic window and onto the tired bodies inside, worn down by expectations and secrets.

"Help yourself," said Cam, who was probably on his third cup of coffee.

Tav shook their head. "I don't want to crash later."

"I don't plan to crash until tonight." Cam winked. "The trick is to not stop." He took another sip and let out an exaggerated sigh of pleasure.

Eli never turned down caffeine, so she poured herself a full mug, then frowned. "Figs?"

"You're learning!" Cam's voice rang with joy. The sound was as comforting as the smell of freshly ground coffee, which always seemed to follow Cam around.

In these moments — if Tav didn't look too closely at the stones protruding from Cam's body — they could almost forget that the world was going to shit.

Almost.

"You went to the Hedge-Witch." Eli turned to Tav.

Tav exhaled sharply. "You followed me?"

Eli's yellow eyes sparked with accusation.

Tav wasn't about to apologize for their actions. If there was ever a time they needed backup, it was now. Eli just didn't want to admit it.

"I know you don't like her," said Tav. They needed Eli to believe in them. There was no way Tav and Eli could close the vortex if they didn't trust each other.

"*Like* has nothing to do with it," said Eli.

"She's going to help us."

"Maybe." Eli tilted her head to one side. A greasy film of distrust slid over the room. "What did you offer her in exchange?"

"I handled it, okay?"

"You handled it." Eli's voice was rough and gritty.

"You weren't exactly here to help."

Eli flinched. "I brought your bike back," she said.

"I hope you didn't scratch her."

"You're welcome, Tav."

Tav took a few breaths. "So the coffee tastes like figs?"

Eli stared at them for a long moment. It felt like a small mercy when she finally said, "Yeah, it does."

"Well." Tav cleared their throat. "We should go, I guess."

The euphoria of the first victory had faded to a bad hangover, and Tav felt a familiar stabbing in their guts.

They were afraid.

"You need to eat," Cam told them.

"No."

"That's what Eli said."

"I don't need to eat." Eli's eyes flashed pure black for a moment before switching back to yellow, like a glitching computer screen bright with broken pixels.

"Well, Tav does. They're at least half human, and they need —"

"I said no." Their voice was louder and harsher than they had intended.

Cam stopped talking, the expression on his face frozen in place. "Okay, captain," he said quietly, with only the barest whisper of sarcasm. "Whatever you say."

"All right girls, boys, and magic toys, time to save the world." Tav grabbed their boots from where they sprawled in the middle of the floor and pulled them on.

"Am I the magic toy?" Eli tapped the hilt of the frost blade and grinned.

Tav grinned back, the adrenalin rush of fear oxidizing into excitement. Like their first time on the cruiser, going a hundred kilometres an hour on a back road, knowing that if they made a single mistake the road would tear the fabric and skin off their body, but loving it, anyway. They hadn't fallen that day, or any day since.

Tav spun the keys around their index finger and then pointed the jagged metal teeth at Eli like a gun, and the words spilled out. "You're something special."

Cam was silent.

THE HEART

The ghost was nowhere to be seen. Eli felt strangely abandoned.

Five blades hung from her hips where there had once been seven. The frost blade, the revealer, that forced the truth from blood and flesh. The stone blade, the shield, a short sword that was a strong defensive weapon. The pearl blade, the divider, that could untether souls from their delicate shells, splitting bodies into their pure material parts. The bone blade, the tracker, with its jagged edges that held on to flesh and scent and memory. And the thorn blade, the ensnarer, that trapped victims in perfumed petals and vicious thorns — the blade that had burned her the night before. Had turned on her.

The glass blade was gone, shattered by the Guardian in the confrontation in the Coven. Eli's fingers played with the empty sheath at her waist — she felt its absence like a lost tooth, worrying the fleshy gap with her tongue.

Eli could feel the gentle heartbeat of the smallest blade, so thin it was almost like a long needle. The obsidian blade: the bringer of death, the harvester of lives, the blade of endings. The assassin. Eli had gifted that knife to Tav, and it now it connected them. Now Tav could use it.

But the blade was tricky and devious, and anyone who touched it was marked, the way smoke leaves traces of ash. The blade was both Tav and Eli now; they were three and one.

Alchemy.

Eli felt the rosebuds in her lungs curling and uncurling their tiny petals in anticipation and anxiety. She needed to prove to herself, Cam, and Tav (especially Tav), that she could do this. That she wasn't falling apart. That she didn't need her blades to be a monster.

(She wondered who she would be without her blades.)

If the blades failed, she would use her teeth, her fingernails, her knuckles.

You're only an energy source, the voice in her head reminded her. The voice was almost bitter, like honey tinged with angelica. *Cam protected you; Tav saved you. What did you do, except lie there, waiting to die?*

How long will your crocodile teeth stay lodged in your jaw? How long until all the blades are broken?

You're falling apart. The Heart is tearing you apart.

You're the centre of everything, and the centre is always empty.

Eli didn't like these thoughts. She liked to move, to sweat, to hurt. She liked the feeling of pushing her body to its limits until the glass and wood hinges creaked, but still, still they held. Her body always held strong. It would hold today.

She watched Tav's graceful movements as they mounted the bike in one fluid motion, legs strong and smooth like a dancer's, and thought, *We will win.*

"You coming?" Cam climbed into the flamingo-pink taxicab he'd commandeered.

Eli didn't take her eyes off Tav, their hands moving lovingly over the iron beast. "No, thanks. I'll ride with Tav."

Tav looked up at the sound of their name. Eli caught their gaze and held it for a full second. Eli felt that she was daring Tav to look away. Electrified by their stare, Eli reached for a hilt. Her fingers grasped only air. She glanced down to where the blade of glass should have hung, unbalanced by the absence of weight. When she looked back up, Tav was frowning into the distance.

Tav revved the engine. "Waiting to grow roots?"

Eli could almost feel the shape of the hilt in her hands, the smooth surface under her rough palm. Grief itched under her skin and made her fingers curl into fists.

"Eli?"

Eli looked up. "I'm coming." She swung herself up behind Tav and breathed in their familiar scent. She hadn't fallen apart yet; there was still time.

"Think you can do this?"

Eli leaned forward, a strand of purple hair brushing against her mouth. "Yes," she breathed. She could feel Tav shiver. Then the bike jumped into action, and they drove closer and closer to the hole at the centre of everything.

THE HEIR

It had begun as a rumour.

Kite knew that every rumour in the City of Eyes was born from a feather of truth, a chipped rhinestone of reality; shiny objects that marked a trail into danger.

Made-daughters disappeared all the time. How did the Coven repurpose the bodies of broken or flawed tools? Eli had been raised on myths that the Heart would devour disobedient girls, but the Coven would never show their preciously guarded secret to a defective daughter. And when Eli had finally touched the Heart they had merged into one. No, that was not where the Coven buried the bodies of their daughters. The graveyard was a secret as well guarded as the recipes for making assassins. But Kite had discovered it.

In her years as a reader, Kite had learned how to listen to silence as well as sound; to understand the turn of a page or the stutter of a wing or the nervous flicker of an essence peeking through skin. Even witches had vulnerabilities if you knew where to look. Even guards and buildings and plants spoke, although not always with tongues.

"You can't come," she told the Beast as he gently gnawed on her elbow. "It isn't safe." He shook his entire body, sending sparks scattering over stone, and did not let go. She relented. "Stay close," she told him. He purred.

They were in the library again. The ball of light buzzed around her head.

"Stop that," she said, swatting it. The light floated away, dimming, and hovered just out of reach.

We could have the best revels in here.

"We can't bring the children here," she told Clytemnestra's essence.

You're no fun, said the light. *You bring* me *here.*

"You have self-control," said Kite. "But if you damage the books, I'll extinguish you."

There's no need for more threats. The light sulked. *But I don't see why I can't materialize. This form is so boring. I can't eat anything.* It hovered over a shelf of loose-leaf pages, yellowed with age.

The Beast growled, a low rumbling like a distant thundercloud.

Kite reached out and let the Beast chew on her forearm. He left delicate teeth marks on her wrist, but would never break the skin. "You're upsetting him," she scolded.

The light ignored her.

Kite closed her eyes and touched one of the walls. She was struck at first by the absence of a pulse, by the empty deadness of a body whose heart had been ripped out by a clumsy surgeon. It was cold. She shivered, her body trembling with the presence of death that she felt in the building she loved.

It needed the Heart.

Kite held her breath as she pressed her mind and magic deeper into the building, looking for a sign of life. A moment passed, and then another. And then she could feel it again — the buzzing, biting, snapping strands of magic that kept this place alive, that threaded through every stone and brick and petal and strand of hair, woven into a nest of knowledge. She breathed out in relief. It wasn't dead yet.

But it was angry and in pain. Sadness coloured her vision, and everything went grey.

The Coven was a distrustful creature. Perhaps once it had been open-hearted and willing to love. Kite liked to imagine that it once offered its knowledge and power to any animal or spore or leaf that reached its halls. But the witches had burrowed too deep into stone, had wormed their way into the ancient structure like ants building an underground network. In response, the Coven had become afraid and selfish, hoarding the magic that the witches fed to it, stolen from stars and bodies that had not come willingly.

Once, it might have been easy for the children to walk into the Coven. Once, no one could have been chained under the earth. But there were all kinds of prisons now.

Kite was the bridge. She just hoped that when the children had walked over her and carved out a new place for themselves in the City of Eyes, they wouldn't forget on whose back their victory had been won.

I'm bored, complained the ball of light. *Why are we here?*

"You're forgetting who you are, Clytemnestra," said Kite. "You'll have to materialize soon."

The ball of light ignored her, instead hovering around the Beast. He whined and snapped his jaws at it. The light danced out of reach.

"Stop teasing him."

You don't tell me what to do.

Kite sighed. She pulled her hand away from the wall. "I think it will take me to the daughters."

The Beast stood up, unfurling long wings. They were thin and opaque, like a bat's wing. She could see the veins stretching across pale skin.

"If Eli comes back, you'll keep her safe, won't you?" She looked to the ball of light, black crystals dropping from her eyes.

You were always such a crybaby, the light huffed. *She'll be fine. Are you sure I can't come? You never let me explore the Coven.*

"It has to be me," said Kite. "The Coven only recognizes one Heir."

Not for long. The light wavered and then flashed again. *Can I do it now?*

Kite nodded, more crystals falling onto her lap. "I'm ready." Her pulse quickened in anticipation of pain.

Stop crying.

The light brightened until the entire room was illuminated. Thick vines wound their way around stone shelves. A staircase of leather-bound volumes stretched upward into the sky. Today the library had wrapped itself into the shape of a labyrinth, an ever-curling spiral of books and pages and insects. Kite sat in the centre of a maze of words.

It could only be her. No one else — except for the mothers — knew how to make or unmake a daughter, understood the delicate magic and will and desire that went into creating a person with crocodile eyes and hands that made every touch sacred. Kite had spent her entire life studying ways to free assassins, and she was driven by more than a desire for power.

The light drifted closer, pausing at Kite's forehead. Then a tendril of light and heat reached out from the glowing core and touched her. Kite stiffened, the pain searing through her flesh. When the light drew back, there was a hole in her forehead, and a flicker of turquoise flame lapped at the wound from inside.

Carefully, lovingly, the ball of light touched Kite all over her body: her palms, the soles of her feet, her collarbones. Slowly, the light undressed Kite from her body. It was nice to be touched; Kite had so little experience with it. And then it hurt, but Kite knew it could have hurt worse, knew that the ball of light was being kind. It was that small kindness, rather than the pain of being torn out of herself, that made her cry pieces of salt like hail. So many manuscripts ruined.

When they were done, there were two balls of light: one whiteyellow like a young sun; one bluegreen like light trapped under the ocean. They hung suspended in the air for a moment, and then Clytemnestra winked out of existence, banished to the Children's Lair, returning to her own skin and flesh and memory.

The Beast stayed.

Kite swam through the air toward the staircase of books, slowly winding up and up, the bluegreen light making everything distorted and strange. As she ascended, a few books snapped at her, pages slicing at her essence — but she could not be cut in this form, and the attack only registered dimly as a sense of sadness. Wounded animals lashing out.

Pity didn't stop her from singeing one into ash, however, when it blocked her path. Some injuries could not be avoided.

She had the feeling, as she always did, that the staircase was being built as she climbed, that she was guiding the Coven as much as it was leading her. Since becoming the Heir, however, there was a difference. Before there was cajoling and bargaining and trickery; sometimes the bookcases led her where she wanted to go and sometimes they trapped her in a dead end. She had played endless games with the library as a child, laughing when it buried her alive in paper and spiders and dirt, elated when she caught a handwritten note from the beak of a vellum crane swooping through the rafters.

Now she had a new power; she could feel it in the beds of her fingernails, in the pins-and-needles sensation in the back of her knees, in the fluttering wings at the core of her essence. If she pushed, she could *make* the room obey. She could use the power the Witch Lord had given her to force her way through.

She didn't want to use this new and coercive power, but she would if she had to.

She thought of Eli — the smell of hawthorn petals, the taste of iron. A girl made from granite and glass, a girl made to cut shadow and shatter light like a sheet of ice.

There was another reason it had to be Kite.

No one else cared for the assassins, and the Coven could feel intention. It was moved by want. The Coven could be rebuilt or destroyed by desire.

Bring me to her kin, thought Kite, her light flickering wildly. *I need them.*

The Coven revolted, throwing books at her; they burned when they fell through her essence, and came away wet and ruined. This was her punishment for daring to ask. She knew there were enchantments set to keep the prisoners in place. But no one could stop the Heir Rising.

Kite's light glowed like a spotlight, and books rose from the shelves, floating around her core.

There was a moment of stillness as the world hung, suspended by her desire.

The thread snapped. Books fell as the staircase collapsed, the pages shrieking as they plunged past her.

Then it was just Kite, alone, hovering in an empty space. Her light didn't mark out the edges. There were no edges. There was only space.

And then a corner. A wall. Her essence started to feel its way into cracks and crevices, casting light on a long, glittering web that hung from the ceiling, glistening with water droplets. The Coven had bent to her will and taken her somewhere new.

It had taken Kite to the graveyard of daughters.

THE HEALER

Eli was different today. Tav could tell. She leaned back, hands resting lightly on Tav's shoulders. Tav would never admit it out loud, but they missed the heat of Eli's chest against their back. Eli was stiff, too, like her balance was off. Not the fluid assassin who moved like a dancer, like mist rising over the water in the early morning light.

I'll have to be strong enough for both of us, they thought. A small smile played at the edges of their mouth. They could feel the magic pulsing in their blood, could see it in their veins and marrow. And now they could use it. Tav leaned their head back and howled at the sky, feeling more alive than they ever had. After a moment, Eli joined in, her hands tightening on Tav's shoulders.

The city was abandoned; only a few night-shift workers and tired parents would be awake. The Hedge-Witch had staked out a perimeter for them, setting charms and traps and enchantments to ward off any humans. There was no telling what protection would be laid on the Vortex, what guards would be disturbed from their sleep. And Tav wanted to minimize the harm done to their city. At the very least, the illusion spells would keep them from being seen.

They stopped the bike suddenly and jumped off, the obliteration-exhilaration turning into spidery twitches down their muscles and tendons. Eli followed more slowly, carefully, as if she might break.

Girls made of glass can break, thought Tav, frowning. *Maybe we should have waited.*

But the next moment Eli was flipping a dagger in the air, catching it, and drawing it across the back of her hand.

"Taste?" Her eyes were jet black, shimmering with the fluorescent light cast by a streetlamp.

"No, thanks."

Eli shrugged. "Suit yourself." She smeared the blood on the lamppost. The light immediately went dark. Eli sighed, "Much better."

"Should you be wasting blood like that?"

"It's mine to waste."

Cam pulled up behind them in his car. The absence of his usual jazz playlist was conspicuous, but Tav was too nervous to comment on it. "Took you long enough," they said.

"Not all of us feel comfortable driving on sidewalks," he said. "Humans have eyes, you know."

"Not tonight, they don't. I have it covered."

His one eyebrow arched elegantly. "You do, do you?"

Eli was licking her wound.

"Focus," snapped Tav. Eli's head shot up like a startled animal's, and her eyes flickered between yellow and back before settling on one crocodile eye and one pure-black eye.

"A little tense, are we?" Cam turned from Tav and toward Eli. He reached out a hand. "Blade me."

Her mouth twisted in a snarl.

"Sorry?" He stepped back. "I thought —"

She shook her head, the anger passing quickly. "It's nothing. It's fine." She handed him the stone blade.

Tav noticed that it looked more at home in his stone-mottled hand than in hers. Tav could see the contradictory emotions flickering in Eli, as different magics competed for control.

They stood awkwardly for a moment, like a couple of teens with a can of stolen beer.

And then black like ink bled over Eli's yellow eye. The temperature dropped, an unnatural stillness settling over their bodies. Tav's arm hairs rose, goosebumps freckling their skin. Tav was sure that even Cam could sense the power that was coming.

Eli was summoning the Vortex. Tav watched as the tension in her muscles was mirrored by a bursting of light and colour, her magic components straining for the home of their birth.

Eli screamed.

They knew better, but Tav automatically reached for her. Cam caught their arm and pulled them back.

"Didn't you say it's rude to interrupt someone when they're tearing a hole in the universe?" His tone was light, but his eyes bored into theirs. "And dangerous."

Tav ripped their arm out of his grasp, heart racing. "Like you would know."

His face closed like a curtain.

The magic inside Eli had turned a sickly greygreen, and was spreading like an infection. Her torso, and then neck, arms, and legs were slowly covered by this new kind of magic. The smell of decomposing gardenias filled the air and Tav found themselves retching.

"What's wrong?"

"Don't you smell that?" Their eyes were running with the heavy perfume that mixed with mould and dust and the faint chemical sweetness of icing sugar.

"Smell what?"

The greygreen was twisting now, turning into ribbons of light and dark, as if filtered underwater, glowing through skin and bone and granite and hawthorn. The Heart.

The made-girl's body glowed with this new, unearthly light — the Heart waking up, reaching for its home planet.

Tav frowned. It wasn't the Heart that would activate the Vortex, it was the fragile shell that was wrapped around it. With the brightness and energy of a small sun, the Heart could burn skin from body as easily as paper. If they reached out now, would Eli unravel onto the pavement into a collection of teeth and petals? They stepped forward again, gripping the obsidian blade.

"What are you doing?" Cam reached for them again, but they dodged his arm.

"Can't you see it?" Tav turned to him, wide-eyed. "She's dying."

"I don't see anything. But I think you should trust her."

Tav hesitated. Ground their teeth together. Took a deep breath and tried not to gag. Kept their eyes on Eli.

"I'm not waiting much longer," they said through gritted teeth. "This could tear her apart."

"It could tear all of us apart. You told me that, Tav. We all know the risks."

The scream ended abruptly, like someone slamming a door. An unnatural silence drifted in the corners and edges between their bodies, thick as fog. The ribbons of light and dark and girl and Heart were wriggling now, a mass of worms writhing with hunger.

The blades started to sing. It was a keening, wailing kind of song; it sent waves of homesickness and loneliness through Tav, who suddenly couldn't breathe. They dropped to one knee. Cam placed a hand on their shoulder. His stones were singing, too. His eyes turned upward to the sky and for a moment Tav could see his eyes turn to two pieces of slate; but then they were human again. They wondered if they had imagined it.

The song ended, and the Vortex opened.

It was colder than Tav remembered. Before, it had felt like nothingness, like the empty space between teeth, or reaching for a hand and finding only shadow. But this time it was cold, and they could see their breath hanging, frosty and glittering with lifeforce.

Sheet lightning flashed in the distance. This was *wrong.*

The blackness

cracked.

They were back on the street, face down, gravel embedded in their knees, a scrape on their shin oozing plasma and platelets onto the cement. The roar of thunder and hail drowned out the harmonies of the city, the sound of their own heartbeat, everything.

Tav rolled over onto their back and stared up at the sky.

It was torn open.

Through the ragged edges of the universe they could see the angry fires of the City of Eyes oozing across the gap like burning sewage. At the edges, flashes of lightning and black clouds reared up as if protecting the Earth. Rain lashed across their face. The world was ending. They were going to die. Everyone was going to die.

What had gone wrong?

This wasn't supposed to happen.

That was the only thought Tav could hold on to as they stared into the maelstrom overhead. This wasn't the invisible passageway between worlds, a hole punched in the fabric of space and time. This was chaos — frayed edges, a tear that was spreading across the universe.

What happened to a world when its magical Heart was gone?

A hand on their arm. Cam's mouth moving, the sounds lost to the tempest. Tav was dragged to their feet. The smell of perfume and rot was gone, replaced by the bitter herb of fear. It took a moment for them to realize it was their own. Cam was pointing, trying to shout, the stones dark in the rain and hail.

Eli.

A small figure hunched on the ground, as if slowly being crushed by the weight of the other world, torn apart by the warring magics outside and inside her. Somehow keeping it open, keeping them in place. As they watched, a spark burst from Eli's spine and sputtered on the wet asphalt. When the ember died, Tav could see that it had bloomed into a single perfect rosebud.

Eli's body was breaking. She couldn't keep this up much longer. It was up to Tav. Drawing the obsidian blade, the other hand clutching their bike keys for luck, Tav walked into the storm.

Wind clawed at their face, and stabs of lightning on the apocalyptic skyline left white lights streaking across their vision. But they could still sense the magic. They could smell it. They could taste it. They breathed it in, and it filled their lungs like a new morning hatching over the horizon.

Tav stretched their arms out, and the wind whirled around each limb, carrying dust and starving leaves and the stinging bite of gravel to burn their forearms. Still, they walked toward the hole at the centre of everything.

They faced the chasm, and through the gaping mouth that had been the Vortex they could see the fiery stars of the other universe, could see the smoky green sky of the witches' world, could almost taste the fossils underneath the Coven.

The other world called to them.

Somewhere deep in their bones, in the graceful arc of their spine, in the cells that pumped oxygen through a body that was also a universe, the magic spoke to them. Their heart beat a little faster; their pupils dilated as if with love; their palms turned unconsciously to face the void that was also a pathway to an alien world.

This was their birthright, if only they would reach out and claim it.

A spike of pain burst through the haze. They looked down, breaking eye contact with the void. They saw a long tooth protruding from their leg. The girl clutching the tooth yanked it out again, blood dripping from ravaged gums, from where she had ripped off her own crocodile tooth to use as a weapon. Tav clutched at the wound and their hand was grabbed by another hand, wet with sweat and blood, sticky as a child's.

"You are the Healer," said Eli.

"I hate that name," said Tav, allowing Eli to press their entwined hands over the wound. Tav closed their eyes and felt the skin stitch itself back together. When they opened their eyes again, a single wisp of steam curled up from smooth skin.

"I can taste the Vortex," they said.

"Spit it out," said Eli, still too weak to stand.

They spat, and the berry-black liquid turned to crystallized salt on the cement, killing the weeds that had managed to survive generations of toxins and human feet.

"They're coming!" Cam stepped in front of Tav, using his body as a shield, wielding the stone blade like it was an extension of his own body.

Shrieks in the distance.

The lightning strikes were coming closer. The lamppost marked with Eli's blood was struck, and it emitted a hissing sound as steam poured over the square.

From under the lamppost a creature emerged. It was forged from metal and brass, its hinges squeaky from decades of neglected rust. An animal? A machine? Soon, three more creatures appeared from lightning strikes, circling the trio.

Tav swallowed, eyes darting from creature to creature, looking for an escape route. Looking for allies.

They were trapped.

THE HEIR

Then —

When she was small, her mother had called for her. "I am going to teach you a lesson," said the Witch Lord. Kite had been curious and unafraid. "I will teach you how to shed your skin and free your essence."

And then she had torn the flesh from Kite's body, until only a quivering bluegreen light remained.

"Now dress yourself," commanded the Witch Lord.

Leaving her skin had been painful, but slipping back into her body was somehow worse, making her head spin and her stomach churn. Kite had dragged herself to the Children's Lair and collapsed on the stone floor, hugging her knees to her chest and spitting up ash. Clytemnestra had the children take turns throwing buckets of seawater over her prone form. None of them spoke to her. They, too, knew that she was marked as the Heir. She was not truly one of them.

Now —

There were no books here.

Slowly, Kite's body unravelled itself over her essence and her feet touched a stone floor. She had learned to master the sickness of transformation. The dizziness no longer made her crawl, and the nausea no longer emptied her body. She crouched on the floor, trembling.

"Beast," she managed, choking on her words and the dirt in her lungs. "Beast."

His soft fur against her damp arm; his tongue on her face, licking salt crystals from her cheekbones.

After a moment she stood. They followed the rumour down narrow pathways and twisting stairs of rotted roots, down into the depths of the earth. Past walls and wards and hand-carved eyes that rolled wildly in sockets of copper and silk. And between luck and want and the lingering scent of human blood, Kite found her way into a network of tunnels that ached with unused magic.

The Beast nipped at her hand, and she stroked him gently. "We're getting closer," she said. "My ankles sing with sorrow."

The air was sweet down here and smelled of lavender and sugar. Kite felt lulled by the scent. The Beast kept trying to take bites out of the air. Kite's fingers trailed through a net of verdant lace and came away wet and sticky. She stuck her finger in her mouth and sucked. The taste was sweet as honey, but with the bitter aftertaste of soured tears — the kind held in too long, and shed years too late, raw pain fermented by regret and denial.

The Beast whined.

Sighing at his impatience, Kite offered him a handful of moss. He shied away from her outstretched hand and refused to eat it.

"Clever boy," she whispered. "You don't want to eat the dead."

She ate the handful of moss and contemplated the garden of a prison. The caverns here were covered in yellowgreen vines and leaves. Blossoms the size of dinner plates studded the lush walls. It was a different world.

There were no guards down here.

She walked along, feeling the moss break down in her body. Something about ingesting it made her feel closer to the furred stone, to the damp pools of stagnant water that welled in leaves impossibly growing underground. Fed by materials no longer needed by the Coven.

Fed by the bodies of shadow assassins, failed daughters. Repurposed by violent magic and fed to the Coven, life giving life. There was something beautiful about the cycle, even as its brutality registered like a faint feather brushing the back of her neck, or a voice whispering in her ear. *My sisters …*

A sudden sickness twisted her stomach, and Kite vomited the tangled mass of green. From beneath the wet, darkened strands, a single rose petal burned red as a morning sky.

Wiping the bile from her mouth, Kite's eyes flashed with electricity and wonder. She reached down and grasped the petal, letting it rest in her palm. It glowed at her touch, as if waking up.

A smile snaked its way across Kite's face.

Sometimes the dead don't stay buried.

THE HEART

The beasts prowled on four paws, their iron bodies creaking with age. A few sheets of metal peeled away from one's haunches, curling into a sharp, rusted edge. Teeth like saw blades. Nails protruding from the spine. Weapons meant to harm.

Eli stumbled to her feet, releasing Tav's hand. She could still feel the beat of their pulse — a rhythm that was dangerously compelling, that made Eli want to bite their wrist and send shivers of electricity through the boi's body. They could be electric together.

Eli took those bright, strange feelings and channelled them into her attack. She launched herself without warning at the closest beast, her limbs rejuvenated by Tav's touch — perhaps they had healed her, too — losing herself to the familiar bloodlust of a good fight.

"Wait!" Tav cried, but their voice was lost in the winds. Another crack of thunder rang out like an omen of death.

But Eli was lost in the dance of battle, muscle thrown against metal, hawthorn tearing at rust. The crocodile tooth, still stained with Tav's blood, punctured the metal torso again and again as Eli wrestled with the creature, hands slippery with blood and oil. Sweat dripped into her eyes, and she could smell the stink of old iron and mouldy gears. She would tear it apart piece by piece, she would fashion a new blade from its corpse —

She was sitting in a pile of scrap metal.

Eli blinked and looked down. Blood pooled under her nails. Four had been ripped clean off. She could feel the scrape of metal in her throat and suddenly felt sick.

She had eaten the creature whole.

Eli didn't remember it happening; she remembered nothing but the fight, the surge of power, the magic of her body that told her she was built to kill. Was there a moment when she had dematerialized and rematerialized inside the creature, tearing it part from the inside? She was more dangerous now than she had ever been.

Nausea roiled through her stomach. Eli leaned over and vomited up a handful of rusted nails.

Then she drew the frost blade and went looking for something else to kill.

THE HEALER

"Wait!"

But Eli was lost to the taste of violence, to the promise of death. Tav pressed their back against Cam's, circled by three of the monsters. Strange magic sparked and hissed inside the metal husks, black as night edged in fiery gold.

"They're animated by some kind of spell," Tav told Cam. "There might be a witch nearby."

"What's our strategy if they show?"

"Don't die?"

"Got it. Great plan, general."

One of the beasts lunged, a paw studded with razor-sharp gears clawing at Cam. He deflected with the great stone blade that was both a shield and a weapon. The sound of metal on stone crashed over the steps. Cam stumbled back. One edge of the blade had cut a ragged gash in the beast's side.

To Tav's horror, the animal was bleeding. The wound dripped black, like ink pooling on the asphalt.

Another darted forward, jaws overflowing with rusty nails for teeth. Tav tried to dodge the attack but felt searing pain as a canine grazed their forearm. Twisting, ignoring the pain, Tav quickly stabbed with the obsidian blade, in case there was an incorporeal trapped in the metal body. The black-and-gold glowing heart of the creature shrunk back at the touch, and the creature let out a ghostly wail, as if Tav had pierced its very soul.

And then Tav knew the truth, and their heart broke with the weight of empathy.

"They're witches," they whispered. These creatures had once been the essences of witches, torn from their bodies and housed in skins of iron.

The imprisoned essences, enraged at their captivity and pulsing with pain, lashed out at Tav and Cam, again and again, mechanical claws and teeth leaving maps of revenge in blood.

The mechanical warriors were playing with them, Tav realized, like a cat plays with a mouse. They didn't want a fast kill, they wanted a long, slow torture. They wanted to draw out their revenge, to punish a world that allowed them to hurt and this human to thrive. They wanted to savour every moment of this half freedom, the same half freedom Eli had shared when she was a shadow assassin, a made-thing allowed to roam the human world; allowed pinches of freedom measured out with breaths and seconds and snowflakes falling on frozen soil. Eli had told them enough, on those late nights when the moon was masked by clouds and a strange moodiness made her willing to talk.

No, this fight would not be quick.

Every second they took to tear Tav to shreds was a moment where these creatures did not have to linger in the dungeons under the Coven where the heavy walls swallowed their screams.

They turned their head in time to see Eli devouring the final piece of essence-infused metal. Fear sparked through their body like an electrical shock. *Please don't die on me*, they thought.

A growl pulled them away from the made-girl, and they barely dodged the wicked claws in time. There wasn't time to worry about Eli. These creatures may not plan to kill Tav fast, but they would maim them if they got a chance.

"We have to go on the offensive," they said to Cam. "I don't know how long the Vortex will stay like this."

Cam brushed a shattered stone from his chest and nodded. "I'll cover you."

The next time one of the creatures attacked, Tav was ready. Instead of drawing away, they moved forward to meet it, forcing the knife through the casing and into the very essence of the broken witch inside the metal husk.

Behind them, they heard the enraged yowls of the other two and the sound of stone and metal being rammed into each other. Cam was protecting them from the other attack. Tav wondered how long he could hold out — even granite could break. Even stones could be ground into sand, and underneath each stone was fragile human skin.

They had to make this fast.

Pulling the blade out of the swirling, furious, fiery mass, Tav brought it back down again and again. Tendrils of essence splashed over their body, burning their skin and sending the smell of charred flesh and metal into the air.

The black-and-gold light went out.

Tav had killed one of metal monsters.

They turned around in time to see Eli appear from inside one of the creatures, metal flying like shrapnel.

Cam's blade went up just in time to deflect a piece of ragged metal from slicing Tav's face.

"Thanks," they said, voice shaking. "Although I think I'd look badass with a scar."

"I'll remember that for next time," he said, smiling through the sweat and dirt.

The remains of the four creatures littered the asphalt like junkyard scraps.

They had survived the attack.

Why didn't Tav feel victorious?

Instead, they felt the sucking pull of remorse. These creatures had lived, had felt pain, had been hurt by their own people, and had died in a place that was far from home. The unfairness of it all swept through Tav like a crashing ocean wave, rising again in a sense of righteous anger at the Witch Lord who had turned them all into killers.

"Eli!" Tav pointed the obsidian blade at the assassin. Eli looked up from the corpse of one body, wild-eyed and grinning. "We need the Heart."

The grin vanished. She nodded and climbed over the debris to reach them. Tav pressed the blade into her hand. "We can do this," they said.

Eli pressed her forehead against Tav's, one hand going to her chest, where the Heart began to glow. Soon, her entire body was bright with white fire. Tav, too, started glowing. They were bathed in light, they were invincible, and the rain now felt like a loving touch from a planet that recognized their sacrifice. Nothing could hurt them anymore. Nothing.

Tav focused on the rift, on the first and greatest tear between worlds. Not to close it, but to make it a doorway. They reached out with their mind, mapping the smooth edges of a wound that had been open so long that it had healed that way. This would be harder to heal, but with the power of the Heart, they could do it.

Closing their eyes, breathing life into their own magic, they channelled the power of the Heart that was willingly offered. They could feel the edges of the Vortex start to shiver, to respond to them. Then it began to change, to shift into something else, something full of colour and life. Something with twisting, tangled vines and pink flowers, feathers and chains and plastic and balloon animals — all of the things from both worlds coming together to make one meeting point of power.

Tav's breath caught in their chest. It was *working*.

A sharp ache interrupted the flow of magic, which stuttered and slowed. Tav could feel the vines and chemicals and organic and inorganic tapestry start to retreat, turning back to scar tissue. They pushed harder.

Another pain, the shock of separation, and Tav found themselves torn apart from Eli, from the Heart, from the power they needed. They looked up, and saw the Vortex was widening again, a gash in the sky.

"What —?"

A hand gripped their arm.

It was Cam.

"They're here."

THE HEIR

Kite picked up the rose petal. “My apologies,” she said, and set it back in against the wall. A moment later, it was covered in a protective shield of leaves. “Wait here,” she said. “We’ll find you.”

Glowing bluegreen, hair dancing around her face, Kite flowed down the green chamber, which she saw now was one of the arteries of the Coven. The farther she went, the more hints of decay she saw. Dried orange peels fuzzy with mould. Tree roots sticking out of the earth, naked and thirsty. Cracks like latticework in stone and glass.

The world needed its Heart.

One petal like a drop of blood nestled in a thicket of thorns; another dried and pressed against a fist of granite. Kite gathered the petals. Then she returned to where the Beast was waiting. He had flattened himself into the shape of a glittering winged snake. Constellations winked along his back.

"Very pretty," she said. "I hope you didn't scare her."

The Beast fluttered his wings like a hummingbird. She petted the smooth skin of his scales. "Thank you for keeping watch."

She pressed the handful of petals against the moss. A moment later, they, too, were wrapped in leaves and vines and roots thick with earth.

And then a girl walked out of the wall.

Long moss hung around her shoulders, and dirt caked her fingernails. She was missing half an ear, and a few fingers. Her cloudy white eye burned with an inner fire.

"Heir," said the girl, inclining her head in a small bow.

"Assassin," said Kite, her hair rippling in welcome.

"How long have I been down here?" she asked.

Kite blinked, and then laughed, the sound of a ship coming home after a long journey, sea spray knocking gently against the bow. "Long enough."

"Where are the others?"

The Beast rose in the air and began swimming around Kite in frantic circles.

Kite reached out and brushed a fleck of dirt from the girl's face. "We haven't found them yet. But we will."

THE HEART

Lightning flashes continued streaking down from the City of Eyes as an army of armoured beasts filled the square. Too many to kill. Too many to fight.

But Eli would try. She couldn't give up now, not when they were so close.

Not when so much was at stake.

Her sense of self-preservation urged her to run, to disappear, to vanish from their lives altogether. But she made herself stay. She made herself listen to the rain on cement and told herself that an assassin didn't run from a fight, she revelled in it.

Eli threw herself at the horde, teeth bared, blades ready. With the pearl blade she tore the witch essences from their shells, and with the bone blade she destroyed their bodies.

Smell of iron.

Taste of ash.

The world narrowed to a pinhole. She heard nothing. Felt nothing.

She was losing herself in the carnage. *What about Tav? What if Tav needs me?*

Who is Tav? The name sounded familiar.

Golden-brown eyes.

Silver earrings glinting in moonlight.

A warm hand against her rib cage.

Eli remembered. She forced through the bloodlust, waking to the roar of the storm and the blood pounding in her head. Tav and Cam were fighting back to back, but their bodies looked small and fragile. She had to help them.

Eli traded bone for thorn, and with a scream of anger, plunged the spiky blade into the earth. This time, it didn't reject her touch. Vines with deadly spikes grew rapidly toward the enemies that surrounded her companions.

The Heart burned, light pouring through her palms and forehead. Eli looked down — one of her hands was starting to disappear, turning into raw energy. She gritted her teeth and tightened her grip on the blade. *Not now. I won't let the Heart take me.*

The ghostly light crept up her forearm to her elbow. She was fading.

The vines were almost there, just a few more seconds —

Her other hand started to flicker, and for a moment she could see through her knuckles. There was a crack in the pavement as a single weed struggled through.

You answer to me. Eli concentrated on the power of the Heart that singed her veins. She channelled that energy into the blade, into the vines.

The blade glowed red, burning her hand like it had before. But this time, Eli didn't cry out. She refused to let go. She kept her hand on the knife, even as blisters began to rise on her palm. She just needed to hold out for one more second —

The thorn blade caught fire. The vines collapsed into ash. As Eli watched, the blade cracked and began peeling into fibrous strips. Eli dropped the blade, her hand burning. The fibrous mass cooled, the thorns retreating into the jagged edges of a blade. She exhaled. It hadn't broken. Not yet.

Eli was shaking. She felt a stinging in her eyes. She reached up to rub her eyes and realized her arm had vanished.

Her gaze fluttered around the square, around the scene of chaos. They landed on a boi with purple hair and golden eyes.

The boi looked at her. Their mouth moved, and Eli thought she caught the word *Please* before the material world fell away.

THE HEALER

Eli was gone.

No, she couldn't be. They needed her. They needed the Heart.

Eli was gone.

Panic swirled through Tav's lungs like snow squalls. They could hear Cam gasping for breath. His rock-covered body was taking a beating, and neither of them could hold out for long.

The obsidian blade was slippery with their own blood, and they were losing their grip, missing easy targets. Fumbling, they almost dropped it.

Do it without the blade.

The witch in the forest. The burning tree. Tav had torn them open with a touch.

Do it again.

They sheathed the blade of dark glass. The next wave of creatures came at them, and Tav reached out with both hands.

The first one opened and collapsed, turned inside out by Tav's magic. They reached for the essence, shuddering at its slimy texture in their hand. They twisted, and opened —

The essence healed, reforming. It hadn't worked. The essence flowed back into the crumpled machine and the creature stood, unsteadily, on dented feet.

It hadn't worked.

Tav reached for it again, and this time not even the metal bent to their will.

The sky turned like a spinning top.

A broken sky overhead. Tav tried to move their legs but couldn't. The adrenalin was gone. The magic was gone. There was nothing left.

"Tav?"

Stones. Granite and limestone and slate. Tav tried to count them. Tried to touch them.

Behind the stones, a bleeding wound in the fabric of space-time. Tav needed to turn it into a door. Tav needed to —

But the Heart was gone, and Tav's magic had been drained.

Lightning struck the ground beside Tav's face and sparks showered their body.

The sound of incantations, low and musical, heavy with the smell of freshly ground coffee and burning vegetation.

The Hedge-Witch.

Tav managed to turn their neck, looking away from the hole in the sky to the land underneath their body. Earth. Their home.

Weeds grew from the cracks in the cement, strangling and roping the metal husks animated by hatred and greed. A stamen punctured a metal plate and bloomed into a sunflower, a giant eye surveying the battlefield.

The Hedge-Witch wasn't alone.

Humans gifted with spells, trained to fight, joined the battle. Tav glimpsed the ghost out of the corner of their eye as two brutal forces came together under a ruined sky.

The Coven's made-army was outnumbered. Seeds burst and grew into new plant life that choked and killed, and the ghost devoured metal and magic in breathless gulps.

It was over. They had survived.

The remnants of a tortured witch army lay shattered on the pavement. Horror flowed through Tav, thick and dark, like a shadow, leaving them cold and trembling and alone.

They looked up at the sky. The Vortex was closing.

They had failed.

THE HEART

Eli materialized back on the pavement, second-degree burns on her hand and wrist. How long had she been gone this time? *What happened?*

Then she heard it — wasps. Horror rose in the back of her throat and she bent over, trying to cough up the fear, but nothing came out. She collapsed, exhausted, and a shadow fell across her face. Eli looked up at the girl who had been walking through her dreams. A smile like a curse, eyes wild with bloodlust. Two blades — one forged from wings and stingers, the smell of paper nests lingering in the air, the other made from screws and nails and broken glass bound together by rust and force.

Eli opened her mouth to ask — *Who*? Or maybe, *How?* But already the blade was descending, and Eli waited for the stimulant of pain or the quiet of death.

The clang of metal on stone broke through the swarm. *Cam*. Eli's eyes widened. Cam had thrown himself in front of the sword, its crusted edge scraping on stone and biting into skin. Red seeped through cuts and scrapes on his bare chest and shoulders.

Eli reached for a blade, any blade, but her fingers, slippery with blood, refused to grab a hilt. Again, the blade rose, but Cam stood firm, the stone blade held tightly in his hand, his hair wild and dirty.

The blade fell.

Eli closed her eyes.

Silence.

Eli opened her eyes again. Cam was gone. The made-daughter was gone. She stared up into the sky and saw that the Vortex was closing.

A moan, somewhere to her left. The call of obsidian and leather.

Tav. She stumbled over to them to — what? Offer a hand, a clump of hair, an apology? She didn't know; she was breaking, she had nothing to offer, no help or words of comfort to give. But still, she came. Still, she made her body move.

As Eli drew closer she could hear Tav repeating one word, over and over, like a spell, a mantra, a swear word, a love poem.

"Cam. Cam. Cam."

Eli looked up at the glittering lights from the City of Eyes, the other world watching them from the slitted eyelids of the rift the moment before they closed.

"It took him," she whispered. "He crossed over."

Tav's eyes flicked to Eli's face. "Are you real?" their voice wavered.

Eli reached down to touch Tav's cheek. "I don't know."

Tav started to cry. Eli tilted her head back and stared up until the seam was once again invisible, a bluegrey sky marred only by bloodied clouds.

Slowly, the reality sunk in: Cam was gone, and they had no way of knowing where he was, and no way of going after him.

THE HEIR

"Do you like it?"

"I love it." Tears pooled in Clytemnestra's wide, sapphire eyes and then spilled over her angelic face. "It's just what I wanted."

The made-assassin was tall and lean, with brown skin and a few freckles like spots of bleach on her left cheekbone. She had coyote ears and her eyes were mismatched — one golden-brown human eye, one pure-white and cloudy.

"Ooh, what's that one do?" Clytemnestra reached out and poked her in the eye. The white rippled, like water disturbed by a fish. The assassin didn't flinch, but Clytemnestra let out a yelp like she'd stuck her finger in a light socket.

"I believe it absorbs magic and uses it to regenerate her own body," said Kite. "A really ingenious design; too bad the witch who made her was repurposed for treason. Something about trying to use her daughter to steal the Coven's magic."

"So she's ours now?" Clytemnestra stuck her finger in her mouth and sucked on the burn.

The assassin turned to look at Kite, tilting her head slightly.

"She's agreed to join us," said Kite. "For a price."

Clytemnestra's eyes lit up, and Kite smiled behind her curtain of hair that today flowed like a waterfall across her face. Clytemnestra loved haggling.

"Let me guess." The little witch clapped her hands together and narrowed her eyes. "You want your freedom?"

The assassin's left ear flicked, and a slow lazy smile spread across her face, showing her wolfish canines that ended in glittering points. "Not just mine."

No one knew how many assassins operated in the City of Eyes. They were supposed to answer to the Coven, but any witch with enough power and insanity could stitch together a girl from beetle shells and eyelashes. Most of them didn't live long enough to do any damage, or to be of any use, but a few did. Those that were caught by the Coven were repurposed, broken down into their parts and fed to the living walls of the witches' fortress.

"The three of us the Heir found and remade rose up against our makers," said the assassin. "But there are others, all over the world. I want you to swear that you will free us all."

Clytemnestra nodded eagerly, saliva beading at the edges of her lips. "If you help us tear down the Coven, I will help you track down every made-daughter in the world and liberate them."

"Make an agreement with me, then," challenged the assassin, staring down the tiny Warlord.

Clytemnestra tore a strip off her pinafore and offered it to the girl. The girl shook her head and stepped back. "I know how this works, witch. None of your tricks. I want a fingernail."

Clytemnestra picked at her thumbnail and offered the calcium-studded flake to the girl. The assassin placed it in her mouth, chewed once, and swallowed. She gave Clytemnestra one of her nails in exchange and Clytemnestra sucked it up noisily.

"It is done," said the assassin.

The tension in the room cracked like a crème brûlée, leaving only sugary sweetness and hunger in its place. Clytemnestra floated over to the assassin and started scratching behind her coyote ears.

"What should we call you?" asked Kite.

"We are the unnamed," she said. She seemed to like the scratching. "We were not born, we will not die, and we will not answer to any name."

Kite nodded. "Your maker is dead," she said. "But the others still have mothers. Their witches will come for them."

"Let them come," she said. "Lead them here, and let your little witches eat them."

"I like the way she thinks," said Clytemnestra. "This will be so much fun!" She raised her arms to the sky and lightning flashed like a jagged scar.

"And they will fight for us?" Kite let her eyes linger on the sinew and tendons on the body of a girl made to kill.

She turned to face Kite. "We will fight to destroy the Coven. After that, we don't promise our allegiance to you, Heir."

The Beast nuzzled against Kite's skirts, and she reached out to scratch his chin. It was hard sometimes for her to feel the intensity that these human and part-human creatures felt, the drive for freedom, for revenge, for love, as if these things were not always shifting and changing and breaking and rebuilding. Maybe it was their short lifespans.

A touch from the Beast always reminded her to live now, and not in a thousand years. It was so easy to lose track of time when you might live forever.

"That's all right," she said gently. "I don't need your allegiance."

The assassin nodded.

"She'll stay here, with you." Kite turned to the Warlord.

Clytemnestra clapped her hands together. "I can't wait for the children to meet her! They will love to play with you!" She twisted her mouth into an approximation of a canine snarl and growled. Then she knocked politely on the closest wall, and it melted away. "Go get your friends and meet me for tea," she told the unnamed girl with coyote ears and a thief's eye. "We will welcome you with a true party."

The girl growled her assent and left.

Clytemnestra turned to Kite. "So, you found a way to put them back together. You *are* a naughty Heir! Mommy won't like that."

"I did as you asked," said Kite. "Have you heard from Eli?"

Clytemnestra ignored her. She tapped her cheek thoughtfully. "If I'm too rough with my new playthings, you can just fix them again, won't you?"

"The Coven was feeding on their lifeforce. If you break one, she's broken."

"It's just a *thing*." Her eyes glittered maliciously.

"Go meet your new allies." The tips of Kite's hair twisted. "I have reading to catch up on."

"You always do that." Clytemnestra pouted. "One day you're going to miss something exciting. Or some*one*."

Kite parted the hair falling over her eyes and let the strands float to either side of her body. "Remember, little one — you don't touch her."

"I remember our bargain. But what if she comes to me? She's *very* special." Awe and greed fought for mastery in her voice.

"She's always been special."

"And *you* were always sentimental." Clytemnestra spun a pirouette.

"You've never been punished before for being naughty, have you?" Kite's melodic voice drifted through the space like warm rain. She leaned forward and caught Clytemnestra by the hem of her pinafore, her sharp fingernails puncturing the fabric. Clytemnestra struggled like an insect caught in a web, but Kite held fast. "I don't think you'd like it very much."

She released the dress, the fabric crusted with salt. Clytemnestra floated up, like a balloon released by a child at a birthday party.

A single pink drop fell to the stone. Salt could burn through flesh.

Then Kite smiled brightly, inclined her head, and slipped out of the room and toward her own chamber, leaving the Warlord to greet the other made-daughters. With any luck, the tomes she had managed to smuggle out of the library would be in a generous mood.

As she walked under stone archways and climbed up marble steps, she thought about the gleam in Clytemnestra's eyes and sighed. Kite hadn't given up her birthright, denounced her kin, and fled her home just to lose her love to a spoiled witch babe.

She was sorry she had to hurt the little witch, but sometimes soldiers needed to be reminded that readers were dangerous.

THE HEALER

Tav was born angry. They had been born on stolen land in a nation that grew strong on blood and sap, devouring the bones of its elders. Their ancestors had been slaves. Anger and hurt were in their DNA.

Fury burned bright inside them, lit up their eyes like gold lanterns; it had made them bold, and sometimes reckless; it had made them an apprentice to a witch runaway and carried them across worlds.

Tav's magic couldn't be separated from their anger. Maybe they were one and the same. Maybe they could use it to save their planet. Eli believed they could. So did Cam, and Clytemnestra, and all those little witches. Tav was the Healer now, a bridge between worlds, an opener of doors.

But sometimes they wondered if the Earth was worth saving.

When cops marched in Pride and Tav's dead sisters were left in dumpsters, when the land was slowly being peeled back, layer by layer, and forest fires burned like a vigil to the god of death, Tav sometimes thought that humanity deserved to be destroyed. Maybe it was better to let the world be destroyed by the witches, sacrificed to a magic that neither loved nor hated, but treated every object and animal and body with the same uncaring indifference.

And now Cam was gone. *Cam*, who had created a drink he christened "The Tavengers" for their nineteenth birthday (grenadine, whiskey, and olives, served in a Thor pint glass. It was horrible). Who sucked at *Mario Kart* but was amazing at *DDR*. Who had filled in the cracks of his broken heart with glitter and gold, and who had showed Tav how to live with grief. Who had crossed between worlds for them.

They hadn't saved him.

"We try again tomorrow," said Eli, cleaning one of her blades.

Tav glared at her. "I need to rest."

"We don't have time to rest. You didn't see what I saw, the Earth —"

"Is dying. I get it." Tav took a sip of bitter tap water and then set their glass down on the table too loudly.

Eli looked up. "You don't understand."

"Death? What, only murderers get it?"

"Don't call me that."

"Assassin. Whatever."

"I'm not an assassin anymore."

"Then what are you?" Tav spun around, letting some of their fury trickle into their words. "Why are you still here? You got your freedom. I thought you'd be gone by now."

Eli leaned forward, crocodile eyes never blinking. Pearl blade clutched with tense fingers. "I'm here because you need me."

"We don't need you. We just need the Heart."

Tav was picking a fight and they knew it. The old Eli had been quick-tempered and would have lashed out or stormed off, leaving Tav alone. (They wanted to be left alone. They didn't want to be left alone.)

Eli, *this* Eli, the one who sometimes turned into light, who spoke to the moon on cloudless nights, *this* Eli stared at Tav for a long moment. She leaned back and lovingly slid the blade back into its sheath.

"I miss the forest," she said finally.

Tav said nothing.

"It's the weirdest part about being this new person, how much I miss the forest. And the Labyrinth. And the wastelands. It's not like missing a childhood home, it doesn't feel like nostalgia. It feels like … like a wrongness. Everything feels wrong. And the magic — it feels weak. Like it's dying. Like I'm dying. I don't think the Heart is supposed to be here. God, I miss the forest so much it hurts."

Sometimes it was easy to forget that Eli, who looked the same as when Tav met her — the same freckles, glasses, and long bangs — was no longer just the made-thing with a spine of thorns raised to kill and to survive at all costs. Eli was the Heart of another world.

It was hard, having to get to know Eli all over again.

"The humans are killing this world all on their own," Tav's voice, harsher than they'd intended, broke the silence. "Do we save it just to let them kill each other, kill the land, burn everything? Maybe we should let it die. Maybe we should end it now, before things get worse."

Silence. This thoughtful, quiet Eli made Tav uncomfortable.

"You should listen to the ghost," she said. "He understands what we can't. He's seen a world die."

"He talks to you?" Somehow that hurt Tav. The ghost had come to *them*, had followed *them*. Besides, Eli — the old Eli, who broke through the surface now and again — hated ghosts.

"Neither of us belongs here."

And where do I belong? Bitterness and hurt pulsed under their fingertips. Again, Tav wished Cam were there, with his jokes and his jazz music and his twirly moustache. He always made them feel better, or at least less alone.

But they had let him down, and now he was gone.

"I thought you said the ghost was dangerous." Tav pushed away their grief.

"He is. But he's also … sad."

"How do you know?"

"He showed me."

Envy flared up again. Why did the ghost speak to Eli and not Tav? Why was everyone abandoning them?

"Cam will be fine," said Eli quietly. "He's made of stone. He's part of the wall."

The grief poured back in, thick and syrupy. "Don't make promises you can't keep."

Eli nodded. "Okay. I don't know if he'll be fine. But I do know that we can't help him right now." She stood up and walked to the window, pressing her fingertips to the glass. The blades glittered at her hips like planets orbiting a sun.

That was the truth, and, like most truths, it bit down on the vulnerable part of Tav's heart and wouldn't let go. Tav's hands curled into fists. They were ready for a fight. They were ready to be held. They waited for Eli to turn around and look at them.

But Eli slowly faded out of existence, leaving only a few fingerprints on the windowpane to prove she had been there. Then it was just Tav alone in an empty room.

Just what I wanted, they thought miserably.

Tav was dreaming again.

The smell of engine fuel and something sharp and green. They rubbed their fingers together and brought them to their nose — they had been picking cilantro.

"I'm afraid," they said. "The world is dying and I don't know what to do. I need your help."

Their mother smiled, her face reflected in the chrome of the bike. "Every teenager thinks that. I thought that. Nuclear destruction, climate change; the planet is more resilient than you think, love."

"The threat of nuclear destruction is real. And so is climate change."

"I know, baby. But we can't live in fear all the time. Here, help me." She tossed a rag at Tav, blocking out the light, blocking out everything.

Like a magic trick, when Tav lowered the rag, the scene had changed. Smell of cinnamon and coffee.

"I'm afraid," they repeated. "The world is dying, and I don't know what to do. I need your help."

"I have helped. And now you owe me."

"Don't you care that the world is in danger?"

"There is no safety in this life, youngling." The leaves of an aloe plant brushed their cheek. Tav shivered from the contact. *Don't run*, they told themselves. *Don't panic.* "Only winners and losers. Living and dead. Which side of that battle do you want to be on?"

"What do you want?"

"You know what I want."

"I said I'll get it for you. Just not yet."

"I hope I can trust you, youngling." The Hedge-Witch's eyes swirled yellow-white and muddy black. Staring into them made Tav dizzy. "You had so much potential once. But now you're very close to becoming a traitor."

They woke on the sofa drenched in sweat. Sun still streamed through the window — it was hard to believe it was the same day they had failed. The same day they had lost Cam. They squinted into the light and thought about the dream. Was it a dream? Or was it a message?

Traitor.

Tav almost laughed. They were definitely a traitor, but sorting out which loyalties they owed would take some time. Did they owe their allegiance to the humans? The human world that only half claimed them, that had made them who they are, forged in fury and pain? To the family that birthed and raised them? The family that adopted them? To the magic world they had barely seen? To Eli?

Tav had already let down the one person they owed loyalty to.

Who cared about anyone else?

It's someone else's turn, they thought. *I'm tired. I don't want this anymore.* They squeezed their eyes shut and wished their magic away. *Give it to someone else.*

They rolled over, pressing their forehead into the back of the sofa, and fell back into a sickly sleep, as light and distressed as a worn-out T-shirt.

THE HEIR

"Your army is growing," said Kite. "The unnamed daughters have reached out to their contacts. More assassins are fleeing their mothers to join you. The daughters will strengthen your numbers."

"It's not enough," sulked Clytemnestra, a paper crown askew on her brow. The flimsy hat had been pulled from a Christmas cracker. The smell of sulfur still lingered in the air.

But the party was over.

"Greedy child," said Kite.

"You're a child, too." Clytemnestra held a party horn to her mouth and blew half-heartedly, the stream of air rippling along the metallic ribbon.

"Yes," agreed Kite, eyeing the shiny material.

A gleam shimmered in Clytemnestra's eyes, the whites thinning to show a blueblack galaxy underneath. Then the whites thickened again, and the doll's eyes returned, with painted irises and dilated pupils.

She adjusted her crown. "You missed the celebrations, but I saved you a party favour."

"A whirligig?" Kite guessed. She recognized a game when she was in one.

Clytemnestra started chewing on the horn. She shook her head.

"A used Band-Aid?"

Another shake.

One more guess. Kite studied the witch girl: Clytemnestra was nibbling eagerly on the plastic toy. Her eyes kept thinning to the consistency of raw egg whites. Kite opened her mouth and let her tongue explore the air. She tasted old blood.

"Something that doesn't belong here," said Kite.

"Yes!" Clytemnestra spat out mangled plastic and giggled. "Just like you, Heir." She waved her hand and the air thickened, swirling around her wrist. Before it was fully summoned, Kite could smell the death and hurt, a heavy stench that made her eyes water. Kite leaned over, choking on the smell, and tadpoles fell from her eye sockets. When she sat up, wiping the slimy trail from her face, there it was.

A sword. An ancient weapon stolen from the moon. Older than humanity. Older than Kite. A malicious creature, its memories long and deep and sharp.

A sword that would turn on its wielder.

No, it did not belong here.

Kite went down on all fours and crawled closer to the magnificent piece of weaponry. Unknown alloy. Alien magic. As she neared the curling, twisted metal spikes and gears that grew from the main blade, the sword spat out a handful of red sparks that smelled of stale blood. One landed on Kite's damp hair, sizzled, and went out.

"Shhh, baby," she crooned. "I won't hurt you."

Some things never wanted to be found. Kite could feel in the hum of the sword how much it longed to be lost, how much it missed the obscurity and comfort of the junkyard.

The best key hungered for its lock.

A sharp pain, but slight. Kite twisted to look up. The Warlord had a handful of bluegreen hair in her hand and was tugging cruelly. Black eyes, comets streaking across the surface. Stars like flames where pupils should have been. A single canine protruded past the small mouth, yellowed and curving to a wicked point. Clytemnestra was beautiful. Clytemnestra was a monster.

The witches stared at each other for a long moment. One royal, one royalty. Both strange, even among their own kind.

When Clytemnestra spoke, her words echoed as if she spoke with a thousand voices.

"You will build me an army that will tear the roots of the Coven from bedrock. You will bring back the discarded and unwanted. The old magic." The paper hat caught fire. The flames danced around her head like the halo of a fallen angel. "It's time for the lost things to be found."

Without meaning to, Kite found herself bowing, pressing her forehead to stone.

THE HEART

"Up for a ride?"

The helmet landed on Tav's lap. They had fallen asleep on the sofa. When Eli had rematerialized, she had hovered over Tav for an awkward minute, wondering if she should get a blanket or not, wondering if she should wake them and ask why they were muttering and turning so fiercely. Wondering if she should hold them. In the end, she had done none of those things. She hadn't wanted to draw attention to Tav's vulnerability.

It's what she would have wanted for herself.

"I thought you wanted to save the world today." Sarcasm dripped from Tav's tongue.

Eli shrugged. "We can do that later if we feel like it. You coming or not?" She held out an espresso shot.

Cam had been teaching her how to use the machine. She didn't tell Tav that she'd cried when she made coffee that morning.

Tav took the petite cup, tossed it back, winced at the taste, and then stood. "Fine. But I'm driving." They didn't change out of their dirty lounge pants and sweat-stained T-shirt. Eli hadn't expected them to.

Eli felt a thrill when she climbed up behind Tav. She could see the anger, hurt, and despair swimming through Tav's body. They were running out of hope.

She knew that feeling. Tav and Cam had been the ones to keep her going when she wanted to give up. Now it was Eli's turn to help.

"Where?" Tav's voice was thick and sharp as a bramble.

"Take a right."

Eli directed Tav out of the city, away from the traffic lights and smells of grease and air freshener.

"I hope you aren't taking me away from town to murder me," Tav said.

"If I wanted to kill you, you wouldn't see it coming."

"That's very reassuring."

"You're welcome." Eli squeezed their thighs around Tav's torso for a moment. She was excited to be in a body again. Every time she came back she revelled in the sense of touch.

The hot leather of the seat underneath her. The feeling of Tav's shoulder blades and rib cage against her chest and arms. The soft fuzz on the back of Tav's neck, purple fading to black. Eli wanted to stroke it. She wanted to drink in all the smells and sounds and touches that her human body gave to her, and nothing — not the threat of annihilation, not a grieving human — was going to ruin it for her today.

"Turn left up here," she said.

"That isn't a road."

Eli leaned forward, her mouth hovering near Tav's exposed neck, and whispered, "Trust me. *Now*."

Tav turned sharply, the bike spraying gravel and dirt behind them.

Eli watched the pulse at Tav's throat, the lively beat of a human heart.

"Stop," she ordered. She watched Tav shiver slightly at the feeling of Eli's breath on their neck.

She had done that. She had the power to make Tav tremble.

Trust me, she had said. And Tav had. Tav *did*.

Without the roar of the motorcycle, Eli could suddenly hear the fierce percussion of Tav's heartbeat thundering in her ears, could hear both of their breathing like an ocean song. And something else — a hum in the distance. Eli smiled.

She climbed off the bike and offered Tav her hand, remembering the first time they had met: Eli had fallen from the sky, ejected from the Vortex too soon. Tav had pulled them up from the pavement.

Now, Eli watched her hand hang between them, bobbing slightly, like a flower in the breeze.

After a moment, Tav took it. Calloused palm and fingertips, with patches of softness, pressed against Eli's skin.

The smile widened.

A low, dense forest. A small path — no more than a deer trail — wound through the branches and nettles. Hundreds of wildflowers wove between twigs and emerged from under stones: Queen Anne's lace and chamomile, creeping bellflowers, blueweed, and cornflowers.

They left the bike, the helmets, the gravel behind. Eli led, and Tav followed. They ducked under thin branches and stepped over fallen logs, half-rotted, swarming with black ants like a net of lace.

After a few steps, Tav dropped Eli's hand and wiped sweat onto their pants. When Eli reached for their hand again, Tav said, "Don't." Eli dropped her hand.

To Eli, every step felt like a gift. Tav was choosing to follow her.

Each step was a love letter.

She kept waiting for her heavy body to fade, for the intensity of colour and anticipation and nerves to recede like a tide slipping away from the shore. But it didn't happen. This time, she miraculously stayed in the here and now. Impulsively, she kicked off her shoes, stripped off her socks, and went barefoot. She could feel Tav staring at her.

She met their gaze. "What?"

Tav shook their head, a slight frown wrinkling the skin on their forehead. "You're just different, that's all."

Eli's thumb brushed an edge of bone, and a haunting wail rang out from the blade. "Yes," she agreed. "I am different."

The woods thinned, opening up into a field that stretched to the edge of the horizon. Eli didn't need to tell Tav that this was their destination.

A sea of purple.

An ocean.

A *universe*.

A field of allium flowers stretched to the horizon. To Eli, it looked like the land was running into the arms of the sky, and the sky was falling down to meet it. Purple and green bled into blue and pink, and it was one picture, one perfect moment, one monument to a planet that never belonged to humanity.

The humming was stronger now, a persistent sound that filled the air, that crowded Eli's mind and ears and mouth and nostrils, that vibrated in her bones and thorns and granite.

An image surfaced in her mind's eye: a girl with cruel eyes. A blade of wasps, ready to tear Eli apart. Panic tore through her body and she froze.

"Bees," said Tav, looking around.

Thousands of bees were swarming the field of flowers, crawling and flying, tasting and drinking the sweet nectar.

Eli exhaled slowly. The assassin was gone, trapped somewhere in the City of Eyes. She was safe — or as safe as she could be in this body.

Barefoot, Eli walked into the purple sea, the heads of flowers brushing against the worn knees of her jeans. The buzzing intensified, drowning out her thoughts and fears, crescendoing and then decrescendoing like an orchestra. Ebbing and flowing like the tides, or the moon. Eli was drowning in purple, in the land that was also the sky, in the sky that was heavy and noisy and full. She was one small flower among many; one star among thousands; infinitesimally insignificant and beautiful.

Tav appeared beside her, a few feet away. Still following. Slower, more hesitantly, stepping clumsily on stems and petals. The smell of sweetness from the crushed plants followed their steps.

Eli led Tav deeper into the ocean of petals. The flowers swished against their legs and arms, waist-high, welcoming them with gentle touches. As they moved, Eli could see only flashes of skin through the pale green stalks and violet petals. Soon they were deep in the meadow, surrounded by flowers and bees.

"I used to come here, sometimes," said Eli. "When I was going crazy, feeling trapped in my body, trapped by the witches and the City of Eyes, lonely in the City of Ghosts, feeling like nothing mattered. I would come out here and lie down in the flowers."

"Thank you for bringing me here," whispered Tav. Eli had to read their lips to understand what they were saying.

Eli reached down into the purple galaxy and emerged with a handful of petals. She threw the petals toward Tav, watching them fall in the space between them.

She waited.

Tav took a single, tentative step toward her.

Eli felt her breathing hasten and lulled her lungs into calm waves. Not yet.

Tav took another step.

Eli swallowed.

Tav was in front of her now, close enough to touch, the smell of gasoline and sweat mixing with honey and crushed grass. Eli's eyes dropped to Tav's mouth, to their full lower lip. She waited.

Then Tav's mouth was against hers, and their hands were in her hair. Eli broke — hands reaching out to encircle Tav's waist, to pull them close, to feel their entire body pressed against hers, to feel that heartbeat as if it were her own, to rub her face against Tav's, to slide her hands up Tav's back —

She pulled back, looking at Tav with their angry eyes and spiky purple hair, fiercer and sadder than the spiky purple plants. The universe of petals stretched out all around them.

"You belong here," she said.

"We belong here," said Tav, and then their mouth was against Eli's again, needy and hot and wanting and asking, and the answer was *yes, yes, yes.*

THE HEALER

Last time had been fingers slipping under sleeves, sliding up her muscular arms. Last time, they had pressed their body against hers on the cold floor of the Children's Lair, kissing her again and again. They had tasted the arch of her neck, flicked their tongue over her ear, gripped her sharp hips with shaking hands.

But they had stopped before it had gone further. Something had held them back. Maybe it was Cam asleep in the corner (although that had never stopped them before); maybe it was the electricity that crackled between their body and Eli's. Maybe it was the way their entire body had trembled when Eli buried her face in the crook of their neck. They had never wanted someone the way they wanted Eli.

It scared the shit out of them.

This time, Eli took the lead. She pushed them down and straddled them, her thighs warm against Tav's. The scent of honey and floral perfume from crushed flowers drifted around them. The hum of bees, and the softness of dozens of insects brushing against their ankles and knees.

Tav admired the curve of Eli's biceps, and let their hands run over the hard muscle. She made Tav feel small and fragile, but in a good way. Tav's eyes fluttered closed for a moment as they wondered what it would be like to fall asleep in her arms.

"Look at me," said Eli.

Tav looked.

Eli pushed herself up to a sitting position. Eyes as yellow as the pollen in her hair. Collarbones sharp as blades. God, Tav wanted to touch them.

Slowly, Eli threaded her arm through one sleeve, and then the other. Hesitated. Then pulled her shirt over her head. Kept her fierce eyes on Tav.

Tav inhaled sharply, letting their eyes touch the freckle on her rib cage, the scar on her breast. She didn't look like a creature made of glass and pearl. She looked human.

She looked soft.

"Now you," said Eli.

A flicker of anxiety. The sun bright and hot on their face, like a spotlight. Tav wasn't used to being nervous. They propped themselves up on their elbows. They could already feel the imprint of stems and leaves tattooing their forearms, the lines cutting through the ink petals and stamens and leaf spines.

"You'll have to help me."

"Okay." Eli swallowed. Maybe she was nervous, too. She shifted slightly. Tav tried not to groan at her weight rubbing against them.

Tav leaned forward, tugging gracelessly on the back of their T-shirt. Warm hands on their shoulders. The feeling of soft cotton skimming their back and arms, quickly replaced with the gentle touch of air on naked skin. When they looked up, Eli was staring at them. Taking in their flat chest, the dark hairs circling wide nipples. The floral tattoos on their left arm. Where Eli was a wave, Tav was a line.

Eli leaned forward, her mouth inches from Tav's. She moved to their ear, her breath tickling their neck. "You are so fucking beautiful."

Tav reached for Eli. This time, they wouldn't hold back.

THE HEART

Tav was narrow and lean. They had more chest hair than she had expected. She liked it. She liked the way they felt underneath her. Eli let her hands skim over the soft hairs, her fingertips grazing their chest. Tav groaned. Eli stroked their chest again, this time with her fingernails. Tav's breathing was hard and fast, and their hands were skimming Eli's hips and lower back.

"I want you," she said, her mouth pressed against their ear. "I want you so badly."

And then Tav's hands were gripping her firmly, crushing her against them. Her bare chest touched Tav's and they both gasped at the sensation. Soft and hard, smooth and rough, skin warmed by the sun and the pounding hearts underneath. Eli found herself starting to move against Tav, rubbing her body against theirs.

She wanted more.

She opened her mouth and bit Tav's neck — gently, at first, and then harder. Tav was moaning, pushing back against her. Then they shifted so they could rub their thigh between Eli's legs. Eli bit harder, grinding against them.

Tav's hand grazing the edges of her jeans, fingers playing with the soft fabric of her underwear.

"I want you," Eli said again.

"You can have me." Tav's hand on the button of Eli's jeans. Their hand shook slightly, and they fumbled the button, missing the loop. "Sorry, I'll just —"

"I can —"

"It's okay —"

Eli's hand bumped into Tav's and they both laughed nervously.

"I can do it," said Tav. "It's hard to concentrate when you're kissing my neck."

Eli grinned. "I know."

Button through the loop. The zipper opening. Fingers slipping into the dark brown hairs that curled over the edge of her underwear.

"Are you sure?" asked Tav, hesitating.

"Yes." Eli fought the urge to shove Tav's hand into her pants. "Are you?"

Tav nodded. "Yeah. Definitely. I think about this all the time."

"Me, too." Eli pressed her hand against Tav. "Do you … want me to do this?"

Tav swallowed. Their fingers played with Eli's hair, tugging gently. Eli's eyes half closed in pleasure. "Yeah. If you want."

"I already told you." Her eyes were still half-closed, and a lazy crocodile smile arched across her face. "I want you. I want to touch you. I want to taste you. I want —"

Tav kissed her, pressing their tongue into her mouth and swallowing her moan. And then Tav, small, wiry Tav, rolled the powerful witch-made girl over until they were on top, and Eli was staring up at dark eyes and hair as purple as the petals around them.

Tav bent down and took Eli's nipple into their mouth. Eli couldn't stop herself, and as she opened her mouth to cry out, crocodile teeth grew from her jaws. Tav stopped and looked at her, their eyes wet and bright.

Then they slowly and deliberately licked the length of a wickedly sharp tooth.

Eli had never felt more alive.

THE HEIR

Kite stared at the sword in wonder.

"From the moon war," she told the Beast. "A legend." She scratched behind his ears and he purred loudly.

"Well, you know what to do. Have a fun trip!" Clytemnestra turned a cartwheel in the air and vanished, leaving Kite and the Beast alone with the vengeful weapon.

Kite had always known that the wasteland and the junkyard were not myths. Stories were never just stories. Eli had survived the wastelands and brought back a dangerous weapon. And Clytemnestra wanted more.

More weapons. More allies. More anger and power from the bodies the Coven had deemed worthless.

The creatures lurking in the wasteland would not be happy to see the Heir. Clytemnestra knew this. But Kite was also proof of the Warlord's power — the Heir Rising answered to her, followed her orders. The Coven was weak. The time to strike was now.

As a messenger, Kite was a symbol — proof that this was a time of regime change. A time of endings, and beginnings.

Out of habit, she reached out with her mind for the familiar tether of power that kept her tied to the Witch Lord. Again, she was surprised and exhilarated when she couldn't feel the chains that had kept her bound for so long. She was still bound, her fate intertwined with her mother's, with her root essence — but she had a little more freedom. A little more privacy. A little more choice.

Every step she took now was another betrayal she couldn't take back. The steps of the Coven turned to fragments of stone and dust. The remaking of the assassins.

She had attacked her mother. Stolen from her.

And now she knew, finally, the terrible fate that awaited all witches who disobeyed or disappointed the Witch Lord — having their essences stolen. Their life-force sucked from their bodies. Their powers absorbed by the tyrant or used to animate dead things. Not just killed, but lost, forever, twisted and used until not a single remnant remained of who they had once been. Kite knew that the Witch Lord wouldn't hesitate to take her essence if she discovered the depth of her daughter's treachery. She could always make a new Heir.

But Kite had some of that power now, too. It sang in her blood and cast flashes of light before her eyes, colours running together and bursting and changing like a human child's kaleidoscope.

Would she use it? Would she dare? If Clytemnestra went back on her promise, and tore the Heart from Eli's body, sacrificing her for the revolution ... Kite pushed the thought away. She had made a promise, and a witch's promise was unbreakable.

But it could be bent, by clever tongues and minds.

As the power to steal essences reared up under her skull, Kite felt the forgotten blade responding to it. The surge of power in both girl and sword (both weapons, in their own ways, wielded by others) cast the acrid scent of burning hair into the chamber. Magic testing magic.

The Beast rubbed his head against Kite and she petted him, humming to soothe his trembling body. Her profane power settled, like silt in water, and the sword, too, let its guard down.

All she had to do was feed the sword her sacred blood, and it would imprint on her. Then, once she freed it from the enchantments Clytemnestra had used to make it docile, it should lead her to the junkyard. It should take her to its adopted home.

Not all things want to be found. The sword desperately wanted to return to exile. She could feel it in the energy radiating out from the alien metal, could see it in the flakes of rust and blood on its edge. Of course it didn't want to be here: there was no space for grief in the Children's Lair, and the sword had been grieving the loss of its home for a very long time.

"Okay, precious, we need to work together, okay?" Kite pressed her forehead against the Beast's face. "I need you to bite me."

The Beast whined again.

"No, no, I'll be okay. You have to do this for us, all right?"

The Beast licked her face. Sighing, Kite stuck her hand into its massive jaw, and scraped her skin against a sharp canine. A single drop of bluegreen blood beaded on the back of her hand.

"Good boy," she told him.

Kite extended her hand over the blade, turning it so the palm was face up, and waited as the drop of blood dripped over the blade. For a moment the black metal had a blue sheen from the wet drop. Then the blood vanished, absorbed by the sword. Linking their bodies together. Blood magic: forbidden magic.

Another law broken. Another step away from the throne, from the promises made by her DNA.

Another step toward chaos, wonder, and freedom.

Licking the wound clean, Kite then reached out with both hands and tore at Clytemnestra's enchantments, clawing the blade free from the suffocating magic. The sword twisted, the metal gears turning, spikes writhing and roiling like snakes, and then it stabbed the air and tore through the fabric of time and space. Kite, her hair moving as wildly as the metal arms of the strange blade, grabbed hold of the hilt. The Heir and the Beast stepped through the tear …

And onto a frozen ocean of black. The sky swirled with purplegrey clouds, and flakes of snow fluttered down like moths to settle on her neck and shoulders.

A small figure huddled on the ice, shivering. Arms wrapped around their torso. As Kite walked forward, clutching the sword, the figure came into sharp focus. Dark hair tousled with wind and pomade. A T-shirt torn in several places. Black skinny jeans.

Kite nearly dropped the sword in astonishment.

"Cam?"

THE HEALER

They were lying naked in a field of purple, petals crushed in their hair. The sweet and acidic scent of a girl made of thorns was fading. The outline of Eli's body was still pressed into the flowers, but she was gone again, and Cam was gone, and time was running out.

Tav sat up and brushed petals from their hair. A single bee landed on their forearm. They weren't afraid of being stung. They reached out and gently touched a golden stripe. The bee danced on their arm for a few moments, buzzing fiercely, full of life and death and hope and fury. Then it flew away again, joining the swarm.

Tav stared at the empty place next to them where Eli had been, and then buried their head in their hands. Eli had blades missing from her belt, and she was vanishing more and more often, becoming more Heart than girl. What if she stopped coming back? Could a body carry that much magic and survive?

Tav dressed, and then waited for a few minutes. Eli didn't rematerialize. Finally, Tav walked away from the field, the forest, the bees, the smell of clover honey and citrus. They climbed back on the bike and drove back to the apartment.

The ride back was long and lonely.

When they arrived at the apartment, Eli was waiting.

"How?" said Tav wearily, dropping their keys noisily on the coffee table. There was no other question. It wasn't Eli's fault she kept disappearing … unless she was doing it on purpose? Tav pushed the thought away. Did it really matter, in the end? They had been left behind, abandoned, and that's all that mattered.

How do you love the Heart of a planet?

"I don't know." Eli looked unhappy; what Tav could see of her face, anyway. The Heart was glowing, and the light obscured the delicate human features of the jar that held the light of a world.

"Not a big cuddler?" Tav tried for a teasing tone but it came out flat.

Eli shrugged with one shoulder.

Tav wanted nothing more than a hot shower and a nap, but there wasn't time for what they wanted. There never seemed to be, these days.

Their voice came out low and quiet. "What if it happens again? When we're making a door?"

Eli looked away. "It won't."

"You don't know that."

"I don't think it will."

"Oh, you don't 'think'? It happened last time! We needed you, Cam needed you, and —" Tav cut themselves off, the anger choking their throat.

Cam had needed both of them. They had both let him down.

"What do you want from me?" Eli moved suddenly, with the languid grace of a hunter, until she was behind Tav. Tav didn't turn around. Eli's breath was cold on her neck, like a winter chill. "You're just angry that I left, aren't you? It wasn't on purpose!"

Tav didn't answer.

Eli vanished and then appeared front of Tav. Tav flinched.

Slowly, Eli stepped back. Tav couldn't see her face through the blinding light that radiated from her torso. Her voice was quiet but steady. "Still afraid of me?"

"I'm not afraid of anything."

"Then I guess we're both liars."

Tav glared at the ball of light, eyes watering from the effort of staring down a sun.

Eli moved away first, drifting back to the window, to the outside world, and away from Tav with the grass stains on their knees and the aorta that leaned to the left.

She's untouchable, thought Tav. Part of them was jealous, wishing that they, too, could sometimes disappear.

Part of them was scared: Tav wanted to grab Eli and hold her in this world, keep her from turning into a tree of light. But not even the Healer had that power.

"A message arrived while you were out," said Eli, as if Tav had been out joyriding. They felt a flash of resentment at this brutal summary of the morning. Hadn't it meant anything to her? It had meant everything to Tav.

"And?"

One finger tapped the windowpane, then two.

"Your friend wants to talk."

"My 'friend'?" Tav's stomach lurched.

Three fingers playing a silent melody on the glass, something only Eli could hear. "The Hedge-Witch lost people in the attempt that failed. She wants her payment now."

All the blood rushed out of Tav's head. Their hand scrabbled against the faded floral-print wallpaper for support. "Now? That wasn't the deal."

"You made a deal with a witch," said Eli. "Their concept of time is … flexible."

"When?" The flowers were starting to blur together, turning into the faces of ghouls and monsters. Tav blinked several times, trying to clear their vision.

"Tonight."

"Okay. Okay." Tav waited for the dizziness to pass. "We have time to strategize."

Eli laughed, and it turned into a cough. She turned around and spat out a single bee. "It's already night."

"No, it's not."

Eli tapped the glass in an insistent rhythm. Tav reluctantly walked over and looked out into the sky that was already turning a deep indigo.

"I don't understand."

"The world is dying," said Eli. "Already the stars are coming out. The witches' world is infecting this one. Time is sliding out of alignment."

Panic raced through Tav's entire body like an electrical shock. They leaned against the glass, fingers splayed like wings. They could see the faint brush of constellations appearing on what should be a bright afternoon sky. *Fuck.*

"There's only one thing to do." They glanced at Eli, wondering how much they could tell, calculating how much they could get away with. "We have to give her what she wants."

THE HEIR

Cam turned around. His eyes were red. The skin on his knuckles was dry and flaky.

"Kite?" Cam's voice wavered. He took a step toward her, and then hesitated. "You're not with the Coven, are you? Did she ask you to find me?"

Kite's eyes roamed over his body. He was agate. Graphite. Quartz. Shale.

And underneath him, a continent of obsidian. The voices of the dead called to Kite from beneath the black glass, and she suddenly understood where she was.

The Witch-Killing Fields.

Her eyes blazed. Had they sent him to harvest the stone?

Is one blade not enough for you, Eli?

"Kite?"

His voice broke the silence like a pebble in water. But it was a small sound, an insignificant ripple, lost in the vast darkness of the ocean.

She met his eyes. Greybrown. Long, artful lashes, like the feathered legs of a millipede. The whites of his eyes stained pinkred from the killing wind. He had come to this world and survived. He had come to this world and been transformed. He had evolved. He had negotiated with the sentient stone that made up the Labyrinth and under-labyrinth, the living wall of the world. He had escaped the Coven. He had found his way here, to the fields of sorrow.

He was dangerous.

She had underestimated Cam. Maybe he did belong here, with the stone that stretched endlessly into the sky. It was Kite who didn't belong. It was *her* essence that would be torn apart by black glass.

Panic swirled through her body like a riptide pulling her out to sea. She clutched the Beast's tail and he whined in protest.

She had never faced true death before, although she had slept next to Eli and her blades since she was small.

She never truly believed that Eli would kill her.

Did she not understand my message? Does she truly think I betrayed her?

Hurt cut through the fear and woke her from her reverie.

"Did she send you to kill me?" Her voice sang across the space between them. Kite stared at the boy and contemplated the engineer of her death. He was strange, and mostly human, but she was learning the worth of human bones and spirits.

"What?" Confusion swirled in his eyes, and he raised a hand to push back the tangles of his hair.

"Did she give you the blade? She must care deeply for you." Kite could understand Eli's attraction — the sharp chips of breccia, the crust of lime. He was magnificent.

His eyes widened. "Oh, fuck. I still have it! What if she needs it?" He held up the knife.

Kite flinched, but she had no lids to shield her eyes from the cruel edge of the assassin, the obsidian needle.

Only it wasn't the assassin. It wasn't a blade aimed at Kite's essence. Cam held out the shield — the stone blade. A blade that could protect as well as harm — but not a witch's essence. Not a magic soul. She was safe — for now.

Kite's seaweed hair relaxed over her shoulders, a few strands stroking her skin. She had self-soothed this way ever since she was born.

"She didn't send you for me," said Kite wonderingly. "She didn't send you here at all."

"What? No, of course not. What are you talking about?" Cam's arm dropped to his side. "Make sense."

Kite ignored his question and walked forward, dragging the heavy sword behind her, its point scraping on the glass and casting a haunting wail into the atmosphere. But Kite wasn't afraid of the music of the dead.

She was afraid of the dead themselves.

"Are you a discarded thing that needs to be found? I will collect you," she promised. "And we will make a home in the ruins of the city for your beauty."

Cam twisted the hilt of the blade, but didn't move away. Humans spooked easy. Kite knew this. When she was close enough to feel the heat of his part-human body, she stopped. The Beast did not, and ran right up to Cam, tail wagging. Cam stiffened, and then extended a hand and let the Beast smell him. The Beast tried to bite a piece of quartz, and then withdrew, whimpering.

"Serves you right for trying to bite me," said Cam.

"He just wanted to taste you," said Kite. "How else do you get to know someone?"

Cam's eyes fell to the sword in her hand, the gears now turning, the iron spokes writhing madly.

"My staff!"

Almost as if it had a mind of its own, his hand reached out for the blade that had awoken when it tasted his blood. The blade that had shielded him from the red wind. The blade that had been traded away for shelter, stolen by the Warlord in the Labyrinth.

Skin touched alloy. Sizzling, then a shriek.

He drew his hand back to his chest.

"It bit me!" A burn mark in the shape of a circle was pressed into his palm.

"You found it," Kite said slowly, understanding dawning.

"Bad stick." Cam glared at the sword. "I didn't miss you, either."

"It follows you," she continued dreamily, "and it can never be lost as long as it is tied to you."

"Tied to me?" Cam made a face. "That doesn't sound good."

Kite noticed that his moustache was drooping and was longer than usual. She flicked away the urge to reach out and stroke it back into shape.

"Oh, it's just an immortal bond between creatures." Kite waved her hand dismissively. "Nothing to worry about. It was supposed to be the compass, it was supposed to lead me there. But instead it brought me to you. Not willingly, I don't think. It seems to hold a grudge. What did you do to it?"

"Nothing! I mean, I rescued it from the junkyard. And then Clytemnestra took it. I —"

"It didn't want to be found," she said, "and perhaps it resents being traded like currency. This sword is a noble creature and should be treated with respect. When we return to the junkyard, it will have a choice to make."

"The junkyard? Why are you going back there?" His eyes narrowed. "*We?* The last time I saw you, you betrayed us to the Coven. And if Eli didn't send you to rescue me, I'm not going anywhere with you."

"Betrayed you?" Kite tilted her head. "Precious, I saved you. I saved *her*."

"She doesn't think so."

"She is scared to trust a witch."

"She should be."

"Yes," Kite agreed sadly. "But I will keep saving her. And I will save you, too, for her." A single strand of hair stretched toward Cam, and the stones on his chest began humming, a melody that sounded like a homecoming. She smiled. "The stones recognize me."

"I guess the stones don't understand that you're a traitor," he said, but his words lacked venom.

"Or maybe they know something the boy doesn't."

Kite walked past him, staring curiously at the smooth glass underfoot. Then she knelt down and stared at her reflection in the dark pane. All at once, a flash of lightning from underneath the stone shattered her image, and Kite felt a scream rising up in her body. She stumbled back, heart racing.

"What's wrong?" asked Cam. "You're acting stranger than usual."

"I can't stay here," she said, hair covering her face like a mask. "This is where the obsidian blades are forged. These are the Witch-Killing Fields. And we have disturbed their slumber. They are awake."

"Who?"

Kite stared into the glass, mesmerized, as her reflection was eaten by ghostly jaws and skeletal hands.

"The broken ones, of course."

His fear cracked. She could smell the moment the adrenalin cast a haze of murky brownred over his body. And then the blade was against her throat, in a split second when his fear decided she was the enemy. But the true threat lay dormant underneath them. Waiting.

Kite let her words dissipate into air, like a small gasp of breath. "That won't kill me," she whispered. Her hair hung limp on her back, wary and waiting.

"But it can make a blade that will. I can chip out a bit of obsidian and end you."

"You could," she agreed. The Beast nuzzled her ankles. She hushed him with her mind. She tipped her head back, throat still pressed against stone, and admired the great fields of the universe flowering with life and death. "Isn't it beautiful?"

Cam said nothing but swallowed audibly. She suspected he had never killed anyone before.

"You know, I was forbidden from coming here as a girl. Too dangerous. I wonder how many witches came, anyway, just to see its beauty. If I had to die, there is no other place I would choose."

A shooting star streaked overhead. The stone was warm at her throat, like the touch of a lover. Like Eli's hand. She always had a firm grip. A few pink shells rained from Kite's eyes and clattered over the black glass. Kite kept her eyes open. Cam stilled, and then set his shoulders back. His grip tightened around the stone blade. He stared into her eyes, the glowing orbs of bluegreen light. His grip relaxed.

"What am I doing?" He pulled on his hair, making it even messier than before. Kite felt the blade pull away from her body, and a rush of cold air replaced its warmth. She let out a breath she hadn't known she was holding. Seawater dripped out of the side of her mouth.

"You were eliminating a possible threat," said Kite.

"I'm not a killer."

"No?" Kite cocked her head. "Then it's a good thing I found you before you got eaten."

"How do we get out of here?" His voice was harsh, grating. The sound forced out of his mouth. "Where are we?"

Kite stood gracefully. "The Witch-Killing Fields. It's where the obsidian is harvested to create weapons like Eli's blade. The power isn't just the obsidian," she told Cam. "I discovered it in my research on how to free a made-daughter assassin. The essences of witches were fed to the ice, and their magic changed. The stone you stand on is a grave, and the ghosts of our dead is what lends the obsidian blades their strength. They are hungry for more witches."

"You wanted to free Eli?"

"Of course. All things should be free." Her voice was light as air, bright as a firefly bobbing in the night.

"But you're the future Witch Lord."

"Yes, that was my fate."

"Was?"

She turned her luminous eyes on him. "All things should be free."

He stepped back and the knife dropped to his side. For a moment, he looked like a lost child stranded on the ice, needing to be rescued. But then the moment passed, and he was a monster again — part man, part stone. A blade edge sharpened by fear and loneliness.

"You can get me back to Eli and Tav?" The longing in his voice was palpable. He was alone, and he was never alone; or at least, he tried to never be alone. They had failed him, Kite realized. They had not sent him across to harvest the black ice. They had lost him. Misplaced him. No wonder he was so afraid.

Kite looked down, letting her hair cascade over her knees and onto the glass. "I can't promise that. I'm not here to help you. I'm going to the junkyard and then I'm going to end my mother's reign." She looked up again through a pool of bluegreen. "Will you help me?"

Cam turned his back on her and stared up at the sky. She wondered if he was looking for his home planet. Finally, he turned back, all the stones on his body shaking as if an earthquake was tremoring through his bones.

"I'll help you, but if you betray us again —"

"Then you will take me back here and trap my essence in the ice. I understand."

He reached out a hand. Kite stared at it for a second, and then grasped the tip of the stone blade instead. A single bubble blossomed from her palm and hung in the air.

"Now you."

He reached out and tentatively touched a piece of hair that had been creeping toward him. It cut like barbed wire, and he hissed in pain. Kite blew on the bubble, and it swam toward his bleeding, burned hand and popped on it. Then she pressed her own wound against his. When she drew her hand away, both were healed, but she could feel the strangeness of blood and sediment in her magic body.

"So." Cam cleared his throat. "Why are we going to the junkyard?"

She smiled, and her eyes glowed with the light of a pulsing jellyfish swimming through an undersea universe. "We are building an army. The unwanted are wanted again."

THE HEART

Tav's shaking hand managed to find the keyhole and turned the ignition. They leaned back for a moment against Eli's chest, and Eli could smell honey.

"Do you trust me?" Their voice was rough with worry.

Eli felt the prick of a thousand thorns as her throat undulated with the lie she wanted to regurgitate. The world around them seemed to freeze; leaves hanging in mid-fall, the moon pausing its rotation for a single moment, tides arched in spikes and curves across the globe.

Their mouth on her shoulder blade. Their hands on her lower back.

Eli remembered the fervor in Tav's voice when they spoke of using magic to take back the city, the way their eyes had burned with hunger when they stared at her glowing body. The Heart of a world.

They would use you. You know they would. They would make you their tool.

But they haven't, not yet.

There's still time. Everyone lets you down, in the end.

"Do you trust me?"

The pain in Eli's body whispered louder than the street. The frost blade burned at her hip. She swallowed.

"Yes."

THE HEALER

Tav felt the surge of caffeine mingle with adrenalin and anxiety. Their hands were shaking. Their heartbeat was amplified in their ears, a heavy bass pounding out the last few seconds between safety and danger. Only this time it wasn't their life they were putting in danger, but Eli's.

She trusts you. She believes in you.

Fuck.

The path was so familiar they could have followed it in their sleep. Their chosen home. The place where they found hope. Love. Power.

No bells rang when they opened the door to The Sun.

The jitters intensified. Tav could hear their teeth rattling in their jaw, and wondered if Eli could hear it, too.

Eli went first. She was, after all, Tav's bargaining chip. Tav's property. Tav clenched their jaw, hating that they had to do this to her. They wanted to apologize, to beg for her forgiveness. But that would come later — if there was a later.

Tav watched as Eli let the tendrils of furious plants wind themselves around her legs, arms, throat, torso. She didn't resist.

She trusts you.

Their eye started twitching. Their heartbeat was deafening. *Fuck fuck fuck.*

"You've been keeping a secret, Tav. I taught you well." Pride laced the Hedge-Witch's voice like arsenic in tea.

"A bargain is a bargain," they said shortly. "You shed blood for us, and I give you the Heart."

The Hedge-Witch's eyes swirled black and white, mixing into cement grey. She stepped forward to inspect the assassin, strands of light blossoming along Eli's veins and the cracks in her chapped lips. "Fascinating. It merged with her organic body?" She walked a slow circle around the girl. "So this is why I couldn't find her. Why my daughter struggled to find her — she'll be punished for the failure, of course. The Heart would blot out any other magic signature. It's more than her." She smiled. "I wondered what would happen when you touched it. It was smart of you to use her as a vessel. The weight of the Heart might have shattered the one who wrenched it from the Coven."

"Did you think it would shatter me?"

The Hedge-Witch raised her gaze to meet Tav's eyes. "You are extraordinary, Tav. I never doubted that you would come home."

The vines tightened their grip on Eli, who still said nothing. Just watched Tav with those yellow reptilian eyes.

The weight of faith was heavier than loss, heavier than pain, than sleepless nights and waking nightmares.

Tav felt the sharp edge of obsidian against their forearm.

"The Coven —"

"I don't want to hear it." The Hedge-Witch raised a manicured hand. "You've been caught up in delusions, Tav. The real battle is here. And it's just beginning. I will lead your people to victory."

"*My* people?" Tav frowned.

"The humans," she amended. "The humans need to be shown the error of their ways. I will make a new world for you. For us. With the Heart, I can —"

"*You* can?" Tav interrupted. "You used to say 'we.'"

Eli laughed shortly. "There is no 'we' with witches," she said. "Only one can rule."

"We are not all the same," said the Hedge-Witch. "I am sorry we will have to destroy your body, daughter of the Coven. You were so useful."

Eli glared at her, and then let her eyes slip back to Tav.

"Why are you so tense?" The Hedge-Witch's voice was soft as sin. "Today we start a new future. You and I together, like we always planned. We'll start with this city — but why end there? We can conquer the entire world. I will rule, of course, but you will be at my side.

We can decide what justice is. We can decide who lives and dies. You will no longer be powerless, Tav. I will give you power."

Their grip on the hilt was slippery, their palm coated in sweat. Hands still shaking.

"I understand you feel empathy for the made-thing," said the Hedge-Witch. "I will let you say goodbye before I use her."

Tav turned to Eli and gently laid a hand on her cheek. They stared into her crocodile eyes. Let their eyes linger on the spot on her neck that they had kissed over and over again, nibbling and biting until Eli had moaned their name.

They leaned forward and pressed a kiss against Eli's forehead. Heartbeat like thunder.

"Goodbye," they whispered.

Then they stabbed her with the obsidian knife.

THE HEIR

The deadly plains stretched to the horizon like a never-ending nightmare. Kite shivered as she stared down at her feet, bare and pale against the dark obsidian. She could almost hear the cries of the dead witches under the surface, and when the light hit the black ice she could see arms reaching up at her, trying to drag her under.

"Kite?"

She looked up, letting the horror bleed from her eyes. Ink dripped down her face, the same colour as the stone.

"Are you okay?" Cam looked at her nervously, tugging at his moustache.

"We need to find the junkyard," she said. "Ask the sword."

"The staff — sword — hates me."

"Then you must free it," she told him.

"How?"

She swirled her hair into a nest on top of her head. Maybe a bird would come to rest, and they could dine on feathers.

"I don't know." She turned around stared back at the obsidian. So beautiful, and so deadly. *Like Eli*, she thought wistfully. "You don't need that, by the way."

"Need what?"

She could taste the guilt spilling from his body like spoiled fruit, could hear the moment he stopped raising the blade, pulled upward by uncertainty and fear.

"We made an agreement. That can't be broken. I can't break that oath. If I do, I will immediately be summoned here for execution. It's what we agreed."

"Eli told me not to trust witches."

"Isn't it a little late for that?" She turned back and stared at the thousands of stones studding his body. Basanite. Siltstone. Mica. "Shiny," she said, and licked her lips.

Cam rubbed a piece of blue granite absentmindedly. "So we free the sword, then it can take us to the junkyard, and then you'll get me home."

"Oh, I never promised that," she said, smiling sadly. Her broken reflection didn't smile at all. "I said I would remake the world. Perhaps at the end of everything, you will find a home. I would never have agreed to an impossible promise."

Forked lightning danced across the earth. It really was like walking on the sky, knowing at any moment you could plunge to your death. Death wasn't something Kite thought about a lot. It was hard to kill witches, and harder to kill the Heir to the Coven. The trembling worsened. She didn't understand why her body was like a violin string being played by a fine bow.

"Have you ever stared at your death?" she asked Cam conversationally. "It's such an interesting experience."

"It's just a rock," said Cam, as if he wasn't half rock himself. He knelt down and placed a palm on the surface. He frowned. "It's hard to hear."

"Stones aren't meant to be tombs, but we keep abusing them," she sighed.

A faint smile played at the corners of his mouth. "The voice of the stone is quiet, but still there. Let me talk to it for a while. Maybe it knows how to break the curse."

"Being bound to another thing isn't always a curse."

"If one of them is unwilling it is. Maybe be quiet and let me work?"

Kite drew back and let him commune with obsidian. The Beast pressed his body against her legs. He was panting heavily.

She missed the library. She missed the Labyrinth. In her own way, she even missed Clytemnestra.

This was the most dangerous thing she had done in her entire life. The absurdity of it overflowed her lungs, and damp air, stringy with seaweed, exhaled from her mouth. A spoiled Heir who knew nothing of war, who knew nothing that wasn't in a book — how could she overthrow the Witch Lord?

Staring at the graveyard of dead witches was depressing. She almost wished she had held grimly on to the fierce playfulness of her child's shape, the way Clytemnestra had. But it had been impossible; she had to pass as an adult, and her shape had changed the way she thought, the way she felt. She couldn't play the way the Warlord played, not anymore. She was a strange thing, a half-grown witch, too old for the Children's Lair and too young for the halls of the Coven.

"Can you make a circle?" asked Cam.

"That's such a lovely idea," she said, watching the stone body bent over the stone universe. "What kind?"

"I don't know, exactly." He bit his lip. "The stone seems to think that we can use the essences of the dead witches to free the blade. But we need to … re-enact our bond, and then break it? Does that make sense?"

"Of course. Rituals have power." She didn't say that she was afraid of what lay under the rock, and that her own essence had already been defeated once, by Circinae.

She was not the strongest of her kind.

"Then let's do it now." He stood. "Lay the sword beside me."

Kite did, watching as the stones on his body began to shake; listening to the sharp hiss of the blade as it came close to the hand that had claimed it and wrenched it from its resting place. "It really does seem to hate you," she observed.

"Thanks for reminding me."

Kite bent down and rubbed the Beast's ears. "Stay out of the way, precious. This could get messy." The Beast barked once, ran a few paces away, and turned invisible.

Kite bent down and breathed on the black surface until it milked over in pearly white. Then she spat on the white and rubbed her hand in the spit. Slowly, she repeated the process all around the boy and the blade, until she had made a complete circle.

Nothing happened.

Pulling on a clump of hair, Kite whispered a few words to the circle, encouraging it to take life. It flared seafoam green for a moment and then flickered out, like a candle being toyed with by the wind.

"I think you need to cut," she said to Cam.

"Okay." He swallowed, and then approached the circle.

"Don't cross it," she said, and he stopped, nodded, and then knelt down. Using one of the chips of quartz on his knuckle, he scratched a thin line over the saliva on the glass. When the circle was completed he stepped back into the centre. The light flared up again, little flames of white and green, but then died down, leaving only piles of white ash like salt.

"Pain," Kite said reluctantly. "All magic requires sacrifice."

"I know," he said. "The obsidian told me. I was just hoping it was lying."

He picked up the sword made of gears and spikes and hatred.

The smell of burning filled the air, and Cam let out a small whimper. But he held on despite the pain and dragged the heavy blade with him. Together, they traced the circle for a third time, cutting deeper into rock.

"It hurts you both," she said. The blade was bleeding just as Cam was, black with an oily sheen of silver dripping between Cam's fingers.

Gasping he dropped the blade, hands burned raw and bloody, face ashen. "Do it," he managed.

She could feel the magic now, bubbling to the surface. The fear inside her flared up, hot and sticky. This magic didn't obey her. It was outcast, destroyed, it wanted nothing and therefore had nothing to lose.

Kite had much to lose.

But she had sworn a promise, and she had a mission to fulfill, and so, compelled, she stepped forward and bit her wrist with an elegant tooth, and let a single drop of sacred witch blood fall into the circle.

The flames raged up, higher than the tallest tree, higher than the Coven.

"This circle is your bondage," she said, sweat dripping down her neck. "Now you must break it, and from one become two."

"From one become two," muttered Cam. "From one become two. From one become two."

And then Kite heard nothing more because the sword had started screaming.

Kite waited several long minutes before Cam walked

through the fire, his body singing a melody of the underworld, of dirt and damp darkness.

He stepped across the threshold and collapsed.

As he crossed the circle, the flame was extinguished, the bond broken. Relief settled in her fingernails like the caress of an insect's antennae. She stepped forward to retrieve the sword.

A hand made of light reached from the cut in the obsidian and grasped her skirt.

The dead witches were rising.

THE HEALER

Tav watched as Eli's eyes grew large in horror, like two mirrors that reflected Tav's dirty face back to them. Then the girl looked down at the sliver of obsidian lodged in her body.

"I don't understand," she whispered, shock blotting out all other sensations like a lunar eclipse.

Tav gritted their teeth and twisted the blade.

Eli groaned in agony. It was an unearthly sound, like a cliff crumbling under a landslide, like a blade breaking on an anvil. The sound rang in Tav's ears and carried with it the memory of rusted swing sets creaking in the rain and stones thrown by older boys.

Tav turned the blade as if it were a key — and opened a door.

The hole they made in Eli's body was clean and bright, a perfect circle through an otherwise ordinary-looking human girl (except for the eyes, of course, which had turned pure black, as if the blood vessels had all burst and bled nightmares).

Eli's mouth closed, but the whimpering continued. The sound reverberated from the plants that covered the windowsill, their leaves trembling wildly. A succulent began shredding itself.

Tav could see a glimmer of black fire through the hole, the lights of fireflies and birthday candles and forest fires and static electricity sparking into life inside the fragile shell of a body.

The fluttering, furious flame of the Heart that had lived for generations under the Coven. That now lived in the vulnerable body of a girl whose touch kept Tav awake at night.

"What did you do?" the Hedge-Witch's eyes burned with excitement. Her sharpened teeth emerged from her lips like a row of knives. "How did you do that? Teach it to me. *Tell me.*"

"Take the Heart," said Tav. "I have cut it out for you." They kept their hand and blade in the frail body as the lifeforce drained out of the girl. The black eyes glittered and went dull.

Tav was killing her, and they all knew it.

"I knew you were special," whispered the Hedge-Witch, excitement pulsing through her words. "I knew when it came down to it that you would get your hands dirty. This is the revolution we need. Sacrifice. Pain. A willingness to betray. To kill. You are truly one of mine." As she reached for Eli, the Hedge-Witch's hands shook with excitement.

She reached her clawed talons inside Eli, seeking the power that flowed through the girl's bones and burned her body to ash. "I can feel the power. I can taste it."

Tav withdrew the blade suddenly and the door closed, skin and hair and stone and hawthorn filling the empty space where the Heart had begun to spill out.

The Hedge-Witch fell back, her hand severed at the wrist. The wound was perfectly cauterized.

"You made a bargain!" she shrieked, saliva dripping from her fangs. She exhaled clouds of crimson smoke that smelled of bleach and foxglove. "Whatever monstrous magic you've been stained with cannot keep you from the bargain you made."

Tav's body was shaking, both from fear and from the effort of holding open the wound without destroying Eli.

She had better be alive.

She trusted me.

"I've fulfilled my end of the bargain," they told their mentor, ally, and enemy. "I have delivered the Heart to your hand." They could already feel the promise they had made fading, the oath fulfilled. The magic was satisfied.

Tav smiled, and knew it was feral. They had outwitted the Hedge-Witch, and they both knew it.

"Clever baby," crooned the Hedge-Witch. "Such a fast learner. But I've been dealing in deception for much, much longer."

The succulent had finished shredding itself and was now a collection of stubby greygreen leaves on the floor oozing lifeblood. The pieces began to twitch violently. And then they began to grow, reaching arms up to the sky and legs down to the ground, shaking out hair matted with earth and cobwebs and coffee grounds.

"I thought that was a new plant," said Tav. "I didn't recognize it. How's it going, you guys?"

They tried not to let their fear bleed over their body and turned, smiling, to face their former comrades growing from the mutilated plant.

Their hand tightened on the hilt. The obsidian blade was now half its size, worn thin by the power of the Heart. It felt small and fragile in Tav's hand.

Their eyes flicked to Eli, who had collapsed on the ground, gasping for breath. As they watched, she coughed up an acrylic fingernail.

They were unarmed and outnumbered.

THE HEIR

There was music playing.

The low murmur of a cello, the melancholy chorus of violin. Every movement under the ice, every ebb and flow of the mass of light that trembled and turned and reached and desired was an orchestra playing an eternal dirge, a melody of mourning and vengeance.

Finally, the dead witches had found someone to gift their revenge.

Kite.

Not just any witch, but the Heir Rising.

They would devour her body and steal her essence. They would take their revenge on anything and everything in their path.

Sometimes trauma blotted out all hope, all futures,

all belief in change. Sometimes suffering only wanted to make more suffering, spreading like a virus. Sometimes destruction was just destruction, and there would be no rebuilding.

The trapped and broken essences of witches long dead were not interested in a new world. They couldn't imagine it. They no longer loved.

Kite could feel their desire to destroy her in their touch.

"Poor things," she said, as she watched the fingers crawl up her leg like a caterpillar, "I can't take you back with me."

But they couldn't be reasoned with now that they had been submerged into rock; they needed and hated the obsidian desert, just as they needed and hated themselves.

"The Witch-Killing Fields were a nursery rhyme we used to sing whenever one of the children went missing. Dead or junked and good as dead. Street myths. Legends. We understood they were true, and we didn't forget you, I promise we never forgot you."

The hand wrapped about Kite's leg and began to pull her into the stone. Kite's essence flared up, hot as molten glass, but the hand was too strong, the fury too great.

Kite wasn't a fighter.

The memory of Circinae's touch prickled up and down her body. A red storm coming to obliterate her light. Fire scorching her soul. Falling, falling forever out of the sky. *No. Not again. Never again.*

She looked desperately toward Cam, but he was still unconscious on the ground. They would vivisect him, too, when they were done with her.

The stone blade was lying beside him on the black ice. If she could only reach it —

Pain seared through her body; the witches were pulling her out of her skin, forcing her into her most powerful and vulnerable state. Without her body holding her together, it would be impossible to resist the resting place of the stone field, impossible to resist the cry from her dead sisters. If they succeeded in drawing her out of her skin, she would be lost. She would forget her mother, Clytemnestra, the library, and Eli.

There was no coming back from an obsidian grave.

Eli. The reckless, confusing, passionate girl that Kite had known and loved all her life. Eli was brave, and Kite could be, too. She could fight back.

She had to try.

Kite pulled back, hair lashing the air, sparks burning from the tips. They scattered across the blackness and continued to burn, casting an eerie bluegreen light over the smooth surface.

Wrenching a handful of strands from her head, Kite whispered a spell over her own dying cells and threw the hair onto the disembodied hand. The appendage released her, as if burned, and a discordant wail broke through the haunting song. Stepping back, Kite could see that each individual strand had wound itself around the hand, lashing the fingers together. The hand collapsed in on itself and fell back into the chasm. She was safe — for now.

The reprieve was short. Looking across the circle, Kite could see other body parts emerging from the lacerations in the stone. Like sickness leached from a wound, the remnants of flesh and magic were oozing out of the cuts in the ice.

And in the middle of the circle, free at last, its bond broken by ritual — the sword.

Kite ran.

The music grew louder and more urgent with every step, the tempo racing to catch the lost princess, who had nothing but teeth and nails and volumes of history to keep her alive.

Fear bleeding into her heart like water damage spreading across a page, Kite hurriedly cast an ancient spell of courtesy. It was one that princes used to cast when they courted the silver trees that grew in a distant galaxy. According to the records, it was like asking someone to dance — they could choose to take your hand or not; they had the power of acceptance or refusal. It made it impossible for Kite to touch the other being without agreement.

The sword had to accept her offer. It was too powerful an artifact to bend to her will — unless Kite used the newfound powers her mother had gifted her. Unless …

No. I won't turn into her. I am nothing like her.

Brilliant turquoise hair coiled tightly around her neck as the witches' teeth bit at her feet. Strange shapes of light and dark stretched from all around her. Kite felt her own light starting to diminish. She was starting to feel like a shadow cast by someone else. A candle being put out.

She waited.

If she was going to die here, she would die like a child of the walls, not an Heir scrabbling for revenge and blame. A clean, honest death, with the brutality bare and unashamed.

Kite caught her reflection in the surface of the blade: her eyes were bright with fire and life, and in the reflection her hair swam around her face like a school of fish.

And then she understood: the sword had accepted her offer of a dance.

Raising the blade with two hands, staggering under the weight of its magic, which thrummed through her body to its own alien rhythm, Kite turned in a slow circle, letting her eyes rest on every flickering essence emerging from underground.

"I'll lead," she whispered.

THE HEART

The hole in her body had closed, but Eli could still feel it. She didn't have to look down to know that her spine was fighting to remain corporeal, that her body wanted to disappear. The ache in her joints and the shock spreading from her chest to her fingertips begged to be relieved. To slip into pure light. To leave this clumsy, messy flesh behind.

Stay, she begged the Heart. *I can't leave them here. Please.*

Eli didn't need the cough that wracked her lungs and choked her breath to remind her that being ripped apart and sewn back together by magic was fucking hard on a body. But she had been made to withstand trauma. She had learned how to carry pain. And she wasn't ready to give in to the demands of her body.

Just a little longer.

After a moment, the feeling of being stretched thin — like an old T-shirt worn by sun and bleach — passed. This time, she didn't vanish. She was still here. Still sore, tired, and angry as hell. But here.

Eli's fingertips rubbed the pollen-scented sprig of purple flowers she had tucked into her pocket. A trinket, a charm, a superstition. Something to give to a valentine in the schoolyard or to press between the pages of a heavy tome. Something to tether her to Tav. To keep her in her body. And it was working.

Excitement and pleasure shuddered down her forearms like a pinched nerve. The café came into sharp focus, and she whipped her neck around to assess the danger and plan her attack.

Tav was exhausted. The effort of creating a door, of holding it open, and closing it without destroying Eli had eaten up every store of energy, every moment of sleep and twitch of caffeine. Eli could see it as clearly as she could see the malicious magic crawling up the windows and blocking out the moonlight.

"I can't believe you let her plant you," Tav was saying, biding time. Stalling. Hoping for a miracle. "What was that *like*?"

There were seven of them. Eli vaguely recognized a man who had been hanging on to Cam that night when she first agreed to the impossible task of capturing the Heart of the Coven. One of the women — brown eyes, perfect eyebrows, purple lipstick — she thought might be the Hedge-Witch's lover. The others were nobodies, cardboard faces, like all the humans she had smiled at or stalked since she was a little girl.

Skin for ghosts, or just empty skin. That's how she used to see humans.

But she was part human, too, and if she looked at her feelings under certain lighting, at just the right angle, she might admit to being maybe, just a little, in love with one.

Maybe.

"You look a little green," Tav was telling the Hedge-Witch's girlfriend.

The purple mouth twisted. Dirt crusted the corners of her lips. "Just give it to us, Tav, and we don't have to fight."

"Where's Cam?" one of the men asked, visibly shaking. "What did you do with Cam?"

"Humans aren't meant to be plants," Eli told the Hedge-Witch. "This will hurt them."

"I don't bargain with made-things," she said, and turned back to Tav. "Why are you so worried about this thing? We'll save the most important pieces for when we repurpose her."

"You don't understand," Tav told their former comrades. "We're trying to fix things. The Hedge-Witch has lied to you."

"You lied to us," said a woman. "You left us."

"Where's Cam?!"

Tav's voice lowered and sharpened. "You need to listen to me. You don't understand —"

They were wasting their time; even Eli could feel the waves of fear and anger that always meant blood. But not from everyone — some were still panicking over their time as a succulent conglomerate. At least one had lost their sense of individuality and was struggling to remember who they were.

But someone was desperately afraid, and Eli had learned enough about humans to know that fear made them dangerous. Anger could be used to build, to remember, to change, to love, or to kill. Fear meant only one thing.

She should know — she had lived in fear for years.

But who was it? Which one was the threat?

"— the mission —"

"— with the *enemy* —"

"— *dying, it's fucking dying* —"

Smoked citrus and vodka, the signature scent of fear fermented into destruction — *there!*

Eli moved. Her body was fast, reflexes honed through years of training. And even weakened, even damaged, her materials came together to create strength. She was stronger than the humans. Stronger, even, than witches. She was Circinae's greatest achievement.

She moved so fast that she blurred out of existence, and the Heart took over for a sliver of a second. Eli ran *through* Tav, rematerializing in front of them, and snatched something out of the air.

Running on adrenalin and instinct, Eli grabbed a blade from her belt and sent it in a perfect line after the taste of orange peel and acetone, acid sharp on her tongue.

The handle cracked the skull of someone in the crowd — Eli couldn't see, and didn't care to — and he fell, unconscious, to the floor.

Silence.

Eli opened her hand. Inside lay an arrowhead carved from obsidian. A witch-killer. A weapon that was forbidden in the City of Eyes. Only the Coven held these arrows and used them to discipline wayward citizens.

The trajectory would have taken it through Tav's heart.

The Hedge-Witch knew that Tav was part witch. She had known, and had never told them. Eli's head snapped up, eyes bleeding blackness. She turned to the Hedge-Witch, glowing with the power of the Heart.

The Hedge-Witch stepped back.

"*You* —" The accusation took over her voice and dried up her words. The light around her body intensified, reaching into the darkest corners of the café, showing the rot under the windowsill — and in the hearts of creatures.

"You saved them," said the Hedge-Witch in disbelief. The plants on the windowsill had frozen. An air of uncertainty settled over the room like a heavy layer of dust. "You put yourself at risk to save them." Colours passed over her irises like sun sliding over oil stains on the road. "You've changed. You —"

Frost blade through the eye. It wasn't made for witches, but it was only the conduit. Eli had new powers, now, and so did her blades. The Heart burned with hunger, flaring up in exaltation.

The Hedge-Witch's drained body fell to the ground in an undignified heap.

"Obsidian!" She reached for Tav, who unsheathed the assassin, the small, thin needle of a dagger that could rend even a witch's essence.

"I'll do it," they said, and walked toward the slippery, silvery essence that was uncurling from the corpse like a snake shedding its skin. They hesitated for a moment, flashes of regret pulsing through their body. Then they raised the blade and plunged it into the essence, not just once, but again and again, until the smoky creature dissipated, falling to the ground as a handful of dried herbs and lavender.

Tav was shaking.

"You … you killed her!" The Hedge-Witch's human lover cried out as if she, too, had been stabbed through the eye.

Tav stared at the dead petals on the floor, grief and anger pooling under their skin.

"Yes," said Eli, stepping forward and placing a hand on Tav's shoulder. They didn't seem to register the touch. "She's dead."

The humans assembled in the room had lost their nerve after the death of their leader. Eli suspected many of them hadn't actually wanted to hurt Tav. They wanted to play with magic, play at a rebellion, but they weren't willing to kill for it.

Part of her felt envious of them. What would it be like, to be able to walk away? To put down her blades?

To hide under the bed and close her eyes and wait for the storm to end?

She had been born into violence and had never had a choice.

Neither had Tav.

They were in this together.

"What do we do now?" a wavering voice cut through the silence.

"I don't care," said Eli. "But you might want to dispose of the body before the cops find out. We're leaving — and we're taking the plants with us."

As she gathered up the magical creatures, a twinge under her left eye reminded her of an unsettling truth.

She had absorbed the Hedge-Witch's hand.

Part of the Hedge-Witch now lived in her body.

Eli swallowed the horror that rose in her gorge, and felt it slide back down into her stomach, slimy and thick as a slug.

"Tav?"

"Hmm?"

The boi with the spirit of steel looked up, a flicker of confusion in their eyes.

"We're leaving." She tried to speak gently.

Tav nodded. "Yeah." They looked around the café, and then laughed once, a hollow sound that pierced the atmosphere of quiet terror. "This place was like a second home to me. But it wasn't real."

Eli pushed a flowering cactus into their arms. "Then let's go make something that is."

THE HEIR

A girl with a sword, her hair a nest of bluegreen around her face.

A boy on the ice, his skin studded with stones. His eyes closed.

And underneath them, the murdered witches were rising from the grave.

It was up to Kite now. "I'm sorry," she told the witches. "I didn't know." But that was a lie. She had known, or should have — the disappearances, the rumours, her mother's growing power. The proof that now ran through Kite's own veins.

She had known, at least, that the Witch Lord killed.

She had not known how. The weight of that knowledge was heavy. The ruler of the world had the power to absorb them and had grown strong on the souls of others.

Kite, too, now had this power. Should she use it? Should she reach out and suck the last drops of life from these wounded remnants of people?

Was she even strong enough to? Or would they crawl over her body like bacteria, swarming her skin and turning her into an empty sack?

She pushed away the temptation and reminded herself what she had to do: *Get Cam and leave. Find the junkyard.* She opened her mouth, unhinging her jaw so it hung long and wide. Fish scales spilled from Kite's mouth, and where they touched the obsidian the witches screamed in pain.

Even an untested Heir was dangerous.

Carefully, deliberately, Kite let the tip of the blade scrape the surface of the stone, and this time it bit instead of freed — it was on her side now. A low moan broke through the harmonies, and the shadows skittered away like darting fish startled by footsteps in the shallows.

A ball of light emerged from the crack, somehow sucking the bluegreen energy from Kite and turning it into shadow. The smell of hatred made Kite's eyes water. As the light came close, carried on a dozen severed feet and hands, Kite swung the blade true. The essence split, sliding around the blade like water, and reformed around it. Kite pulled back, the essence following her like it was trying to cut in on their dance.

The gears on the blade started to spin, capturing a strand of essence. The gentle hum of a record spinning and the dead thing was pulled through the machinery of the weapon. The undead creature spooled on the ground like a long thread.

The blade turned ice-cold under her touch, and Kite spun around in time to see the Beast, visible once more, sever a hand from an arm.

More witches crawled from underground, and now Kite could see obsidian teeth and fingernails. The dead couldn't leave the Witch-Killing Fields, but they could trap Kite here forever.

There were too many of them.

Kite's eyes, minnows in the shallows, darted from the ghosts to Cam lying prone outside the circle.

Pressing her lips to the hilt, she breathed her power into the blade, which shivered at the warm sensation of her breath on its metal.

"Ready?" she asked the Beast. His tail turned scaly and clubbed. She took that as a yes.

And then they ran, sword and girl and creature, cutting through flesh and essence until they stood beside the boy with the stone blade.

Kite wrenched her hair back with one hand and swung the sword with the other. Eyes closed, she sent her desire into the blade edge like a question, like a plea.

It slid through her hair easily, and the severed strands fell to the ground, blackening and charring, the tips burnt and splitting. Her neck felt exposed and vulnerable.

"A sacrifice for safe travel," she murmured, as a small rip in time and space appeared before her. She bent down and wrapped Cam's hand around the stone dagger, then stabbed the ancient sword into the seam.

"Take us away from here, please."

The metal like a kiss on her wrist. A turn of a knuckle, a hiccough, and then they were gone.

Behind them, the ghosts began eating her hair. She could feel it, even as the rest of her body was taken away from the Witch-Killing Fields.

THE HEALER

Fatigue weighed on their arm hair and eyelashes. Tav rubbed their stinging eyes and let Eli guide them out of The Sun, one of the few places they had ever felt truly safe.

"Thanks for not killing me," said Eli lightly. Her hand on their elbow was gentle as the wind.

"Don't you mean 'repurposing you'?" Tav tried a smile, but the betrayal of their former friends darkened their mood like a packet of black cherry Kool-Aid powder in clear water.

"Yeah. I like my current purpose."

"That's too bad, I was hoping I could give you mine." Tav flicked their hair out of their eyes. It was getting long, the dark roots making the violet more vivid by contrast.

"And that was … to fight injustice, or to get revenge on everyone who fucked you over?"

Tav shrugged. "A little of both."

"I appreciate your honesty."

"I didn't think an assassin would be too judgmental."

"We're a very open-minded group."

This time, the smile was genuine.

"It's okay to be angry," said Eli, looking at the horizon rather than at Tav. "I've seen how it works here, what it can do. You don't have to hide from it. It doesn't mean you're going to turn into her."

"I know that." Irritation checkered their voice. "I don't need you to tell me how to survive in my own world."

"Well, you might want to learn how to duck."

A surprised laugh, light as a cirrus cloud. A few more steps. Her hand on their arm, keeping them steady.

"So, what are we doing with these? Opening a flower shop?" Tav looked down at the armful of plants, the wild magic so bright it hurt their eyes.

"The City of Ghosts is so passé," said Eli. "It's time to go back to the source."

Tav stopped. "The journey across worlds could break you," they said quietly. "It almost has before."

"I know that."

Tav studied Eli's face. Her eyes flickered between yellow and black like a bumblebee.

"Tell me." Their voice was hoarse and gravelly.

"Tell you what?" Eli met their gaze with wide eyes, but the hard set of her shoulders gave away the tension under her skin.

"Eli."

"Tav."

"Please?"

"Is that the magic word?" Eli laughed. Tav ached to hear the emptiness behind the sound, like a tin can kicked by a child.

"In the allium field —"

"Don't. That's not fair."

"None of this is *fair*. But you can't keep acting like you're still working alone, Eli. Because you're not."

The hand fell from their elbow. Eli adjusted her glasses.

"I'll tell you," she said finally. "Once we get away from here." She let out a long sigh. "I think this experience has ruined espresso for me for good."

Tav shook their head. "That's the real tragedy here."

At the bike, they hesitated. The desire to appear strong struggled with the desire to lean against a solid body and close their eyes. To let someone else lead for once.

"You want to drive?" they asked.

Eli's eyes like yellow saucers in her face. "Is that a trick question?"

More smiles, quick and guilty, like awkward laughter at a funeral. But they had to smile. Everything was falling apart. Everything was absurd.

Eli hesitated. "Where should I take you?" She didn't need to say it out loud — Tav knew the apartment might not be safe anymore. The number of shelters they had was dwindling.

A memory, sweet and sharp, cut through the haze. A girl who fell out of the sky.

Tav put a gloved hand on Eli's shoulder and squeezed gently, then offered her the word that had gotten Eli into all this trouble in the first place.

"Anywhere," they said.

Eli grinned. She revved the engine, and they tore off down the street.

Tav wrapped their arms around her and held on tight. Eli hadn't disappeared. Somehow, she had stayed, despite the power of the Heart that had burned with the light of a planet. Eli had trusted Tav to tear her open, and then she had saved them.

She was incredible.

Tav tightened their grip, as if they could keep Eli's body together by sheer force of will. If now was all they had, they were going to hold on to it. As the engine rumbled and the tires spat out gravel from underneath them, Tav closed their eyes and focused on Eli's heartbeat.

Now. Now. Now.

THE HEART

Eli took them to the river. This was the place where everything had changed — when a human had seen through her glamour. Had really seen her. And not fled.

Tav had never been afraid of what she was. Eli had to trust in that bravery now.

Eli flowed over the rock like the river below them. Tav followed. The water pirouetted into eddies, shaping arabesques out of foam. Water communing with land.

Eli could feel Tav's eyes on hers, could feel the intensity of their gaze. For a moment she lost herself in the Heart, her body fluttering into immateriality and back like a line of laundry tossed by a cruel wind. "Don't," she said automatically. "Don't look at me."

"Okay." Tav turned to face the river. They waited. Eli closed her eyes and listened to the human heartbeat next to her, felt the warmth from the rock under her legs mixing with the heat from the skin beside her. So much life. So much death.

So many things to break.

She looked down at the river, at the split stones and the edges of land worn smooth by water. Carved into a new shape. Falling apart.

Everything died, in the end.

Finally, unwillingly, Eli broke the silence. She spoke quickly, forcing the words from her lungs like a surgeon deftly tugging stitches from an old wound.

"It *is* repurposing me. The Heart. It's not meant to be in a flesh-and-blood body. Even a magic one. Even a body built to be stronger than any born creature. I'm falling apart. That's why my blades keep rejecting me. I'm scared every time I touch one that it won't recognize me." She swallowed. The truth left an ashy and bitter coating on her tongue.

Tav waited.

"I'm used to being breakable. I've never been invincible. I mean, I sometimes felt like I was, but I've been hurt before. My body is vulnerable to strong emotions. The magic that burns bright in me burns fast, and I get tired more quickly than many other people. I am fast and strong and then tired and weak. I'm thorn and glass and bone and blood. I'm all of it. All of their strengths, their weaknesses, their fragilities — that's what I was made of.

"I'm me, and I've always been me, and I'm *more* me now than I was when I was trapped by Circinae and the Coven. I'm her, and I'm the Heart, and I *love* this body. But the Heart is too much; it's more powerful than me, and the longer I'm carrying it the more I'm losing myself. It doesn't want to … you know? It doesn't want to hurt me. We agreed. We joined. It came willingly. But it can't help being what it is, and my body isn't strong enough. I'm running out of time, Tav. And I'm worried I'm going to fall apart before we fix this. Before" — her voice cracked — "the Earth dies. And the next time I vanish, I might not come back."

Across the river, a leaf fell from a maple tree and into the water. It was caught up in the liveliness of the flow, and danced its way downstream, a sliver of white and silver shimmering against the dark for a brief moment, and then it was gone.

Tav exhaled heavily. Their heart was beating faster, louder, drumming in Eli's ears.

What were they thinking? *Weak. They're thinking I'm weak. They're regretting —*

"So we go back to the City of Eyes," said Tav. They turned to face Eli. Their words rang with conviction. They gripped Eli's shoulder, their fingernails digging into the soft skin around her clavicle. "We bring the Heart home."

THE HEIR

The land was smooth and red as a wound.

It was getting easier to cut into the material of the universe. Kite knew this meant that the City of Eyes was falling into ruin. Reality was becoming nothing, meaning falling into dust. A world without its Heart beginning to fall apart.

The Beast was panting heavily, and he bled from a dozen scratches. Kite wished she had left him behind.

"Oh no," Cam groaned, turning onto his back. Kite could see the way his body struggled to breathe, to cling to life. Humans were nothing if not tenacious. She had learned that years ago, when a girl child had clawed her way into the Children's Lair. "Not this again."

Kite leaned over him, her eyes glowing like headlamps. "Are you dying?" she asked curiously.

Cam opened one eye, then the other, and then shut them again. "It's creepy when you look at me like that." His voice was thin, as if his vocal cords were vibrating through sand.

"Like what?"

"Like I'm a specimen for you to study."

"Aren't you?"

"I'm a person." He opened his eyes again and glared at her. "Personal space?"

Kite drew back, head tilted to one side. "Are all humans this touchy? I thought it was just Eli."

Groaning again, Cam sat up. "My pebbles are all dirty." He frowned.

"I didn't know humans cared that much about cleanliness."

"Well, I do. I have a reputation to uphold." He sighed deeply and then winced. "I think I cracked a piece of limestone."

"I expect you'll erode away eventually," said Kite.

"Are you always this morbid? No wonder Eli likes you." Cam stumbled to his feet.

"You carry the shield." Kite nodded at the knife in his hand. "Eli must think highly of you."

"Wasn't much use back there, was it?"

"It's not the blade's fault you fainted."

"Breaking a blood bond takes a lot out of you."

"I've never tried it. I believe it would kill me."

Cam stared at her. "That could have killed me?"

"Most things can." Kite reached up to play with her

hair and found nothing. Her hand hung in mid-air like a marionette on a string. "Humans are very fragile."

"Well, unlucky for you, I survived."

"It's not unlucky. You're much more useful alive."

"Thank you?"

"You're welcome." Kite smiled sunnily, her sense of existence spreading through her limbs to her extremities. Away from the obsidian plains, she felt full of life and magic and chaos again, and it was wonderful. "Does almost dying always feel this good?" she asked.

"I'm going to pretend you didn't ask me that." Cam began polishing a pyrolite with the dirty hem of his shirt.

"Let me." Kite reached out and trailed a damp, slimy finger across his arm. Drops of seawater glistened where her skin touched his.

Cam said nothing, but he held still so she could polish each individual stone. She missed nothing: not the tiny pebble of sandstone, not the cracked limestone, not the dolomite. At her touch the stones seemed to calm, as if her very touch was a lullaby.

Under the bed of her finger Kite could feel the liveliness of the stones. She could feel the trace of their home, which, in some small way, was her home, too: the Labyrinth had sheltered her and the other children when no one else would. Just being near Cam was a comfort.

Finally, he was as clean as he was going to be. He stared at the desert around them in resignation. "So, a thousand steps in a straight line, or do you have a shortcut?"

"A shortcut?" Her voice trilled like a sparrow's. "To what?"

"The junkyard? That's how we got there last time. A thousand steps in any direction, the junkyard is the portal. Right?"

Kite stared at him in confusion, her eyes swirling with grey mist. Then they cleared to a polished aquamarine beryl. "The sword brought us home. It would not mislead us." Her hand stroked the blade affectionately, and it warmed to her touch.

A silence followed her pronouncement. She looked down at her feet, cool against the sand. Her pale feet contrasted with the dull redbronze of the land.

"This isn't the junkyard," said Cam. His words fell like dying stars burning through the silence. "The junkyard is gone."

"Nothing is ever gone," said Kite, staring at the blade in her hand. Crimson light glinted off its strange black-and-silver surface, dazzling her eyes. She looked up.

Desert stretched out in every direction.

"It's so … quiet." Cam shivered. The stones on his body did not shiver with him. They made no sound, but instead held themselves unnaturally still as muscle and sinew moved underneath.

He was right. Where were the buzzing trees, and angry insects, the ferocious flotsam and jetsam that had washed up on the shores of time, falling from the outskirts of victory? Where was the wind running its hands through her hair?

Understanding unfurled itself like a plant starving for sunlight.

Kite saw the moment his eye snagged on a speck on the sand that was black like a beetle's carapace. Grasping it in one hand, he pulled out an umbrella. Sand poured over his feet.

"There should be mountains of things. Before, it was —" He waved the umbrella around, shedding sand.

"That was probably hundreds of years ago," said Kite, trying to make her voice gentle.

As his shoulders slumped and his eyes started to flutter shut, she realized she had used a too-gentle voice. Adjusting her voice like a musician tuning a guitar, she continued, "Time passes differently here."

He woke up. "Right. Time pockets or something." Cam looked around helplessly. "So everything's gone. There's no one to help us."

Kite shook her head. The lightness of her hair threw her off balance, and a dizziness spread through her entire body. She stilled her movement, turning herself into a statue. "For someone so good at listening, you really are terrible at looking."

THE HEALER

Tav heard the words fall from their mouth and knew they were true. The only way to save Eli was to return the Heart to its world. They had to go back to the City of Eyes.

Once, they had dreamed with the Hedge-Witch. They had wanted to steal the Heart and use its power to change the human city, to break what needed to be broken and build something new. But the power of the Heart was not a weapon — it was a living creature, the soul of a planet. It would burn any body that tried to hold it for long. And they weren't going to sacrifice Eli for anything. That wasn't the revolution they wanted. The Hedge-Witch had taught them this with her betrayal.

How you do something is just as important as *what* you do. And Tav was not a tyrant. Just a boi with anger in the shape of an arrow — both a weapon and a sign pointing the way forward.

Tav's anger had never just been anger.

It was justice.

It was heartbreak.

It was connection.

It was love.

You don't sacrifice the people and futures that you want to save.

Their voice strengthened, threads of confidence and decision weaving into the words. "We return the Heart to the City of Eyes — but not the Coven. We give it to someone else. To the wall. To the wastelands. To the forest."

Eli's words were so soft that Tav had to read her lips. "What if it doesn't work?"

"It will work." Tav's grip tightened. "If I have to cut it out of you myself, it will work."

"But the Vortex —"

"We'll find another way to heal the rift," Tav cut her off. "Without the Heart. Clytemnestra is waging war on the Coven as we speak. There are other magics we can use." They hesitated, and then offered what they were pretty sure was a lie. "My magic is getting stronger, Eli. I think I'll be able to heal the wounds without the Heart."

Eli sighed. Fingerprints on her glasses. Hair tucked behind her ear, a few strands falling loose. Tav wanted to reach out and stroke them into place.

"No. We need to heal the world first. We go to the source, Tav. Where this all started: the Coven. The Heart's magic is weakening in this world — it doesn't belong here. That's why we failed. If we keep trying, we'll keep failing. We need to be in the City of Eyes. We need to heal the tear between worlds while we still can. We finish what we started."

Tav glanced at Eli's frost blade, the sharp edge shimmering like sun on ice. They didn't need the confirmation of the blade of truth to believe Eli's words. Growing up in a city of lies and secrets, of diversity posters and slurs dripping from wide smiles, Tav had learned to recognize the truth when they heard it — the clean shine of skin scrubbed smooth by soap and friction.

They had to go back to the Coven.

They knew it was the truth — but they didn't have to like it. "You want to keep fighting? You just said this is killing you!" They didn't like the note of fear that rang in their voice. But Cam was gone, and the scent of allium nectar was the only thing keeping the nightmares at bay.

Eli carefully extricated Tav's hand from her shoulder. To Tav, it felt like she was slipping through their fingers like smoke.

"Eli, it could destroy you."

Eli reached out a hand and gently brushed a strand of curly black-and-violet hair from Tav's face.

"I know, Tav. And I really don't want to stop existing. But I have no idea how to separate myself from the Heart. Even trying could kill me. And we can't fix the world without the Heart." Her eyes narrowed, and her voice grew heavy with emotion. "I've already lost one home, one family, one way of life. I won't — I *can't* — lose another."

Tav's dream poured from their memory and danced before their eyes:

A frozen river torn in half, fragments of ice like a string of diamonds gleaming under the silverwhite glow of the moon.

Feathers like black flames, crackling with edges of purple and gold and green.

A crumpled body with a sprig of hawthorn growing from its chest.

A nightmare or a prophecy? Tav didn't know. But they knew the flow of a river could not be stopped for long. They knew they had power that no one — not the Hedge-Witch, not Eli, not even themselves — understood.

They *would* save her.

"Okay," Tav said. "Jesus, this is crazy, but okay. We get the children to help us. We channel the magic of the Coven through the Heart, and we finish this. And then — then we figure out how to remove the Heart and keep you alive. Okay?"

"Okay."

"Promise me that we'll try."

Eli turned her reptilian eyes on Tav. She placed a sweaty hand over Tav's, their fingers interlacing like a woven daisy crown.

"Okay," she said. "I promise."

Eli pulled her hand away again, spat into her palm, and pulled a few strands of hair from her head. She offered the sticky promise to Tav.

Tav shook their head. "I trust you. I don't need it bound by magic."

Eli's hand hung outstretched, shaking slightly. Then she took it back and wiped it on her jeans.

Tav fell back into their thoughts. It made sense. The Coven had torn open the world and only from there could it be mended. And once that was finished, they would save Eli. They would find a way.

They were going back to the City of Eyes. To the world of witches and dark magic and deadly daughters.

Tav's heart quickened. They were going back. To chaos and danger and colour. No more secret 2:00 a.m. struggles for a city that didn't care. No more furtive magics and missed phone calls and guilt. No more trying to be human. No more following rules and obeying orders.

They couldn't deny that the call of the witch world was strong. It claimed at least half of them. Already adrenalin was surging through their body at the anticipation. The fierce trees. The hungry stone.

If they were being honest, they knew all along it might come to this.

If they were being even more honest, this is what they had always wanted. A city in the sky. A world of power and light. The taste of magic like honey and lavender dissolving on their tongue.

A homecoming.

THE HEART

A homecoming.

Dread spread through the network of veins and capillaries and arteries that made up her ragged body of magic and flesh, pearl and granite. Eli could feel her eyes growing glassy and wet. She reached a hand up to brush a tear from her eye. She rubbed it between thumb and forefinger and brought it to her nose to sniff.

The substance was thin and smelled of formaldehyde. The Heart was corrupting her tears. She was becoming less herself with every passing moment.

Eli didn't want to go back. She had only just started to make a home for herself in the City of Ghosts, with Tav and Cam and the promise of sunlight every morning, with logic and laughter and honeybees.

But the Heart's power was waning. Earth was not its home, and it pined for its daughters, for the silver sap of the forests and the rhythm of the stones dancing under the earth. If they returned to the City of Eyes it would be replenished, its full power returned. And if her fragile body could hold that power long enough, they could heal the rift. They could save the dying Earth, and the many ecosystems and lives on that planet.

Eli never wanted to see the Coven again. The long white hallways, the traces of chains, the histories that whispered of control and hopelessness. Returning meant revisiting the spaces that had hurt her. It meant giving in to memory. *You are a tool. You have value.*

But it was the only way she could heal the rift between worlds.

"So how do we get there?" Tav asked. "I'm drained, and we can't use the Vortex."

Eli licked the formaldehyde from her hand. "Oh, don't worry about that. We have help."

The succulents shook their spiny leaves at the sky.

THE HEIR

Kite watched Cam as he looked around the barren landscape. The skin around his eyes crinkled and then smoothed again. He reached down to pull a cracked dinner plate out of the sand. He brushed it clean, and then set it down again, carefully, as if to avoid cracking it further.

He was fascinating. Kite was mesmerized by the way he played with his moustache and rocked back and forth on his heels. His face was alive with feeling. And he never tried to hide his emotions, either: he let confusion and fear and wonder play across his face and body and sing through the stones on his skin.

"What?" Cam frowned at her.

"Sorry?" She tilted her head, feeling the swish of her shorn hair brushing her ears. A gentle, low hum filled her ears. The strands were mourning.

"You're staring at me."

"You're just so good at being human."

"Um. Thanks?"

"Are you setting a dinner table? Are you expecting company?" Kite sat cross-legged before the single porcelain plate. A pattern of blue roses stretched around the edge. She thought the crack through the centre added elegance to the otherwise too-symmetrical piece.

"I don't know. No, I'm just ... I don't understand. How are we supposed to find allies here? Everything is buried."

Kite, following Cam's example, reached into the sand and drew a tarnished silver spoon from the earth. She placed it beside the plate. "So is much of the wall."

"So?" He tugged on his moustache. "You have the sword. Is there even anything else useful here?"

The wind picked up, an insistent hand tugging at stray threads and souls. A warning.

"That's not how you behave at a dinner party," scolded Kite, retrieving a gold-and-glass goblet from its place of burial and setting it upright at the place setting. It was fuzzy with mould.

"I didn't ask to come to your dinner party. I'm not even supposed to be here." Cam kicked a patch of sand into a glittering gold arc. Then he sat down and put his head in his hands.

The stones made a gentle keening sound, and then fell silent. Even stone could get lonely sometimes.

Kite hummed softly, bringing forth a melody of remembered waves and the perfect curve of a fish spine.

She set a stainless-steel fork on the other side of the plate.

Cam looked over at the girl with the halo of bluegreen hair, her fingertips dusted with gold sand. She picked up the plate, polished it on her sleeve, and set it down again.

"What are you doing?"

"Waiting for you to find them. You seem to have a better affinity for the buried than I do."

"Don't hold your breath. I'm the useless one."

"What do you mean?" Kite began polishing the goblet.

"I'm not like Eli or Tav. I'm not magic. I'm not good at anything except parallel parking and using my body as a shield. And making jazz playlists. And now I'm trapped in your world and I'll probably die, and my body will be perfectly preserved in this junkyard forever."

"There are worse places to be. You'd be in good company."

"Yeah, that plate looks really chatty. I'm sure we're going to be best friends."

"Is that something you need? Friends?"

"It's what everyone needs."

Kite turned her lamp-like eyes to him, those bright and pupil-less orbs of undersea light. "Witches are taught to need power and nothing else. My mother taught me that the first time she threw me into the wilds as an infant and told me to not come home until I had proved my value."

"That's … intense."

"No," she sighed, "it was perfectly normal. I sometimes envy you humans — all the feelings that I can see on your body, the intensity of mortality, how much you care about Tav and Eli and the stones that are now part of you. Everything matters so much, and it's always *now*. For witches, there is rarely a now; there is always later, and time doesn't matter. Love doesn't matter. Death doesn't matter. Only power matters."

"That sounds … lonely. Do witches get lonely?"

Kite's mouth twitched slightly. She did not understand.

Cam shifted a little closer to her. "If only power matters, then why are you here?"

"Oh, that's an easy question." Kite smiled brightly, and then paused to lick sand from her forearm. "The time is now."

The plate, fork, spoon, and goblet picked up the melody of Cam's stone-sutured body.

Kite stood, gestured toward the place setting, and then skipped aside, so light on her feet that she left no footprints in the sand.

Witches were more magic than substance — especially when they had been weaned by the Witch Lord.

Cam inhaled sharply. "I can't do this."

"You can."

"What makes you so sure?"

Kite let her hand drift to the sad, short hairs on her head, and soothed them with slow, gentle strokes.

"Because I've seen what humans can do. And because Eli trusts you."

Cam's face hardened, and in the sharp line of his cheekbone Kite could see the stone that lived under the skin, as well, the layer of hardness he had used to protect his soft heart and fragile bones. Armour woven from laughter and music and moustache wax.

Witches were not the only creatures who could cobble together a life from scraps. Kite saw in the tremble of Cam's throat that he had crafted a life out of bits and pieces, and this mosaic of identity had become strength, flexibility, survival.

So many bodies struggling to survive.

It was time for them to *live*.

Like Kite, the wastelands could feel Cam's emotions, could hear his knuckle bones rubbing against one another, the friction generating heat and energy. Could smell the sweat of his body mixing with the calcium of stone. There was no one in the worlds like him.

He crawled closer to the place setting, tucking his legs under him. The sand swirled up at his movements and stuck to his slick sticky salty skin. Humans carry places with them.

He closed his eyes, and Kite watched with interest as his eyeballs twitched and jerked under the lids, as if they were dancing.

It made Kite want to dance, too.

So she did. She swayed in place, her hair rippling around her ears and neck; her arms waving like leaves fluttering in the wind. She moved, and she watched him.

She watched his breathing slow, his heartbeat drop to a gentle murmur. She watched as Cam pressed his palms to the sand. She watched as he sank deeper and deeper into the earth, until he was waist-deep in sand.

But the sand didn't take the goblet, the plate, or the spoon. Instead, objects began rising from underground. More plates — plastic and glass and metal, with gold leaf edges, scratches, and stains. Forks with tines missing, chopsticks, tiny silver dessert forks that had fallen out of fashion.

Cam gasped, and his heart rate accelerated. Kite could see his pulse twitching like a fish tossed up on shore, writhing under his skin. His face was pale, and he was shivering.

Kite caught him before he fell, and he slumped to one side. She pressed her cheek to his and let her hair heal his fever. Finding the lost took a toll on a body, and humans were not invincible.

She needed to remember that.

"You're okay." She repeated the words she had heard Eli speak. "You're going to be okay."

"They're angry," he whispered.

"They should be. They have not been treated well."

"No, we haven't."

His eyes snapped open. Kite peered into their red depths and saw her own eyes, glowing turquoise lights, reflected back. And something else, swimming in the murkiness of his pupil —

A few grains of sand.

A smile tremored through her entire body, and she felt her essence burning with a brighter light.

"Stop that." Cam winced and drew back, shielding his eyes from the light. But Kite couldn't hold in the excitement and anticipation that swam through her arteries.

"You said *we*," she whispered back. "We."

She would not have to force them, not have to ensorcell the bitter and broken lives in the junkyard. She would not have to steal their stagnant magic like a spider lurking in a web. Only now did it occur to her that Clytemnestra might have wanted her to fail — she must have known the lost things would not trust the Heir. Perhaps the Warlord wanted to get rid of a potential threat. Or perhaps Clytemnestra fully trusted Kite's power, trusted in the violence of her pet Heir. But there would be no fighting or force, and no one would die today on the lonely wastelands of a heartless world.

They wanted to come. Because of Cam.

"You are amazing," she told him, and kissed the top of his head.

He blinked in astonishment and then grinned. "Parallel parking is harder than you think," he told her.

"I've never wanted to learn."

Other creatures were rising from the ground: bone-white trees slashed with deep red; monsters made out of aluminum and peach pits, and more stones than a rocky beach, their jagged edges glinting in the light.

This was an army to tear the Witch Lord from her throne.

"They can take us back to the Labyrinth," said Cam. "Is that safe?"

"Of course not," said Kite. "But we'll go, anyway. Just … wait."

There was one more loose end before they left. Kite

found that she was a little sorry to be returning to her home of marble and glitter and Lycra. There was something lovely about the bronze desert, something comforting about the moraine of fury and passion that lived underneath the sand. But it was time for the ugly things to be seen, and for the pretty shine of power to be worn away.

Kite walked back to the sword. It had protected her, saved her, risked its life to fight off the dead witches for her. And maybe she had the power to compel it, or to drink its magic and become as strong and sharp as a blade herself. But Kite was not the future Witch Lord. She was a second-hand witch, a daughter who had learned how to cheat at games without getting caught, a reader who missed her books so much it hurt.

She would not use the power her mother gave to her.

Kite brought her face close to the blade's edge, so close she felt the desire to press her skin against it and give her life to it. "You are home, my love. Thank you for saving me. We are going into battle now, on the other side of the world. Will you come with me and risk your metal again, or will you stay here?"

A long moment followed her question. The blade darkened, and red patterns swirled across the alien alloy.

The sword was thinking.

Kite waited patiently, her hair gently swaying around her face.

A flash of light. Kite stared down at the sword, and saw her glowing eyes burning in the silver. Then there were a hundred eyes opening across the blade.

Kite flushed with pleasure. Tenderly, she reached out and slid her arm against the edge, leaving a thin line of silverblue in her skin. Kite watched the sword drink her blood and murmured to the blade, so low that no one could hear her, "Thank you. I will make sure you are not lonely."

"Are you ready?" Cam asked quietly. Kite stared at him. A piece of algae drifted across one of her eyes, briefly obscuring her vision. She blinked, and sent it skittering back to the corner.

Kite wondered what he saw when he watched her bent over the blade, singing to its sharp edge, letting her blood bead along the surface. Was he curious? Aroused? Jealous? Kite had never been able to reach inside the skull of a human and unravel their thoughts.

"Does that matter?" she asked, frowning. Was she ready to see the world change completely in a few sharp moments? Was she ready to face Clytemnestra, or Eli, or her mother? What did it mean, to be ready?

The sword warmed under her touch.

"It's okay," Cam repeated her words back to her. "It's going to be okay."

Kite felt the laugh taking flight from her chest like a murmuration of starlings. The human was comforting her! No wonder Eli had fallen in love with one. They were so different from the daughters of this world.

Her grip tightened on the blade, and her hair whipped across the back of her neck. "I'm ready."

The portal opened willingly.

THE LABYRINTH

The Labyrinth was angry.

For millennia, the Labyrinth had lived only to eat, ravenously hungry for magic and flesh. But as the years wore on, it grew sick of the taste of blood that was spilled in its halls. Then it had offered shelter to the lost and lonely. It had nurtured little witches and strays of all kinds, keeping them safe from the prying eyes of their parents.

The Labyrinth was growing weary of being forgotten. Of watching little witches turn their backs on it.

Cam felt its loneliness. As he fell through the darkness of the portal that had opened up in the wastelands, through the very mantle of the planet, images crowded his mind.

He watched a witch girl with flashing eyes and a devilish grin step through a shadow door and leave forever. He missed this girl and wondered what happened to her. The iron masks of the Coven overlaid the image of the young girl stepping through the door, forever leaving.

How they hurt us, he thought. *How they abandon us.*

The images changed, and he saw his grandmother's face. Cam felt a pang of remorse that he had never learned to speak Vietnamese fluently. The Labyrinth felt this pain with him. Flashes of streetlights and broken glass and running shoes collided with images of dying bodies trapped in the wall, slowly rotting, caught in the stone like a bone caught in a throat.

What do you want? he thought, and already the question was changing to *What do we want?*

A glittering world, bleeding into the galaxy.

A body pressed against his.

A wall, stretching across the City of Ghosts, reaching outward to the stars. A body of stone. The spine of the planet.

We, too, desire to be free.

Cam felt the blood slow in his arteries, magma cooling and transforming into andesite.

All magic requires sacrifice.

The portal through the core had asked a lot of the Labyrinth, and the living stone needed something in exchange.

Something, or someone.

Part Two: Homecoming

THE HEIR

The portal led back to the Children's Lair. There was an affinity between the strange hoarding of the children and the junkyard. Between the children themselves and the discarded magics of the wastelands.

The sword glowed like a burning ember in Kite's hand, scaring away a few shadow spiders that had gathered to greet her.

"Hush," she told the sword. "Leave them alone."

She looked around her at the collection of things she had brought from the forgotten side of the world: puppets and playthings, shoes and arrowheads. She had brought an armoury for the children, living shields and weapons longing to destroy. The thirst for revenge was palpable, and the walls around her shrunk back, trying not to touch the sharp edges of broken dining sets or the toxic chemical fumes of banned toddler toys.

"What's happening?" Fear broke through Cam's voice, and she reached out for him instinctively.

Her hand met stone. "It's okay," she whispered, luminous eyes watching a boy turning to stone. "You're still beautiful."

"Kite! Help me!" But the stones were growing, stretching over his skin, pulling him into the wall. "Don't —" His words faded to the sound of gravel on sand, and then there was silence.

Cam was gone.

The walls had claimed him.

A sense of dread gathered in her essence, making her hair lie flat and sticky against her forehead. She hung her head, wondering if Eli would forgive her for misplacing her friend.

"That's where he belongs," she murmured, trying to convince herself. He would be happier as part of the Labyrinth. It had freed him once, and it was right that it should reclaim his body.

"Where did the strange boy go?" asked Clytemnestra, who burst into the room with dirt on her chin and a velvet cape draped across her shoulders. "The sharp one who glitters? I wanted to play with him."

"He's gone home," said Kite. She looked at the mischievous child who was also the devious Warlord.

Kite had grown accustomed to the frayed hems and yellowed lace, the dirty knee socks, and scuffed Mary

Janes. She wasn't sure what to make of Clytemnestra's red-and-gold costume. It looked like she had interrupted playtime. The scent of baby's breath and hemlock was overpowering, and Kite slithered away from the girl, turning back to the comforting taste of found things.

"We don't need him," said the Warlord. "We have our army." She picked up a rusted Campbell's soup can and then yelped. "It bit me!" She stuck her finger in her mouth and threw the can back on the pile of junk — now treasure.

"All things bite, little one."

"They don't bite *me*." She scowled.

"Are the daughters ready?"

The Warlord's eyes sparkled with wickedness. "We have many daughters now. More came when they heard of our cause. So many bad girls, runaways from home!" She adopted a sing-song voice. "They're going to be in so much trouble. They're going to *be* so much trouble."

Clytemnestra waved her hand and the wall behind her melted away. Made-daughters and dirty children entered the chamber.

"Finders keepers!" cried Clytemnestra, diving headlong into the collection of things from the wastelands.

"You have to ask their permission," Kite told the soldiers. "They have their own spirits and thoughts. Some will want to fight on their own. Others will mould themselves into arms."

"We are already armed." The unnamed stepped forward, her pale eye like milk froth.

"Then don't make a bond with a wastelands survivor." Kite's fingers skittered up and down the moon sword. "But there is … power in it." She hadn't meant to say *power*, she meant something like *companionship* or maybe *love*, but the words slid off her tongue like oil and left her with the only word burned into her memory by the Witch Lord.

The unnamed nodded and turned to the assassins. "Speak to the objects, if you wish." She had clearly become their spokesperson.

Kite watched as the girls sifted through each stone and toy and metal contraption. She looked at the new girls, the runaways who had abandoned their mothers to fight for freedom. She felt a little in awe of their rebellion.

The gentle hum of insect wings rubbing together made its way to Kite's ears, and she turned to see one girl who had hung back, uninterested in forging a bond with something that did not live in her blood. Kite's eyes brightened at the body before her — all muscle and sinew and tendon. Muscular biceps and thick thighs. A powerful body. Kite's eyes shifted upward, catching the steel eyes that had no pupils but seemed to glow with an inner light. Then the assassin turned slightly, and the swords strapped to her back took Kite's breath away —

Thousands of iridescent insect wings, like a stained-glass window in a cathedral, only with more venom. Hundreds of Phillips-head screws and broken bottles — green, brown, and blue. A mosaic of death. A work of art.

"You're the Heir." The girl's eyes met Kite's.

"For a little while longer," Kite agreed. "Your design is ingenious. Artistic. I've never seen anything — anyone — like it. Who was your mother-maker?"

The daughter hesitated. "I'd rather not speak her name."

Kite nodded. "Names have power. I understand." Her eyes lingered on a dragonfly wing at the sword tip. A familiar smell hung around the daughter, and Kite tried to remember —

A bloodcurdling cry from behind her caught Kite's attention like a butterfly in a net, and she turned to see Clytemnestra wrestling with another child over a piece of chain mail woven from candy wrappers and aluminum foil.

"I saw it first!" whined the Warlord.

"I *got* it first!" yelled the boy.

The chain mail wrenched itself away from both of their greedy claws and affixed itself to one of the junk-made monsters that were assembling themselves from the flotsam.

Clytemnestra stuck her tongue out at the other child, who threw a spitball at her.

Kite turned back, but the daughter was gone. Her signature scent still lingered in the air, and now she could recognize it.

The daughter smelled of espresso and rusted nails.

THE HEALER

Tav sprinkled the dirt of another world over the ground, and Eli used her knives to mark out a circle to try to contain their cut. They wanted to make a small incision in the material of the universe, not another bleeding wound that would only quicken the Earth's death.

Eli rubbed one eye with the back of her hand, smearing dirt across her forehead. She was sweating, and her body had started fading again, the light of the Heart under her rib cage pulsing with anticipation of the return. She turned to Tav.

"Do you need me to —"

"I don't think so," Tav cut her off. They had started to understand that Eli's magic was a limited resource. And unlike most powers, they weren't sure that Eli's would regenerate. They would save her magic until they really needed it. "You're here, I'm here, and so is part of the Hedge-Witch. It should open for us without you having to use the Heart."

"Okay." Relief frayed the edges of the word.

"Ready?"

"Never."

Eli and Tav smashed all the plants at once. The flowerpots shattered on the rock, shards of pottery covering the ground. Dirt on their ankles and knees.

A silence, a breath, and then a shoot of bluegreen uncurled from a crack in the stone beneath their feet. From the shrapnel of pottery emerged a small forest of vines and leaves, reaching upward.

Trying to get home.

"Hold on to me," said Tav. Eli gripped their arm. Together they watched the enchanted succulents breach the sky, tearing through cloud and atmosphere and the laws of physics.

Tav brought their mouth to Eli's ear. When they spoke, they were rewarded with the assassin's shiver at the feeling of their breath on her body. "You know, the Hedge-Witch was right." Mischief danced in their eyes. "You really have changed."

"Oh, fuck —"

The doorway cut her off.

THE HEIR

The world trembled. Kite felt the earth shaking in excitement, felt it shiver and quake and laugh. Felt the lungs of the world strain for breath, gasping for air. Felt the blood of the world, every drop of water, begin to boil.

Kite could feel it in the small of her back, in the cycle of magic that slipped through the fine hairs of her arms and along the curve of her calves.

The smell of burnt sugar, and warmth like honey flowing over her body, flowing into her very essence. The bluegreen lights that twinkled under her skin brightened.

Her hair started growing, lapping up sustenance like a plant photosynthesizing.

Excitement surged through Kite.

Eli was back, and she was in danger.

Kite had to find her. Her hair whipped around her neck and Kite's eyes danced with light as she sought out the Warlord at the centre of the war party.

Clytemnestra had felt it, too. She was wearing only one shoe and a helmet forged of candle wax and barbed wire. She didn't even try to stop a tiny child from running off with her other shoe. Her gaze met Kite's.

"She's here," said Kite. "Take me to her."

"Who?" Clytemnestra began combing her hair with a plastic fork. Her hair flowed, long and golden and thick, brushing the floor.

"The whole world has to know the Heart has returned. We've all felt it. The Coven will be coming for us."

"Oh, don't worry about that." Clytemnestra rolled her eyes and stuck her grubby hands in pockets filled with sweets, Barbie doll shoes, empty wrappers, and crayon stubs. "They already have."

A flash of gold. The signature scent of overripe plums and sugared dates. Kite caught the card that Clytemnestra tossed from the bottom of her pocket.

Dread twisted in her liver like a worm on a hook. The Beast whimpered and pressed against Kite's legs. He was mammalian again, with six canine legs and a long, whip-like tail.

"An invitation from the Witch Lord," she said softly, her hand gripping his fur. "To a masquerade." She looked up. "Those things are bloodbaths."

"Of course they are," said Clytemnestra. "Even grown-ups know how to have fun once in a while." Eagerness and excitement slipped into her tone, and she lowered her voice conspiratorially. "Who should we send to the slaughter?"

"An invitation," Kite repeated, turning the card over in her hands. It was made of pure gold, the lettering written in dark blood that refused to clot. "So we've worried her."

"We had better find some nicer things to wear," said Clytemnestra, eyeing Kite's ragged skirts. "The Witch Lord wants to parley."

THE HEART

She was standing on a cliff looking out over the ocean. It was black as ink, as if all the books in the world had bled into a single bay. Eli knew that if she touched the water it would leave a stain.

The cliff was silverwhite, reflecting the glow from the crescent moon that hung overhead in a mocking smile. Looking down, Eli stared at her filthy and bloodied toes (one was missing a toenail — it had been ripped clean off) marring the raw beauty of the rock. *Monster. Human.* Something that didn't belong here. Had never belonged.

She looked up again, drawn to the call of the moon, to the whispers of home and the intoxicating hurt of a lost homeland. She frowned; she had been wrong, it wasn't a crescent moon, it was a quarter, and it illuminated the entire bay. The water shimmered as if a coat of gasoline covered the surface. She could almost feel the slime against her tongue.

"I wouldn't swim, if I were you," said a voice.

Eli forced herself to turn around slowly, wincing as each step rubbed the skin from her soles, exposed flesh scraping on sharp stone.

A crow cocked its head at her, eyes like two black buttons, shiny and empty.

"What would you recommend?" Eli switched to her own black set of eyes, and saw a strange, struggling magic fighting to escape the feathered cage. Dark red and black, like dried scabs.

"Flying, of course." The bird landed on her shoulder. "I thought your mother taught you how to fly."

"She pushed me."

"Sometimes fledglings need to be pushed." He drove his beak into her shoulder. She cried out, grabbed the bird, and bit the head from the body. Then she stumbled back in horror as a smoky magic uncurled from the corpse.

"Thank you for freeing me, little bird."

A gust of air, hot and malicious, burned Eli's eyes. They watered, stung with grit and heat.

The redbrown sand rose in a cloud and started to form a familiar shape.

"So you've come back to me. What an obedient daughter."

Eli stumbled back. "They killed you."

"Killed?" Circinae's essence slowly moved toward the wayward daughter, a cyclone of possession and intent. "What a romantic notion. You've spent too much time with the humans. I'm disappointed in you. No, daughter, they didn't kill me — they transformed me. They trapped me. But here, I am free. And you are mine again."

"I'm not your daughter."

"I made you!" The storm formed a hand and reached for Eli, but it passed through her body. "What did you do? How did you do this?"

"I am not yours. I'm not anyone's!" Eli reached for the obsidian blade but found the strap on her belt empty. Panicking, she grabbed for the glass blade, her hand drawing nothing but a broken hilt. She dropped it on the rock.

"You're right," marvelled Circinae. "You're no one. And your power is running out. You broke the beautiful machine that I made. You are an abomination." Heat surged, and boils erupted on Eli's skin. Eli's blades were gone, her magic was gone, and the memory of her mother was going to destroy her.

No.

Not today.

Not yet.

Circinae saw the change in Eli's clenched jaw and the slitted pupils of reptilian eyes. The essence coiled tighter, a snake of fire and hate. "What are you going to do, broken thing?"

Eli smiled grimly. "Take your advice."

She launched herself off the cliff.

Overhead, the gibbous moon burned like a dying ember.

THE HEALER

Tav felt a surge of adrenalin mixing with something else — the dangerous sweetness of nicotine, the promise of caffeine, the heat of a backyard fire piled high with old tires and planks of rotten wood.

They had never used this much magic before. They hadn't known it was possible.

They had created a door between worlds.

That knowledge itself was intoxicating, but the magic, too, had affected them. The sky was brighter, the stones of the wall sharper. They could hear their bones shifting position, their stomach digesting, their skin cells replicating.

Where was Eli?

Panic rose in their throat like bile. They looked around the stone room, one of the many chambers of the mad playhouse where witch children plotted treason.

No Eli.

Wait. There —

A glimmer of light on the floor, like an electrical current. The light shuddered down a body that was half there, half gone. *Flick.* A mouth. *Flick.* A hand. *Flick.* An ankle.

Tav had taken Eli back to the City of Eyes and the Heart had taken over, subsuming her body into light and power. Eli was suspended between corporeal and incorporeal states, between a body and a world.

Between life and death.

Without thinking, Tav moved forward, reaching for the stuttering, breaking, unstable body of the girl they loved.

The Warlord popped into the room, trailing clouds of purple smoke. She hung in the air between Tav and Eli, blocking Tav from the Heart.

"Oh no no no no nooo." Clytemnestra clucked her tongue and waggled her finger at Tav. "The Heart is sleeping. Let it rest."

"We have to wake her," said Tav. "She said dreaming was dangerous in the City of Eyes."

"Oh, it is. Very dangerous. Eli's a naughty girl!"

"Then we have to wake her. Help me!"

Clytemnestra frowned, and then placed her chin on a chubby hand. "How do you wake a world?"

"She's a person," said Tav. "She's a girl, she's —"

"She's the Heart," said Clytemnestra harshly. "The Heart of this world. You can fuck a world, you can love a world — but it can't love you back." She shifted her face into an approximation of sympathy. "This is something all children have to learn," she crooned softly. "It can never love you back."

Anger choked Tav's lungs and throat. They coughed violently, and black phlegm splattered over the witch. Steam rose from the tiny wounds Tav's mucus had inflicted on the Warlord.

Clytemnestra calmly wiped her face with the back of her sleeve. "Come," she said. "There's someone who wants to see you."

"Eli —"

"I will watch over it," she said. "And I know more than you, little one. You're just a baby, aren't you?"

"I don't trust you."

"The feeling is mutual." Clytemnestra offered a coquettish smile. She waved a hand and the far wall shimmered like a mirage, and then melted, the rock pooling on the floor and hardening into waves of magma.

Tav gritted their teeth. "I'm not leaving until she wakes up."

A storm cloud formed over Clytemnestra's head. "You're ruining my fun!" she stomped her feet and snorted. Smoke spiralled from her nostrils. Electricity shimmered over her head as tiny forks of lightning spat sparks at Tav.

Tav didn't back down. They stared at the storm forming around the Warlord, and then through it — into the white magic edged with peach and coral. Then, as they had done with the magic of the world, and with the many strands of magic running through Eli's body, Tav reached into the core of the storm cloud and grabbed a handful of cream-and-pink thread.

Clytemnestra shrieked. The storm vanished. When Tav opened their hand, revealing three apple seeds.

"It's rude to touch someone else's magic," said the witch primly.

She swooped down and gobbled the seeds from Tav's hand.

Tav remembered feeding chickadees like this in the winter. Their mother would take them cross-country skiing in the woods, their skis leaving smooth ribbons in the fresh snow.

"This time, I forgive you, because you are a newborn and don't know any better," said Clytemnestra. "But if you touch me like that again, I will eat your eyes."

So there were rules, social etiquette, even in the savage city of bloodlust and revenge. Even among thieves and warmongers.

The regicidal girl was staring at Tav like they were a new kind of insect she wanted to stick under the microscope.

"I don't know what you are," she said, and ran her tongue over her teeth. "But you are *interesting*."

Tav wasn't sure they wanted the attention of the volatile Warlord.

"I'll play," Clytemnestra announced. "I haven't been dream-diving since the seven seedling stars hung like pearls in the sky. You'll need that" — she inclined her head at the sliver of obsidian that was cold as ice against Tav's forearm — "in case any of the monsters in her head come out."

Tav nodded. Together, they turned to the ghostly outline of a girl made of light and a power that was corroding her flesh.

THE HEART

Eli was standing on the island.

It had once been a haven for her and Kite, an escape, a fantasy. Make-believe. It had once bubbled with life — the clear brook, the crustaceans and fish and insects that came to worship Kite's hypnotic hair. The song of the trees like a sacred hymn.

Now the water ran red with the blood of the humans she hadn't saved. It was too late. She had failed.

"Miss me?" Clytemnestra turned a few cartwheels in the air, her Cupid's bow mouth pursed into a perfect kiss.

Eli rummaged through her memory for scraps of linguistic shrapnel. "I never miss." She tapped the glass blade, and the sound of a thousand chandeliers echoed against the stone walls.

Walls? Eli scanned the shadows of the trees but saw nothing. Where *was* she?

Was this real?

Did that matter?

Clytemnestra halted midturn, legs over her head. Her eyes widened, like pieces of white quartz. Eli could see herself reflected in those eyes.

"You're losing so much," scolded Clytemnestra, staring at the glass blade that had no scars, no scratches, no flecks of witch blood staining its surface. It was clean as fresh snow, as clean as the day Eli was crafted. "If you lose yourself to the Heart, I'm going to be in big trouble with that sexy boi of yours. They want their plaything back."

"I'm not anyone's *thing*."

Clytemnestra smiled, an upside-down grin that looked like a clownish scowl. "We're all *things* in here."

"In where?"

Her cartwheel completed, Clytemnestra landed on the island. Where her feet touched the ground, yellow daisies burst from cracks in the rock, grew several feet tall, withered, died, and vanished. Standing at her full height, she only came up to Eli's waist. Eli reached for the obsidian blade, but it was gone.

"Looking for this?" Clytemnestra ran the blade over her fingernails like a file. Eli froze, and then opened her mouth, crocodile teeth overflowing her small jaw.

"I was just borrowing it!" Clytemnestra squealed and threw it in the air. Eli grabbed it and slid it back into its leather skin, but something was already in there.

Trembling, Eli pulled out a piece of honeycomb. She ran her thumb over the wax hexagons and tried to remember what she was doing here.

"You should be more careful." Clytemnestra wagged her finger.

"What game are you playing?"

"Which one?" Clytemnestra giggled and then floated up until she was at eye level with the assassin. "It's almost time. I hope you're ready."

Eli narrowed her eyes. "I'm always ready."

Clytemnestra clapped her hands together excitedly, sparks flying from the friction between her palms. They sizzled against the earth and died. "Having you around is so much fun. So many new deadly games! But don't stay here *too* long," she added. "I've heard the Earth is dying. And so are you."

Twelve mirrors circled the girl and the witch. A dozen little witches blew a dozen kisses. Eli flinched, her eyelids snapping closed and then opening again.

Clytemnestra was gone. Eli stared at her reflections, girls with stringy, dirty hair, their bodies covered in cuts and bruises and oozing sores.

Hand to her hips. As her fingers fell across pearl and stone and thorn, the blades vanished one by one, until she was completely alone in a prison of glass.

THE HEALER

"She's still asleep," said Tav. "Try again."

"It was boring," whined Clytemnestra. "You do it."

"I don't know how to!"

Red liquid pooled under the ghostly girl. Panic pounded in their head. Tav reached forward, ready to break the rules, to twist the Heart and *make* it give Eli back —

"It will kill you faster." Clytemnestra waved her hand and a gust of wind knocked Tav back. "Stupid boi. Besides, the blood isn't hers. She must be reliving that time she killed a human by mistake — oopsie!"

"So what do we do?"

"Oh, let's let *her* take care of it. She's getting used to playing in the mud with the rest of us."

"'Her'?"

They smelled her before they saw her: salt and brine. Body moving like an electric eel.

"You." A hand on obsidian.

"Me," Kite agreed, playing with the ends of her hair. "You brought her back. That was dangerous." It sounded like a compliment.

"She's dying." Tav drew the blade and watched the blue witch warily.

A tremor of light flickered through Kite, and her eyes glowed with intensity. "We won't let that happen."

A single word can be a key, can open a door in a wall you didn't know existed. It can draw two people together; can shift space and time and meaning. Enemies can become allies. Rivals can become friends.

Tav saw the conviction in her face, heard it in the deep ocean timbre of her voice.

We.

Their grip loosened on the hilt. "No, we won't."

Kite flowed over to Eli and circled the body of light and bone and raw power. She sighed, breath like bubbles spilling from a brook. "If she doesn't wake soon, she will become the Heart."

"So? Who cares?" Clytemnestra was kneeling on the ground, half a dozen spinning tops twirling around her. She pulled another one out of a pocket and spun it, but her finger slipped and the top skidded across stone and stopped beside Tav. Clytemnestra scrabbled over on all fours. Tav placed their shoe over the spinning top, pressing it into the earth.

"Say please."

Clytemnestra peered up at them through spidery eyelashes. "Cruel," she said admiringly.

Tav clenched their jaw and moved away. Clytemnestra picked up the top in her mouth and crawled back to her play area.

"She's just a child," said Kite gently. "The oldest child in the world. Let her play."

Tav ran their hands through their hair and tugged on the short spikes. "I don't like feeling useless."

"Oh, we will use you," Kite reassured them. "But not yet."

She leaned closer to Eli's face and stared at her eyelids before the girl vanished again. Carefully, she reached out and stroked the air around where her forehead should have been.

"Oh, baby," she whispered, salt crystals forming in the corners of her eyes. "What have you gotten yourself into?"

THE HEART

"Where am I?"

The sand stretched out, red as blood against a black sea. Sheet lightning like camera flashes lit up the empty expanse of the sky.

"You're here." Kite smiled, and Eli felt a new shoot grow from her rib cage. She looked away.

"There are no stars."

"You're angry with me." Kite said this calmly, as if observing a scientific experiment.

Eli tried to swallow but the words caught in her throat. She spat on the sand: a black feather, a dead honeybee, and a single withered petal.

Both girls stared at the earth for a long moment. And then Kite moved with the deadly grace of the tide, sweeping the sand and sky and world with her, swallowing everything in a single step. Eli closed her eyes. She had forgotten what it felt like to watch Kite walk toward her, as if Eli were the centre of the world.

The made-girl smiled, hand resting lightly on her chest, on the Heart of the world. She started laughing. Her eyes opened, the lids sending sparks sputtering over the sand; they caught the edge of the petal and burned it to white ash.

Kite stopped. She was an ice sculpture, beautiful and untouchable.

Eli kept laughing. There was something repressively funny about being this beacon of light, of power, even as it was killing her. The laugh turned to a hacking cough. This time she spat up blood and phlegm. She wiped her mouth with the back of her hand and then faced Kite.

"Looking for this?" The Heart glowed, making visible the delicate arches of bone and glass underneath her skin.

"Not yet," said Kite. "Soon — but not yet." She started walking again, but the spell was broken, and she was only a girl getting dirt on the hem of her skirt.

"When?" Eli let her hand fall to her side; the glow dimmed.

A flash of lightning made Kite's face appear ghostly white. Maybe they were both ghosts. "You'll know."

"I'll die, you mean."

"Maybe."

Kite stopped a hand's width away from her friend, lover, sister, enemy. Where the black surf touched the land, salt crystals formed intricate designs. A wave brushed across Eli's feet, salt stinging the sores on her skin. She winced.

"It hurts you," said Kite quietly.

"Salt cleanses the wound. You taught me that."

"You had many wounds." Her eyes were glassy and wet with the dampness of the sea that she always carried — or were they tears? Eli had no way of knowing. *Such a human thought*, she reprimanded herself. Witches didn't cry. Witches didn't grieve.

Tav grieves.

Kite knelt down and carefully gathered the bee, ash, feather. She rose and offered them to Eli.

"Don't give these away." A smile slipped across her lips like an arpeggio.

So many times, Eli had opened her mouth and swallowed for Kite. Blood, berries, sea urchins, flower stems. Now she stared at the sickly greenwhite hand and its offerings.

Kite's eyes filled with pearls and wept, the tears clattering like hail over the sand. "Don't give *them* away. Eli."

The black feather. The vision of Tav with wings like night. Or had that been a dream, as well?

Maybe it was the invocation of a boi with anger in their eyes and gentle hands. Maybe it was the sound of her name, and the rightness of its shape in Kite's mouth. Eli closed her eyes and opened her mouth.

The bee felt like velvet as it slipped down her throat. The ash was still hot and warmed her cold body. The feather fluttered in the back of her throat before slipping back inside. She closed her mouth again, her teeth grazing Kite's fingers.

Kite leaned in, and Eli vanished.

She was still there — she was always there — but also somewhere else; the world looked faint and incomplete, and she felt that she could see through it, or move through it. What would happen if she vanished entirely? How would the City of Eyes hold her ghostly form?

As the Heart, Eli could only see Kite as an essence. The seafoam green that Eli had seen only once before, when Kite and Circinae had fought over a girl trapped in a box of black ice, suspended between worlds.

A tendril of Kite's essence reached out, shyly, like a new bud. *May I touch you?*

Eli could feel the question; could feel the electricity dancing around their strange incorporeal bodies.

Yes.

Kite reached into Eli's translucent body and grabbed the Heart. She squeezed. Hard.

Pain seared through Eli's bodies — Heart, flesh, magic, human. She blacked out.

She was back in the Children's Lair. The beach and the sea were gone. Eli looked up at the stars raging overhead, burning with greed and desire. And somewhere out there, the chosen point of orbit for the witches' world — the City of Ghosts.

She could still feel the ticklish sensation of feathers at the back of her throat. Eli pushed Kite away and stumbled back, clutching at a wall adorned with thick vines and chokeberries.

"You didn't used to dream," Kite said. "When —"

"Get out," gasped Eli. "Leave me alone. And stay out of my dreams."

Kite left, trailing pearls in her wake.

Only later, when Eli looked down at her healed feet, did she realize that by wrenching her out of a dream Kite had probably saved her life.

THE HEALER

"You're awake!" Tav threw their arms around Eli without thinking, pulling her into their embrace. "You scared the shit out of me."

They needed to feel her body against theirs, needed to hear the thud of her human heart, needed to run their hands over her body to check that she was alive and here with them. Eli stiffened in their arms, and then relaxed. Tav buried their face in Eli's neck, smelling laundry detergent and ripe hawthorn berries.

"Sorry," murmured Eli into their hair. "But it's not my fault you're a worrier."

Tav pulled back, eyes searching Eli's. "The risk. We can't —"

"We have to. This doesn't change anything. I'm back, aren't I?" Eli's eyes swirled black and yellow. The spiralling pupils made Tav dizzy, and they had to look away.

"You two are *so boring*," complained Clytemnestra. "I liked it better when you were trying to knife each other."

"We can always play target practice with you, if you'd like." Eli pulled the frost blade from its sheath and tossed it in the air. She caught it with the blade down. When she opened her hand, Tav expected to see a deep cut, but she was unmarked. The blade had chosen not to harm her.

"We have to get to the Coven," said Tav.

"Of course you do. Isn't that why you're here? You didn't want to miss out on all the fun. I know you" — Clytemnestra pointed at Tav — "know how to have a good time."

"What fun?" broke in Eli.

"Oh, it's going to be the best game." Clytemnestra wriggled with excitement. "We're going to destroy the Coven. You came just in time for the war."

"The Earth —"

"Can wait," said Clytemnestra. "Tonight is for harm. You can heal tomorrow — if there's enough of you left." Her smile was cruel and taunting.

"There isn't time —"

"When the Coven has fallen, it will be safer," said Tav quietly. "We can wait until then, can't we?"

Light flooded Eli's body. "Hurry up and finish your war. We have work to do."

Quick as a cobra striking its prey, Clytemnestra lunged for Eli. She snatched Eli's hair and forced her head back, so their faces were pressed together.

"I don't take orders from you," she hissed. She laughed, and it echoed through the Labyrinth. Then she vanished, her laughter still dancing in the room.

THE HEIR

Kite could still feel Eli's teeth on her fingertips. The thrill sent shivers of excitement up her spine. Strands of hair like twisted seaweed drifted in front of her face. The walls melted away before her, welcoming her into their secret chambers and passageways. The sacrificial tears were devoured by stone. Kite plucked a few hairs and added them to the offering. She didn't want to owe the Labyrinth a debt — it had saved Eli twice now.

She's back.

The Beast nipped at her ankles with love bites. He was still invisible. Kite's excitement was contagious; she could see it in the aquamarine swirls of light that bloomed from each step, from each breath; she could see it in the walls that darkened with seawater as she passed, trailing a finger on the damp, cold surface.

She pressed a palm against rock, and mossy seaweed studded with black pearls crawled through the cracks. The Labyrinth was reshaping itself around her emotions, studded with shells and sand and the fossils of crustaceans.

Kite watched as her joy spread down the corridor.

It stopped.

A small hand, no bigger than a child's, was pressed against the wall. Slowly, the seaweed began to dry, matting like unwashed hair. The shells crumbled into dust. The water evaporated, leaving only traces of salt like frost on the pure white alabaster.

Clytemnestra.

"*Feelings*," the baby witch growled, fingers arching into claws.

Kite's hand dropped to her side. "Must you?"

"Yes." Clytemnestra picked up a piece of fossilized seaweed and ate it. "Did you tell her about the Witch Lord?"

Kite's hair fell limp against her shoulders.

"Good."

"You seem very pleased that the Witch Lord knows the Heart has returned and suspects that we have it."

"She's scared, and she's making mistakes." Clytemnestra ripped a toenail off and started picking her teeth with it.

"You mean the invitation."

"The invitation will open a door."

"Only for the delegate. Then it will close."

"And while she's distracted, we go through the library. You will open that door for us."

And let the children rampage through the stacks. The thought made Kite sick.

"You know, I've heard things. Rumours." The Warlord hovered closer, until her lips were an inch from Kite's ear. Her breath was hot and sticky. "Whispers about the Witch Lord's powers. Powers she could share with the Heir Rising."

Kite stepped away, her hair swirling up in a protective layer around her face. "I'm not the delegate you want."

"Oh, I know that. It was never going to be you — a watered-down copy too afraid to use her powers. I thought I might have to sacrifice one of the children. But now I have a better idea: we're sending the human."

"Whatever happens, you can't let Eli near her."

"I promise."

Kite arched her neck elegantly, letting beads of water run down, catching on her collarbones. "I need to talk to her."

"No. You talk to the human monster. I'll make sure our little assassin is safe."

"I really think —"

"Stick to your books," said the Warlord, "politics isn't your style."

Kite chewed on a piece of her hair and then spat it out. She met the little witch's gaze. "No manacles this time."

“Cross my heart.”

Kite nodded once, and then swept past Clytemnestra, head held high. After a few steps she heard a yelp.

“Beastly creature!” the witch shrieked. “When I catch you, I’ll eat you!”

Kite’s lips curved into the shape of a scythe. “Good boy,” she whispered.

THE HEART

“We didn’t come here to fight a war,” said Eli.

“Didn’t we?” Tav’s eyes shone with fervor. “Don’t you want to see the Coven burn for what they did to you?”

“Yes. But —”

“We will, Eli.” Passion burned in their voice, and they grabbed Eli’s wrists softly. “We will make them pay for what they did to you. We will make everyone pay.”

Eli felt the Heart warm under Tav’s touch, felt its magic creep along her forearms toward the boi with an obsidian blade and nerves of steel. A boi thirsting for power and destruction. What would happen if the Heart was transplanted into Tav?

Eli pulled away.

"You're scaring me," she said, and turned away from the hurt and confusion in Tav's eyes.

Stay away from me, she thought. *This Heart could kill us both.*

THE HEALER

Eli pulled away, and Tav saw fear skittering from the corners of her eye like a daddy long-legs.

The draw of the Heart like the whispered promises of schoolchildren in the dark. If Tav reached inside her, they could take it.

They could almost see Cam shaking his head at them, his eyes grey and sad.

Cam.

They had forgotten about Cam — they hadn't even asked the witch-demon to look for him.

They hated themselves in that moment.

A glimpse of red like a single autumn leaf caught their eye. "Eli?"

"It's fine." Eli was fumbling with her shirt. Her hand came away slick with blood. "The fault lines —"

Tav stared at the bared torso on her friend and lover. A crack was forming, a fissure in her body. Through the break in the skin Tav could see the glitter of a granite rib cage.

"Not now," Eli muttered through gritted teeth. "Not yet —"

She collapsed on the floor. Her glasses fell from her face, a jagged crack splitting across one lens.

Tav fell to their knees, fumbling with Eli's shirt, pushing the fabric out of the way. They pressed their hands against the fissure and tried to ignore the warmth of the Heart that would soon need a new home.

A trickle of gold flowed through Eli's veins and arteries. As Tav tried to focus on knitting skin and bone together, a single droplet of worldblood touched their hand.

Images burst across their brain:

A field of jewel-green moss hanging from silver birch branches, blossoms blue as heartache with gold centres opening to the moon. Skin.

An ocean, inhaling and exhaling against a cliff face. Lungs.

A wall of granite and quartz growing through the core. Skeleton.

A planet with a heartbeat.

The afterimage of blue-and-gold petals lingered on the backs of their eyelids.

Sorrow hung around their neck like a stone.

Now Tav understood why the Heart kept calling out to them, why it seemed ready to abandon the girl who had rescued it from the Coven's chains.

If Eli died, the Heart would die with her.

Unless it found a new host. Unless it was somehow freed. And Tav could free it, could tear the light and magic from the corpse of a made-thing. Could open a door in the magic of Eli's making.

Tav stared at the small body of the girl who was the life of a world.

It wouldn't be a surgical incision, small and neat. It would destroy her.

Whispers swirled through their brain.

You're stronger than Eli.

You're more powerful.

With this power, you would become a god.

They stared at the perfect curve of Eli's ribs, at the loose petals in her chest cavity. Purple-and-black smoke curled around their wrists and lingered in the beds of their fingernails. Slowly, the skin grew together, tendrils of flesh and bone reaching out, growing, healing. The scent of burning rose petals.

Tav drew back, and the whispers stopped.

Eli was breathing, but still unconscious. Tav pressed their forehead against her stomach.

I can't do this without you.

"You can't help that thing," a low voice crawled across the space. Tav shuddered — they hadn't heard anyone entering the room.

"What do you want?"

"The help you promised me," said the Warlord.

"When she's better."

"The children will look after her. And it's you we want, not her."

"Me?"

"We need you." The little girl's voice was grave. "The world needs you."

Tav swallowed, watching Eli's chest rise and fall softly with the pattern of her breathing. If they did this, if they helped the Warlord, then Eli could stay here and be safe.

"If I come, you won't make her face the Witch Lord? She won't have to fight?"

"No, she won't."

Relief bubbled up in their chest like seafoam. They turned, facing Clytemnestra.

Clytemnestra was twirling a lollipop so fast it was only a blur. But she had prepared for war — her teeth and fingernails had been sharpened to wicked points, and her buckle shoes had sensible flat heels.

Tav met her porcelain irises and nodded. "Whatever you need, I'll do it."

The Warlord's eyes burned pure white with anticipation, flames dancing where pupils might have once lived. "Haven't you always wanted to meet the Witch Lord?"

THE HEIR

Kite turned the invitation over in her hand. The stolen magic swirled up inside her, and when she turned the card at a certain angle to the light, she could see the glossy fingerprints of the Witch Lord's power that called out to Kite's essence. After all, they were the same.

She thought about loyalty, luck, and lineages. She wondered what it might be like to no longer be the Heir, to no longer have her existence tethered to another body. One corner of the card snagged on the roughened skin of her thumb and made a quick and calculated cut. Hissing in pain, Kite stuck the finger in her mouth and sucked the algae leaking from the wound.

The Beast sat on her skirts.

"I'm sorry my love, I wasn't thinking." Kite offered

the wound to the creature, who lapped up the last green droplets on her finger. Steam rose from the wound — the Beast's saliva was cauterizing it.

"Thank you, darling." She bent down and kissed the Beast's head.

Soon she would see her mother again. Soon, the Witch Lord would know of her betrayal. Kite wondered if she was strong enough to resist, or if her mother would drain her essence as she had so many other witches.

She felt strangely calm. She had done it: she had helped Clytemnestra raise an army. She had shattered the steps of the Coven, freed the made-daughters, and brought the lost things home.

Each betrayal lead to the next. Kite had not known she was capable of this rebellion, this recklessness, this intoxicating choice.

Eli had shown her.

Eli.

She had to keep Eli away from the Witch Lord, whatever the cost.

The Beast barked once, and Kite patted his head. "You're right, precious, we have work to do."

Pocketing the invitation and wiping the grime of power on her skirts, Kite walked through the wall. As the stone and vines unfurled themselves before her, ushering her deeper into the Children's Lair, Kite felt like a mourner going to a funeral. With a shake of her head, she shed those thoughts like rain. She couldn't get lost in her head now.

She had one more task to complete before returning home.

Kite's homecoming would be a death sentence.

The room was filled with scraps of crushed velvet and silk scarves riddled with holes. A crow was nesting in a pile of half-finished crochet projects. In one corner a rat was chewing on a bedazzled denim jacket. A mahogany vanity stretched across the far wall, the large and stately glass mirror tarnished and spiderwebbed with cracks. Mechanical birds and windup toys of all kinds littered the floor, and Kite had to make her way carefully through the clutter to reach the boi sitting in the plush pink chair, staring at their shattered reflection.

The silver earrings that lined both ears were glowing in the light of the moon. Their hair had been styled to one side, the undercut sharp and clean. The violet tips of their hair looked like embers glowing in a dying fire.

Tav was beautiful. Kite could see why Eli had fallen in love with them.

"Clytemnestra asked me to get you ready for tonight." Kite moved without making any sounds, but her presence filled the air with the smell of sea salt. Beside her, the Beast licked his forepaw. Kite reached down and stroked his head.

"I didn't know the Heir followed orders." Tav was playing with an empty perfume bottle, the glass tinted a delicate pale pink. Kite could smell the lingering notes of black orchid and pomegranate.

"She leads the children, and I am a child."

"But you're not a soldier."

Kite smiled, watching her mouth split in the broken mirror. "No, I'm not a soldier."

"And Eli?" Tav almost choked on the name.

"We will keep Eli safe."

"Safe like when you tried to kill her? Or safe like when your friend chained her up?"

"Safety is different in this world, earth-creature. And witches don't have friends."

"We call chains 'safe' in our world, too, witch."

"You're starting to sound like Eli," Kite observed.

Tav placed the perfume bottle back down on the vanity.

"Why is she sending me?" they asked. "Because I'm replaceable?"

"Because we don't understand you. Which means the Witch Lord won't understand you."

"Understand me?"

"We don't understand what you are. What you're made from. How a human has the powers that you have." Kite could hear Tav's heartbeat accelerate as she spoke, in excitement or fear. Did they know where their power came from? Did they have secrets that only Eli had tasted? Kite imagined opening the boi's rib cage to see what was inside, like unwrapping a gift or smashing a pinata.

What would she find at the core of this creature? A human heart beating blood and oxygen through an animal body? Glittering onyx and amethyst like the core of a geode waiting to be cracked open? Smoke and feathers?

"Stop looking at me like that." Tav swivelled in the chair to face the blue girl. The obsidian blade hummed in warning.

"Like what?" Kite's hair coiled in on itself, drawing closer to her scalp. The memory of the Witch-Killing Fields was too close.

"Like you want to vivisect me."

"I only want to vivisect things that interest me," Kite said earnestly, hoping Tav could hear the compliment.

"Is the Witch Lord going to vivisect me?"

"Maybe." Kite let her eyes slide over Tav's neck, shoulders, chest. "But she'll want to play with you first. You'll be an enigma for her, a mystery she'll want to unravel herself."

"I'd rather not be unravelled."

"Then don't give up your secrets," said Kite, leaning forward and reaching over Tav for the perfume bottle. Her skin brushed against Tav's, and she could feel the ice and fire burning in their veins. The dark stain of frostbite spread down Kite's forearm from where the two had touched, the skin mottled purple and blue for a moment before fading back to bluegreen. Kite shivered, but not from the cold. She drew back, the pink vial clutched in her hand.

"If you keep the Witch Lord curious, you may still be alive when the children come with their justice. Don't let her get bored with you."

White teeth. Dark eyes flashed gold. "I'm never boring."

Another shiver. The desire to be burned by them. Kite brought the pink bottle to her mouth and licked the tip. Bitter coated her tongue and reminded her why she was here.

"Let's get you dressed for your audience with the Witch Lord." Kite dropped the vial and enjoyed the cacophony as it smashed on stone. Then she knelt down and gathered up the pieces, using her magic to knit the broken glass together with velvet and copper and spiderweb. She had always enjoyed making things.

"Why isn't Clytemnestra sending you?" asked Tav. "Wouldn't the Heir be an enigma?"

Kite stilled, like a raindrop halting its slow descent down a windowpane. "I can't." The Beast cowered between her legs. He didn't want to see the Witch Lord, either.

Flashback of agony and cruelty. The way her mother had torn her from her body, had touched her essence. *I can teach you ...*

Promises of power and promises of pain. Kite remembered the helplessness of lying in the dirt at her mother's feet. Not once, but many times. Many small wounds, many needles pricking a skin and telling it to become numb. But nobody was ever truly numb. Even skins that souls could slip out of like nightgowns had memories. Kite's body remembered the lessons her mother had taught her. Those lessons had sent a little girl running into the Labyrinth, hiding out in the walls.

The Witch Lord had underestimated the children, had underestimated her own daughter. The Witch Lord had been lonely for so long that she could not comprehend what companionship might feel like. Kite hoped Cam had found companionship in rock. He had seemed so lonely when she had found him on a sea of black glass, as discarded and forgotten as all the lost things in the wastelands.

Kite wondered if she should tell Tav that she had dinner with Cam, but as soon as she had the thought it slid across her mind like a water skimmer on a pond. Then it was gone, and there was only here and now.

"Did it tempt you?" she asked lightly, wanting to understand this human. She rose with the vest she had made, black with gold embroidery and glass buttons. It smelled of crushed orchids and fruit.

"What?"

"The Heart. Did it tempt you?"

"No."

Kite heard the lie and was surprised by it. Humans thought lies made them safe.

Witches knew how to wear the truth as the brightest and strongest shield.

"Magic requires sacrifice," she told them, helping them slip into the sleeves. She crouched in front of them and slowly buttoned up the vest, listening to the song of their heartbeat harmonizing with every exhale. "You will have to decide what you are willing to give up."

"I'm not going to sacrifice anyone. Or anything."

"Then you'll die." Kite's fingers brushed the thin fabric of Tav's shirt and felt rough skin and hair underneath. Bluegreen lights danced along her fingertips and across the back of her hands.

"I'm sure the Warlord would be pleased."

"No, she likes you."

Tav laughed, short and harsh. "Yeah right."

Kite frowned, confused by their response. "Of course. She loves puzzles."

"And what about you?" Tav looked down and their gaze met bluegreen pupil-less eyes. They ran one finger along the edge of the obsidian blade strapped to their forearm. Behind the sliver of black glass, leaves and petals were marked into the skin with faded blue ink. "Do you love puzzles?"

Kite reached out, a wave caressing the shore. Her hand on Tav's wrist, the skin damp and soft as seaweed. She felt the bite of fire, and then her hand was on the blade, and she pressed the pad of her index finger against its ravenous tip.

The blade wouldn't cut. Kite's body ebbed away from Tav, the ghost of a smile playing across her face.

Eli's blade had refused to harm her.

"Me? I prefer stories."

THE HEALER

Tav's smile grew.

"There's one more thing you need," said Kite.

"Better armour?" Tav fiddled with one of the glass buttons.

"Yes." Kite pulled out the final piece.

"It's a masquerade?" Tav stared at the twisted metal dangling from Kite's finger on a copper spiderweb.

Kite's laugh was like church bells ringing underwater. "Every day is a masquerade in the City of Eyes. This is just the prettiest poison. Are you ready to play?"

"No."

"That's the right answer." Kite smiled, and behind the gleam of white teeth Tav could almost smell the dead animals that had willingly crawled into her mouth. They half wanted to offer their own throat to the luminous creature. A bite like hers would make you forget a thousand touches. "Now, close your eyes."

"I'd prefer to keep them open."

"Then you don't like to be surprised."

Tav allowed Kite to approach them, to lift the mask and tie it gently around their face. "You are ready to kill me," Kite observed. "I can see the intention in your twitching liver."

"I don't want to kill you," said Tav, wondering if that was the truth.

"Then I hope you don't have to."

Kite was right: they were ready to kill. Tav wanted the Witch Lord dead. They felt the bloodlust rising behind their eyes, staining the world wine red. Power, sweet as candied almonds, spilled over their tongue.

Purple smoke uncoiled from their mouth.

"Stop that," said Kite, flicking her hand and breaking up the smoke. It crystallized into glittering pieces of confetti and fell to the ground. "The Beast doesn't like smoke."

"I'm sorry," said Tav. "I didn't mean to."

Kite leaned forward, the dampness of her breath brushing their neck. "You don't have to apologize to me. But when you use your magic, you should always mean it."

Tav wondered if Kite and Eli had practised kissing under a cobalt sun, if Kite had flowed over Eli's body and made her moan the way she had moaned against Tav's chest. Seaglass and skin, hawthorn and hands.

Tav turned their head slightly to breathe in the heavy smell of salt. Kite's bluegreen light flared up, bright and pure as a star.

Wait —

Something was different.

The edges of Kite's essence burned white and gold and pink, and small sparks shed from the distressed soul of the lonely witch girl.

And another scent was creeping under the fragrance of the sea, like a single piece of rotten fruit in an orchard.

What was wrong with Kite's essence? Tav opened their mouth to ask, feeling their heartbeat quicken.

"Kite —"

"*Look*," the blue girl whispered. Her breath clouded the mirror, and when the fog faded, the glass had been repaired.

Tav stared at the face in the mirror: the purple hair like a crown of thorns, the glittering eyes like flecks of mica. Their face was obscured by the black iron mask that arched and curled into playful twists — only to end in jagged edges. It was a face that would draw blood.

It was a face that demanded sacrifice.

"Beautiful," sighed Kite; and that was true, too.

"It's the face of a witch," said Tav.

THE HEIR

Kite breathed again and the reflection vanished. "Welcome home."

Tav said nothing, but the light in their eyes shuddered.

Kite ran her finger along the obsidian blade. "You can't take her with you, precious."

"Of course not. Why would Clytemnestra want me armed?" Tav sighed.

"You won't live long enough to speak with the Witch Lord if you come bearing a witch-killer."

Tav nodded, and slowly unsheathed the blade Eli had gifted to them. "Keep it safe," they said. "It's part of her."

"I know," said Kite, accepting the black needle.

A moment of charged silence fell between them.

"I think you'll live," Kite said finally. "You have the mouth of a survivor."

"Well, I haven't died yet, and I love a challenge." Tav ran a hand through their short hair. "Oh, but there's one thing I need. If you want me to put my neck on the guillotine for your rebellion."

They tossed the keys in the air. They glittered once, and then a giant magpie swooped down and swallowed them whole. The bird landed on Kite's shoulder. Kite took a single feather from its wing and ran the edge across her mouth.

"Done," she agreed.

"Thank you." Tav looked down. "Take care of Eli for me, okay, boy?" They leaned over and scratched the Beast's scaly ear.

Kite stilled.

Not even witches could see the Beast when he became invisible.

"What are you?" Without thinking, she placed a hand on Tav's chest, reaching for their lungs, or maybe a chest cavity filled only with stardust. Tav inhaled sharply, then placed their hand on Kite's. Kite gasped as a circular burn spread over her skin, leaving traces of ash and frost. Tav gently placed Kite's hand on her own knee.

"You have to ask," they said. Their voice was hoarse, as if their vocal cords had been singed by the contact.

"I'm sorry. I will."

Kite stood and looked around for a moment, taking in the plastic toys and the piles of fabric. The spilled eyeliner pooling on the vanity. The crystal vials of potpourri and almond extract. The room looked like it belonged to a mad king or an unsupervised child.

There were crayon drawings scribbled on the wall.

Kite twirled the feather between her thumb and forefinger, aware of Tav's gaze.

"We will, you know," she added, bending over and picking up the Beast. "We'll take care of her."

Then she walked through the wall and took another step toward regicide.

THE HEALER

Kite had left the invitation on the vanity, pinned with a jewelled broach in the shape of an owl. One of the bird's eyes was missing. Another souvenir from the City of Ghosts, another trinket for the children to play with. Tav was sure the broach had been left intentionally — for all her dreamy slowness, Kite was an important part Clytemnestra's revolution, and she had experience with the curiosity of children.

Tav pinned the broach to their vest and picked up the Witch Lord's calling card.

Tav could see the magic burning in every fibre, and the smell of gunpowder and gardenias was overpowering. They understood: it was a password, a key, a summons that would bring any one creature into the Coven. A portal.

Tav wondered if it would let them leave again.

The vanity looked like something that had been picked up at a flea market, stuffed with costume jewelry, and left out in the rain for a few weeks.

Cam would have loved it.

If he were here, he would have insisted on doing their makeup so that under the mask was a second one, fierce and fantastical. He would have offered to come with them even though he knew he couldn't. He would be standing here, beside them, making jokes to hide the worry in his eyes.

Cam will be okay, Tav told themselves. *He's part of the Labyrinth. He's probably back in the under-labyrinth. After all of this, you'll find him.*

"Don't bleed on your mask," said a high-pitched voice. Tav turned around. A tiny girl in an oversized T-shirt, clutching a broken Game Boy, stood in the centre of the room. Her feet were bare.

"Who are you?"

"That's a rude question to ask," said the girl. "You're leaking."

Tav brought a hand to their face in time to catch the black feather that fell from one eye.

What the fuck? They dropped it and looked up at the girl. "What are you doing here?"

"We came to watch." Another child appeared, naked and sticky with popsicle juice. "Clytemnestra told us to give you a gift and then leave. But we're staying." They both giggled.

"I always like an audience." Tav bowed deeply. The children giggled harder. "It's showtime, kids."

They twirled the invitation around in their fingers for a moment and then brought it to their lips. They kissed it gently, tenderly, letting their body communicate how much they wanted to know the other party. Their lips left a stain on the gold paper.

The card shimmered, glittered, and the kiss caught fire. Tav released the edge and it hung, suspended in the air, burning.

Where the paper peeled away, shedding sparks and ash like a snake shedding its skin, was a hole.

A perfect circle of nothing.

A pathway.

Through the hole Tav could see glimpses of white light, could almost hear the laughter of insects. The smell of plum skin and vinegary wine was stronger now. They could almost taste the burnt perfume of the Coven. Of the Witch Lord.

"Don't forget your toy," said the little girl, tossing something sparkly in the air.

Tav caught the keys, glittering silver under the light of the Earth's moon. The second the keys touched their palm, the air in front of them rippled like heat waves. Black and chrome. Their Kawasaki Vulcan 900. The mermaid spray-painted on the fender, the paint fading and chipped. They'd have to touch it up when this was all over. Tav reached out and stroked the bike, the soft leather of the seat soothing their fingers. They were already feeling less alone. *I missed you, girl*, they thought.

Tav grinned at the children. "Thanks, kids," they said. "If I don't come back, you can keep my shades." Tav nodded their head at the cheap aviators they had left on the vanity.

"If you don't come back, we'll probably all die," said the popsicle child, licking juice off a dirty elbow.

Tav wasn't listening. The familiar bite of adrenalin had woken them up, and everything was sharper, clearer, brighter. The glow of recklessness and danger warmed their bones. It was time for another story. It was time for a terrible mistake.

Tav grinned as they swung one leg over their motorcycle.

It felt good to be back.

THE HEART

Darkness. Warmth. The Heart was an acorn, an embryo, a spore. There were no dreams in this place, only stillness and the promise of rest.

A shrill voice cut through the silence. *Wake up. We need to wake up.*

The Heart stirred but resisted the call. It was sinking into oblivion, losing itself in the synaptic dance of a human brain.

The voice came again, sharp as glass. *Wake up* now.

Eli wrenched her eyes open. A headache stabbed at her temples and gold lights flickered at the corners of her vision. But she was awake, and whole — at least for now.

She was also alone.

Eli stared up at the bruised sky through spiny gothic spires. Her vision was blurry. She fumbled around for her glasses and jammed them on her face. Then she rose on unsteady legs and asked the walls, "Where's Tav?"

"Oh, they've gone to a fancy dinner party. Sorry you weren't invited!" Clytemnestra popped into the room. She was juggling skulls and seemed in high spirits; high treason suited her.

Eli stopped breathing. "You sent them to the Witch Lord."

"They agreed to be our delegate. You missed so much while you were convulsing, lazy girl!"

Eli ran a thumb over the pearl blade. "You're playing a dangerous game," she said. "Inviting the Witch Lord into your home. If you open her portal, she might just come through it." The movement of the skulls in the witch's hand was making her dizzy.

Clytemnestra grinned. "I wouldn't be interested in playing if it wasn't dangerous."

"Can you stop that? I can't think." Eli waved a hand at the spinning bones.

Clytemnestra stuck her tongue out. "You were more fun as a child."

Eli's blade pierced the skull of a squirrel, pinning it to the wall behind the witch. The other bones crashed to the ground as Clytemnestra lost her rhythm.

"I take it back," said the baby Warlord as Eli crossed the room and wrenched the blade from stone. "There's still some fun in you."

"So you're sending Tav as an offering."

"Our *delegate*. An exciting distraction while my tame Heir opens a back door into that cranky old building."

"Don't talk to me like I'm not from here," said Eli shortly. "I know what 'delegate' means. What I don't understand is why you want to use *Tav* as bait."

"Because" — Clytemnestra spun a pirouette — "the best bait bites back. Don't worry, your girlfriend will be there to look after them."

Eli's stomach dropped. "I'm going after them."

"Sorry, sweet prince, we're not sending the Heart into the hands of the Witch Lord. I'm sure your friends will be fine. And if not, Kite gave us some delicious chaotic magic to blow things up. There will be revelry soon enough. I promise to save you a piece of the Coven to destroy." Her voice was sweet and sticky as candy.

Eli suddenly realized that Clytemnestra was trying to comfort her. Never had the little girl ever offered to share. This was her attempt at kindness.

The knowledge only made Eli more anxious. Why was the Warlord keeping her from Tav? She was the most powerful thing in the world — the Heart — and Tav might need her.

"Am I a prisoner?" she asked quietly. "Is the Heart your plaything now?"

"No!" cried Clytemnestra, and then she shrugged. "Well, yes. But you knew that when you retrieved it for me. You knew that when you came back here. You could have gone to the Coven, to the forest, to the home your ruined witch-mother left abandoned. You could have gone anywhere, but you keep coming here. You keep asking Tav to bring you here."

"I didn't ask —"

"Maybe not with words, but with your material. With your thoughts. With your desires. You came to me, even though you are not a child. And we have sheltered you, because you have something that belongs to us." Her eyes shone with fervor, and when she blinked, flecks of rust speckled her face.

"The Heart doesn't belong to anyone." Eli stepped away from the girl warily, hands hovering instinctively over thorn and bone.

"It belongs to my world." The witch bared her teeth. "And we are taking that world back. You might be dressed like a made-daughter, but you are our Heart. And I forbid you from going anywhere near the Witch Lord." The air around her head crackled with thunder and lightning, and hot pink sparks burst like fireworks around her forehead — a garish halo. The scent of chemical smoke filled the room.

Eli's eyes flashed, and behind the yellow slits of a reptilian monster were the storm clouds of a distant planet. She looked around her prison. "No chains today? Don't tell me you're getting soft."

"I made a promise." Clytemnestra quickly crossed her heart.

"Then you can't stop me."

Clytemnestra rolled her eyes. "It's too late now, sleeping beauty. If all goes well, my sisters and brothers will soon be flooding the Coven. If it goes badly, I'm sure we can get you a memento of your dead lovers." Gone was the attempt at appeasement, the offering of scraps of war. The witch was bored of this game. Her patience had run out.

So had Eli's.

The pearl blade clutched in one fist, the divider, that would tear the witch's essence from her body. Eli drew another dagger — the ensnarer, a tangle of rose thorns. An offensive pairing, and a brutal one.

Long yellow teeth spilled from a thin mouth.

She pointed the pearl blade at Clytemnestra.

"I haven't had a challenger in decades," said Clytemnestra, delighted. "We never thought you had it in you."

"I don't work for you. We work together, or not at all. And I'm getting out of this cell one way or another. I'm no one's prisoner."

Clytemnestra narrowed her eyes. "*You* have always been free to go, but the Heart stays here with me."

Eli felt a twinge of pain from a recently healed wound. But Tav's magic was strong, and it would hold.

"If you want to pull apart my body, you'll need to come closer," she said softly, keeping her stance light, her grip firm on the blades.

"After all these years, my pretty little assassin, I thought you would know." Clytemnestra vanished and then reappeared behind her. "I'm faster than you." Claws raked Eli's back.

Again, she disappeared, and then reappeared in front of Eli's face, knocking the thorn dagger from her hand. "I'm stronger than you. And I'm —"

Eli pressed her forehead against Clytemnestra's, the Heart of the world flaring up under her skin. Clytemnestra shrieked and pulled away, a burn mark spreading across her face. A whisper of a smile flitted across Eli's face and then faded.

Slowly, deliberately, Eli unbuckled her belt of daggers and let it fall to the ground. Her eyes swirled with smoke and light. She took a single step toward Clytemnestra, letting her body flicker in and out of existence.

"I'm still here," she said, her body fading except for her head, disembodied and grotesque. "But you can't hurt me."

A hand rematerialized, gripping Clytemnestra's curly blond hair. The little witch was thrown against the wall, cracking her head against its unforgiving surface. A thin trickle of white liquid flowed down her neck like milk.

Clytemnestra vanished, sliding into invisibility. Eli only laughed. "Cute trick, but you can't hide from me."

A scream of rage, and then both bodies fully rematerialized, Eli's teeth embedded in Clytemnestra's leg. Eli tossed the tiny body aside like a rag doll and fell to all fours.

"Let me go, and I won't have to kill you."

A pause, a silence heavy with the weight of a thousand eyes watching and waiting. Then a single, high-pitched giggle. Clytemnestra started laughing, kicking her arms and legs in the air like a toddler having a tantrum. Then she sat up, brushing her golden hair out of her unnaturally blue eyes.

"Oh, you *are* fun." She floated up, up into the sky, staring down at the pile of blood and bone and pearl and death crouched on the earth. She burst into flames, the white fire encasing her entire body. "Let's play."

THE HEIR

Take me to the library.

The thought pulsed outward from Kite's body like a tsunami, and the wall before her ripped open, scattering stones and clumps of dirt and shattered eggshells. A blue robin's egg fragment caught in her hair. She stepped back in surprise at the violence with which the passageway had opened up before her.

Always, before, the stones had slid coyly to make room for her body, or had simply melted away, had reformed around an elegant passageway leading to the archives. The walls had even offered phosphorescent moss and flowers to light her path. It had welcomed the witch with the touch like soapstone and the eyes like lotus blossoms. The Coven loved the girl who had made a nest out of scraps of poetry and old letters.

She had meant to ask nicely, to make a wish and offer hope to the sentient structure that stretched across so much of the world. (How much? No one knew. The Labyrinth had never been mapped. It was alive, and kept growing, moving, and changing.)

But the command had been regurgitated from her body automatically. The sweetness of overripe bananas filled her mouth — the alchemical creation of a ruthless Witch Lord. Stolen magic. The essences of dead witches. The walls did not know their touch the way they knew hers, and crumbled before the threats of the Witch Lord.

Sorrow flooded Kite's limbs, making her hair lie flat against her back. She did not want to be the Witch Lord's arm. She did not want to use fear and force to move through the world.

She needed to end this, and soon. The hallway was dark, but Kite didn't need sight to find her way home.

Kite entered the Coven for the last time.

An army of children and daughters and discarded things followed close behind.

THE HEART

Eli felt the coiled fury in her body start to unwind, sending tremors down her limbs. Her teeth ached from the vibrations that rocked her body like a heavy bass, a pulse that sounded like life.

She had been built to be a tool, a weapon, a machine. She had spent her life in cages made of blood and fear and promises. But she had broken free from the Coven, free from her mother, and she wasn't going to leave one form of bondage for another.

"You can't stop me," she told the Warlord, and the humming in her bones grew stronger.

Clytemnestra sharpened one fingernail on a glittering canine and then winked. "Didn't your mother teach you it's bad manners to tell lies?"

Eli was on her like a cat on a bird, her bloody mouth on the hem of Clytemnestra's skirts, dragging her *down, down, down.* Sheet-lightning pain burned electric and hot against her skull, and fingernails like razor blades carved patterns into her skin. The skin there was so weak, so fragile, and the blood dripped into Eli's eyes, obscuring her vision. But her magic eyes saw through the blood, through the pain, to the scared, trembling essence of her enemy, and before Clytemnestra could complete her victory, Eli tore a piece of fabric from her dress and swallowed it.

"You've ruined my dress." The little witch pouted. "I hate you! I *hate you*!" The temper tantrum made her essence boil and steam, and the scent of sulfur and kerosene filled the room.

"It was delicious," said Eli.

She tucked a few loose strands of hair behind her ear, getting blood on her hands. It was rust orange and dried immediately on her palms, rough as sandpaper. Eli rubbed her hands together, sending flakes spitting like sparks. She noticed that Clytemnestra flinched when one landed on her ankle.

"Hate you," Clytemnestra whispered, her Cupid's bow lips barely moving.

And then the little girl exploded.

A piece of cerebellum landed on Eli's face, still animated by the girl's essence. Eli realized in horror that it was sucking at her eyes, at her magic sight, trying to devour her ability to see her attacker. Desperately, Eli wrenched at the dark-grey mass, trying to ignore the feeling of wet intestines as they wound their way up her ankles.

No one used magic like this. It was forbidden.

There was a reason Clytemnestra was the Warlord, a reason she had lived so long as a child, a reason the Coven had never repurposed her.

She was hard to catch, and harder to kill.

Panicking, hands slippery with blood and meaty flesh, Eli stuck out her reptilian tongue and licked Clytemnestra's brain matter. With a shriek, the cerebellum released and fell to the floor, where Eli stomped on it ferociously (not that it mattered to the magic essence inside, but it felt really good, anyway). Then Eli set about chewing through the intestines that were ensnaring her body, using her crocodile teeth to tear and bite.

At her feet, two eyeballs lay on the ground. They looked like they were made of porcelain, with painted irises and pupils. A doll's eyes.

"Maybe I'll wear you as a pendant," Eli told the left eyeball, as she tossed a piece of intestine to one side. "I seem to have misplaced the last one you gave me."

The eyeball rolled away quickly.

"You know why this is forbidden, don't you?" Eli asked, recalling Kite's lullabies as they fell asleep together on the island, the legends and myths Kite recited from memory. The stories she brought with her from the library, from the Coven's archives of history and knowledge. "A witch is weaker when her essence is torn."

She knew this to be true; she had felt it in the thinner, frailer magic that touched her body, as if Clytemnestra had been watered down with tears and rain. Another word rose to mind, like the drifting waves of Kite's hair brushing across her stomach.

Gestalt.

Her belt of blades lay on the floor, stained with something dark and wet. The frost blade rang out — a single clear, high note. It was time to end this. The pieces of Clytemnestra hurried to join together, liver and tongue squelching over stone.

Eli waited for the Warlord to put herself back together.

Clytemnestra, mostly reconstructed but missing a few parts, lunged at Eli with teeth and nails. Lacerations etched themselves into Eli's back and legs and shoulders — but wood and stone are strong, and the witch's magic was weakened.

Eli flickered in and out of existence as the adrenalin from pain merged with the excitement of the fight, the pleasure of giving in to a body that was strange and wonderful and monstrous.

Catching hold of Clytemnestra's hair, Eli pulled the little witch close to her. Eli's body glowed with the power of the Heart. She was a girl lit up from the inside, like a glass jar humming with fireflies. She looked down at her body and could see through her skin to the thorns and granite and black pearl rustling and glittering and growing inside, illuminated by a power greater than any single being.

The Heart didn't need a blade. The lights crawling under Eli's skin swarmed over Clytemnestra's body, and then delicately, the way a lover plucks a flower, Eli reached out and tenderly tore the witch's essence from her body.

Clytemnestra's screams would echo in the room for years to come.

The tension broke like a storm breaks over the horizon, flooding the sky with darkness.

The crumpled mess of hair and keratin stained the floor, while a ball of white light shivered in a corner, shuddering wildly.

"I'll give you privacy to dress," Eli told the ball of light. "And don't wait up — I'll be back late."

She retrieved her blades from the floor and buckled them around her hips. A smile split across her face like stitches breaking over a wound, and then she was gone, running through the Labyrinth, looking for the door. She would find her way back into the Coven. She would be there to face the Witch Lord.

After all, Tav needed her.

THE HEALER

Tav revved the engine and laughed, feeling that familiar rush of power between their legs. No matter how far across the galaxy they travelled, this would always feel like home.

"Time for our grand entrance, girl," they told the bike. It seemed to whine in anticipation. Tav swore the mermaid winked at them.

The door grew large enough to fit the human and their mount and Tav rode their faithful metal steed into the war chamber of the Coven, where beauty and deceit glittered like shards of ice.

As Tav crossed over from the Children's Lair and into the Coven, they could see the magic swirling in the space, an oppressive light thick as fog seeping into their nostrils and mouth, filling their pores with the smell of power.

Tav careened through a ballroom of marble and black quartz tile made to look like a giant chessboard. Huge chandeliers made of pink crystal tinkled faintly overhead and cast a pinkish-red hue over the room. They felt themselves immediately drawn to the pulsing light that emanated from a throne on the opposite side of the grand chamber. The light was intoxicating and alluring, pulling them in like a spider wrapping insects in sweet-smelling web before eating them alive.

They drove toward it, toward the Witch Lord, toward the trap made for a baby Warlord.

A trap that would be sprung by a human who could use magic, a creature no one seemed to understand.

Witches flittered out of the way of the gleaming monster as Tav raced through the chamber, leaving a trail of pretty destruction in their wake — spilled pearls and flawed diamonds, plates of food upended onto the shining marble floor. Tav slammed on the brakes and turned sharply before the raised dais where the throne stood, leaving tire tracks on the white marble. They patted their bike once and whispered, "Thank you," before dismounting.

A scandalized silence followed their entrance, as the court waited to see how the Witch Lord would deal with this disturbance.

"You must be our honoured guest," she said.

The throne was so bright that Tav had to look away from the burning star that was the elaborate centrepiece of the game.

"I must be," Tav agreed, offering a short bow — making sure to show their neck, a sign of vulnerability that told the witches they were not afraid. Kite had coached them on these small, specific gestures.

They waited.

Out of the corner of one eye, Tav saw a single, flawless pearl roll across the floor.

The court held its collective breath, a garden of stone and glass statues.

The Witch Lord made them wait.

The light began to ebb, bleeding out of the throne. Behind Tav, the murmured sounds of velvet brushing against skin filled the ballroom. Hushed voices whispered to one another; songbirds opened their shining beaks and sent clean, pure notes from pillar to pillar.

"You may stand," said the Witch Lord.

Tav stood again and met the gaze of the only person in the worlds who frightened Clytemnestra.

Their eyes widened and they fought to keep from stepping back and showing weakness. Struggled not to react to the confusion and horror that coursed through their entire being.

Sitting on the throne, her hair writhing around her face like a curse, was Kite.

THE HEART

Eli looked for the magic purpleblack signature she now recognized as Tav's. The City of Eyes was full of magic threads that glittered and burned, filling the world with colour and light. She could see the silverwhite glow from Clytemnestra's essence. It was angry, but it would take a while for the Warlord to stitch her body back together and regenerate the damaged cells.

Eli could see a thousand threads stretching between bodies of water and bodies of land; between spongy flesh photosynthesizing and skeletal and muscular frames running on oxygen; between rock and bone and glass.

Only three threads of light connected to Eli —

Smoky purple with the sheen of midnight: Tav.

Gold painted with aquamarine starlight: Kite.

The third was mossy green and bronze and reminded Eli of fossils and music. *Cam's alive*, she thought, relief flowering under her rib cage. *He's probably a lot safer than we are right now.*

These threads were pathways between Eli and the people she loved, the people she had chosen to tether herself to. These were not lines drawn in the sand, not fault lines dividing tectonic plates, not chains to enslave her. These threads were a string between two tin cans, the kind human children play with. These threads were a climber's rope: something to hold on to.

Eli reached out and strummed first the purple thread, and then the gold. The first note was low and rich, a major chord on a piano. The second was high and wailing, like a violin that's been deliberately left out of tune. Then she strummed the third thread: silence, but gentle vibrations, as if the instrument was muffled by dirt. Eli didn't know what that meant. But they were all alive, at least for now.

She followed Tav. No one should have to face the Witch Lord alone.

The thread wound through the mad labyrinthine dollhouse of the Children's Lair, the signature fading and then flaring up again, sometimes disappearing entirely. But Eli's body, fused with the Heart, could always find it.

Eli followed the thread through rooms filled only with neon shoelaces and disposable cameras, through rooms that were giant pillow forts, soft blankets twisted into arches and portcullises. Through rooms that were bare stone with manacles in the wall, the rusted iron wrapped in flowering vines.

Each step took her closer to Tav. Closer to the Witch Lord. Closer to war.

The signature flared a fierce indigo, and Eli stopped in a room that was like a Barbie playhouse — if Barbie was both a princess and a dragon.

A hot pink vinyl beanbag chair sat in one corner, covered in swaths of fabrics and costumes. Gold and silver buttons spilled from a tulle tutu and onto the stone flooring. The shredded remains of a jean jacket decorated the floor like petals thrown over a bridal procession. A great vanity of mahogany took up one entire wall. It was covered in windup toys and robotics.

Eli had never been to Clytemnestra's chamber, and she fought the urge to give in to curiosity and look around — to rifle through the piles of silk and velvet and Lycra, to run her hands over the glittering diamante bottles of perfume and bubble solution. To steal an oxidized copper button or shoe buckle.

Eli moved closer to the vanity, to the great mirror that reflected back a girl with pure black eyes and knives that sparkled under the light of the lava lamp that perched on the edge of the armoire.

Gasoline and lavender. Traces of Tav. Eli closed her eyes and breathed it in. They had been here. They had stared at their reflection in this mirror as they had dressed for battle.

And then they crossed.

The door had closed behind them, but Eli could feel the seam. It was still healing, still leaking the smell of caramelized fruit and fear. Had Tav purposefully left it open for her to follow? Or was it simply that the fabric of a world with no Heart was thinning and fraying, the edges unravelling? The air felt thinner. Eli felt it would be easy to fall through the living walls and find herself in the forest, or the wastelands. The world was beginning to collapse.

But the Heart was home, if still hindered by a human-magic-machine body, still trapped in the shape of a flawed daughter. It was easy for the Heart to undo the loose and gaping stitches of the most powerful witch in the world.

All Eli had to do was let go, to release herself in every exhale, to fade into light and magic. It was a disappearing act that no one else in the galaxy could do.

The Heart slipped through the fold in the universe and followed the faint trail of smoky purple toward justice — and judgment.

THE HEALER

Kite sat on the throne, her claws curled around alabaster arms made out of shells and pearls and gleaming fish scales.

No, it wasn't Kite — it was Kite reflected in a warped mirror. Pupil-less eyes a little paler, with a tinge of coral; fingernails and teeth sharpened to deadly points.

But she smelled like the sea.

Tav understood, then, why it was so important to keep Eli away from her. Not just to protect the Heart — the Heart was a beast that hungered for revenge and freedom, that would drink the essence from this beautiful shell without hesitating — but because Eli was a liability.

Eli had been ready to meet an enemy, a monster, a nightmare — but not one that looked like a friend. Not one that took the shape of her lover.

The Witch Lord's frostbitten lips twisted into a cruel smile. She was enjoying Tav's discomfort. She must assume the dilated pupils and quickening of their carotid artery was from fear. But Tav was too shocked to be afraid.

Tav found themselves remembering Kite's touch and shuddered with disgust and desire. The Witch Lord's hands looked like Kite's. Would feel like Kite's. Would taste like Kite's.

All those years that Eli had pressed her body against Kite's. Was it all that different from touching the Witch Lord?

Kite's a different person, Tav told themselves, guilt crawling up their throat. *It's not her fault.*

All the pieces were falling into place: what made Kite's relationship with her mother different from Eli's; why so few witches had trueborn daughters, and instead cobbled them together out of orange peel and rusted hinges. Kite was not her mother's child — she was her clone. They shared an essence. Kite was the Witch Lord's extension and a replacement body. A second skin. A second set of eyes.

The horror of having a daughter so you could use and even steal her body rocked through Tav's bones like an earthquake, and the taste of rotten fish filled their mouth. Aftertaste of pity. Eli's mother had been greedy, selfish, and brutal. But a small part of her cared for her daughter. Kite had never been loved by anyone except Eli.

Movement made Tav's eyes flick from the Witch Lord to her throne, and they realized suddenly that nothing about it was dead — fish and crabs and anemone writhed and twisted, trying to escape the magic net that bound them in service to the Witch Lord. Tav swallowed the sickness in their mouth and felt the darkness settle in their stomach like lead.

"You have been honoured with an invitation to our celebration," said not-Kite. "Will you not drink with us?"

A figure swathed in white, eyes spinning like pinwheels behind a mask of blood-red silk, carried a thimble crafted from crystal. To the naked eye it appeared empty, but Tav could see the struggling drop of a witch's essence, greenblack, trapped in the vial. Where was the rest of the witch whose essence had been drained to feed the elite of the world?

They struggled not to visibly react, not to pull away or flinch. They kept their eyes wide open, like their mother when she put in contacts in the morning.

"What are we celebrating?" Tav asked, accepting the crystal, trying not to stare as a thread of acid green, light and airy as cotton candy, curled over the lip of the cup.

"The unification of the City of Eyes. The return of the wayward children to their kin. We feed together, and we will never go hungry."

As if on cue, a thousand hushed voices repeated, "We feed together, and we will never go hungry."

Tav nodded. "We feed together, and we will never go hungry." They raised the vial to their mouth and then stalled. "This glass is empty," they said, raising one eyebrow. "Did one of your servants get thirsty?"

After a strained moment, like the agony before the snapping of a violin string, not-Kite laughed, a harsh sound like a ship scraping rock. The rest of the Coven echoed her, a laughter like electronica and static, recorded and mixed and twisted into strangeness.

"It is a symbol of the power we will drink from our enemies and from our prey, to grow strong. Only the strong survive."

The crowd echoed: "Only the strong survive."

Silence fell. The Coven waited for Tav to drink.

The Coven waited to feed. The Coven was hungry.

Tav smiled and raised the vial, keeping their eyes on the Witch Lord's glowing orbs. The faint pink tinge was like a drop of blood in a cup of milk.

"To you," they said, and raised their voice. "To strength. To unity. To power." They turned to their bike, the inanimate contraption of gears and glass, filaments and spark plugs. "With the gift of this drink, and in honour of the Witch Lord, I christen you Ariel." *For you, Cam.*

They smashed the glass over the motorcycle.

The drop of essence from a poor witch, long since forgotten by her sisters, crawled into the skin of the motorbike. Ariel purred, the engine revving on its own. It was good to have a body again.

Tav knelt down, exposing more of their spine for a brief moment before looking up at the statue of the Witch Lord who seemed to emerge from the throne like the figurehead of a ship. If she was angry that Tav had not fallen for her trick, she did not let on. Her face was as blank and beautiful as tumbled amazonite.

Tav spoke, willing their words to sound as light and creamy as the gauzy fabric that cascaded from the Witch Lord's ethereal frame. "Will you honour me with a dance?"

The Witch Lord smiled. The needle-sharp teeth like sickly saplings promised imprisonment and starvation. She leaned forward, arching her long neck closer to the boi and their bike. The stench of salt was suddenly overwhelming, and Tav's eyes began to water.

The Witch Lord waved a hand lazily, and a throng of witches materialized before the throne. They wore masks of silver and copper, satin and lace, slate and shale, adorned with scalloped shells and razor blades, colourful feathers and strips of duct tape cut into tassels. The witches were soft feminine, butch, androgynous, hard femme, hipster masculine, and genteel dandies.

And underneath their fleshy exteriors, Tav could see the curling smoke of purplegrey, the coiled yellowgreen, the airy and shimmering pinkgold essences pulsing and dancing and fluttering through every eyelash and strand of hair.

"Choose," said the Witch Lord.

Tav turned again to take in the full brunt of those alien eyes, brimming with power — and something else. Calculation. Curiosity.

Clytemnestra told you that she likes to play games. You can't let her get bored. Clytemnestra's sending her soldiers into the Children's Lair now, this very second.

What if Clytemnestra's plan fails? What if we fail?

What will happen to Eli? To the Earth?

They already knew that this creature was not capable of mercy.

Panic flared up, hot and thick in their lungs. Tav bent over, gasping for breath. White candle wax splattered over a shining black square of polished onyx.

The witches watched silently and waited.

Tav stood and shook their head. "I choose you," they said simply. *Keep her interest. Buy them time. Kite will come.*

The Witch Lord frowned. The assembled witches seemed to become even more still, even less alive. Then she hissed, and steam poured from the gaps between her teeth.

Ariel revved her engine again in warning, or perhaps in fear. She remembered the wrath of the Witch Lord. Tav placed a hand on the warm leather seat, but the bike would not be soothed. The vibrations jumped to Tav's hand and jittered up and down their extended arm.

"You are not worthy," the Witch Lord finally said, each word falling like a guillotine.

Tav had made a mistake. They had been too bold, too daring. The Witch Lord wanted a game, but they wanted to run it. Tav's request had been too much of a challenge.

The air was thick with salt.

Tav's vision swam behind a veil of tears.

"I'm not worthy," they repeated, lowering their head. Maybe if they grovelled, they could draw out the execution.

A single tear fell from the damp, mucous membrane of their human eyes and plunged toward the ground.

Tav, keeping their eyes downcast in a show of reverence, watched the trajectory of the water droplet. It glittered under the pink chandeliers like a black diamond bathed in rose perfume. When it touched the onyx tile, it didn't break. Instead, it wobbled for a fraction of a second, and then extended, stretching across the tile, shifting, fading, changing, until the single tear was gone.

In its place was a glossy black feather.

The smell of salt retreated. Tav glanced up — the Witch Lord had pulled back in surprise. She rested her elbow on the writhing spine of an eel and contemplated Tav again, looking them up and down.

She waved her hand and the witches vanished, flowing back to their poses behind pillars and next to tapestries. Everything in the room was art, a decoration for the Witch Lord's palace.

Tav remembered the taste of witchfire, the ash and despair that had lingered on their tongue for days after escaping the Coven with the Heart. They wondered where the witches of the first ring were lurking, those closest to the throne, and most deadly — were they hiding in the underbelly of the Coven, waiting to strike? Were they leading malicious magics and enslaved essences into the Labyrinth?

Were they dressed in furs and wrapping paper, watching Tav behind masks of barbed wire and begonia, hiding among the sycophants?

The Witch Lord flowed down the throne, and Tav's lungs struggled for oxygen as the sea washed over them.

"You should be careful what you ask for," she said, and offered a hand.

Tav took it. The Witch Lord's hand burned like ice and the kind of loneliness that turns geometry protractors and broken rulers into weapons in girls' bathrooms.

Tav flinched at their touch, at the way the Witch Lord seemed to find their most painful memories and play the bruises like a world-class pianist. They knew immediately that the flinch was a mistake — the Witch Lord smiled, and Tav thought, *If she keeps smiling like that, I will find myself headless, and the witches will feed.*

But that will not curb their hunger.

Dimly, they realized that an orchestra had materialized, cellos and violins playing themselves. A waltz played at an impossible speed. The pink lights burned brighter, and a headache split across Tav's skull.

"I'll lead, Messenger," said the Witch Lord. Their voice was a net scouring the ocean floor. It sounded so much like Kite's — a soprano and mezzo intertwining to create a hypnotic harmony. Her hand on Tav's waist left the tingling itchiness and pain of jellyfish stings. She leaned closer, her lips to Tav's ear. "You should not have trusted the Warlord. I don't think you will enjoy this."

The dance began.

THE HEART

The Heart looked around the ancient cavern, feelings she was unaccustomed to stretching through every synapse in her cramped body.

Fear. Confusion. Panic.

Witches drifted through the space, glowing with life-force. Giant pillars of black marble rose out of the tiled floor like oceanside cliffs.

To the Heart, the witches were like dandelion seeds cast about by the wind. No more important than a pebble, no less important than an ocean. She turned away from the revelry to the living, breathing, feeling, hurting, hating structure itself.

The building that had once been the Heart's reluctant prison.

The Heart looked up into the vaulted ceiling. Cracks snaked through the stone. Ruin was everywhere. No amount of gold leaf paint could hide it. She drifted away from the chessboard adorned with pieces of lacquer and gold. She needed to face the place where she had been imprisoned for so many revolutions through the galaxy. The darkness that had kept her bound and had isolated her, had choked off her freedom. The place where her power had been drunk like thin, sugary sap.

She walked through walls, shells, the carcasses of animals of all kinds.

The roots caught fire. Her tree-daughter was screaming, the pain arching up and down the bark of her spine. The Heart was helpless, unable to rescue her.

The pain would teach her to behave, to stop reaching out with wishes and seed and shadows. To stop trying to touch every part of the planet.

Mouths on her limbs, sucking, draining the pure, raw honey of lifeblood from her trunk. Draining the world.

The memories surged like a shot of adrenalin, the stinging bite of a needle in skin and the aching hurt of trauma that was never past, and always now.

Now. Now. Now.

Gasping for breath, fumbling with the alien shape of bronchioles and trachea, the Heart flowed through this strange, dark space that smelled of hatred and apathy and something else … something familiar …

Sea salt. The island. Hands stroking her hair. The golden leaves from ancient sycamores raining over her body leaving patterns like gold leaf pressed into her skin.

Eli turned and saw crystals of salt on the cavern walls, like fingerprints left by a wayward Heir who dared to love a made-thing.

The panic stopped, and in its absence was a void that quickly filled with numbness. The exhaustion of a soul in pain blotting all out all other colours, feelings, thoughts.

"We're okay," said Eli. "We're okay."

"No," said the Heart. "We're not."

Eli flickered into existence for a moment, scraping her hand against the sharp edge of a shell trapped in dirt. She stared at the trickle of blood and thought how strange it was that after all this time, after all the magic that had gone into her making, she could still bleed.

"We're not okay," she said again, closing her bloody hand into a fist. The truth settled onto her body like starlight over the fields of the moon civilization that had once shone across an entire world. When she opened her palm again, the scratch had been closed by a seam of quartz that glittered under the dim glow of phosphorescent moss.

Not all wounds are empty; some grow gardens.

THE HEIR

The Coven was falling apart. Dead leaves littered the ground; vines were withered and moulding on the wall. Kite reached up and touched a white starflower. The petals burst from the stamen in that final exhale of death and crumbled to fine powder as they fell. She raised her stained fingers to her nose and breathed in. Smell of rot and fear.

Without the Heart, the Coven was dying.

All that knowledge, all those handprints and memories and passions, ground under her feet. Lost forever.

She licked her thumb, grimacing a little at the acidic taste of an empty home. It wasn't too late. There was still time to save it.

Kite closed her eyes and pressed her body against the wall. Behind her, the army waited.

Water began to leak from the stone; just a trickle at first, but then a steady stream, flooding the hallway. Higher and higher it rose; tiny crustaceans and little electric blue fish swam eagerly in this strange new world.

Leading the rush of water and foam, the froth of algae and dead skin and water skimmers, Kite made her way toward the ballroom, ready to face her wicked, twisted destiny.

THE HEART

The stale air of the caverns tasted of melancholy, as if the Coven itself was in mourning.

Someone was going to die, and the Coven knew it.

And not just anyone — so many lives had been sacrificed to the Witch Lord's greed, her thirst for control, her need for power.

The one marked for death was someone the Coven loved.

Eli stumbled forward, trying to keep herself together, trying to stay invisible, just a breath passing through a lung. Shadow and light.

Water lapped against her feet. Not bile excreted from an old stalactite; not the tears of a crystal.

Water.

And there were waves. There was movement. The water was moving as if guided by a little moon.

Eli only knew one person who could call the tides, who could coax tears from sand and dirt. Only one person who walked through the Coven with gentle footsteps.

How could the Heir defeat her own mother? How could she give back her birthright, the power she had been born into?

She couldn't.

Eli didn't know what was going to happen, but she knew, deep in the unfurled buds of her being, that Kite was in attendance tonight, and that she didn't expect to come out of it alive.

What was Clytemnestra playing at? Why had she sent two sacrifices to the Witch Lord? Kite and Tav. A girl with salt on her tongue and a boi with oil stains on their jeans.

Eli could lose everyone she loved tonight.

We could lose more than that. The Heart's thought pooled like warm honey in her mind. *We could lose the whole world.*

Eli was a ghostly figure of shadow and light that sometimes flickered with the hint of bone, the coy arch of a rib, or the playful curve of an eyelash. She was the Heart. And her planet was dying.

Eli wondered what would happen if she surrendered to the honeygold warmth that flowed through her veins, letting her skin and stone and glass evaporate into dusk and earth. Maybe the world could be saved. Maybe it wasn't too late to save the forest and the walls and the deserts from the Witch Lord's destruction. Maybe if the Heart returned, it could pulse new life into the crumbling core.

But that wouldn't save Kite or Tav, and the Heart was still a body, still a girl, still a lover. The Heart felt the human fear that sang through her marrow like a melody.

The Heart turned around and went back — back to the room with the pillars of ice, back to the decaying cavern, to the mouth of the beast, to the lair where the Witch Lord puppeteered the death of celestial bodies.

Eli had one last thing to do before she died.

THE HEIR

Kite used to tell time by the paper cuts on her hands, using the marks to remind herself to raise her head from the books, to go for walk in the woods, to lie on the secret island she shared with her secret friend. Now the webbing between her fingers was smooth, and her wrists were forgetting the weight of leather and fibre.

As she brought a drowning to the Coven, as she came to bury and to save, she kept seeing glimpses of paper cranes stamped in a forgotten font; of tulips and roses blooming with ink; of a staircase that was ridged like a spine.

When she had a vision of paper and vellum, Kite closed her eyes and pretended she was a salmon swimming back to its place of birth. She brought a flood that was salty with the bodies that had lived and died in the Coven since the first animal breathed on their planet.

She worried about water damage. Mould was death to a book.

No, there wasn't time for her fears, and she had to trust in the library, in the knowledge that changed and hid and let itself be forgotten and remembered again. She would trust in transformation.

The water was up to her knees now. She brought the flood. She brought destruction. She brought change.

Behind her came the children with plastic forks and ceramic shards, barbecue lighters and slingshots; buttons and doll's eyes for ammunition; dirty hands and flexible spines and an innate knowledge of how to shatter.

Behind her came the daughters, their eyes carved from alabaster or plucked from taxidermied lynxes, their bodies sparking like electric eels or glowing with phosphorous; girls like blades, needles, arrows, shields, and shells; girls who smelled of chamomile and acetone, sumac and sesame and gunpowder. Girls with axes woven with stained glass and barbed wire, with spears of smoke and flame, with harpoons crafted from stinging nettle and porcupine quills dipped in ammonia.

Behind her came the discarded things, the monsters of scrap metal and succulents, creatures of corduroy and rust and shadow. The other objects who had followed

Kite away from the wastelands had bonded with the soldiers, and many of the children and daughters now wore crowns of asphalt or breastplates of crystal and tire tread.

As they moved through the tunnels slowly filling with water, their footsteps wrote stories with eddies and waves, the white froth in their wake a prophecy for someone else to read.

The Heir walked toward her execution with the grace of a single water lily in a stagnant pool.

THE HEALER

Tav and the Witch Lord twirled through the ballroom as hundreds of sycophants dressed in broken glass and tarmac watched, their eyes gleaming like polished stones.

"What are you?" the Witch Lord whispered, eyes glittering like winter frost under an angry sun. Tav's eyes watered under the harsh brightness. There was something horribly compelling about her — Tav could smell the dead fish on her skin, and yet felt the urge to lean closer, to catch every word, to let themselves shrivel and blister under her gaze.

"What are *you*?" they responded, watching the multihued essence writhe within its shell as if trying to tear itself apart.

The mood changed. The room darkened, the crystal chandeliers shaking violently. The sound was a warning. The Witch Lord's eyes turned storm grey, and a bolt of lightning flashed across them.

"You have not yet earned the right to ask me a question, sacrifice," she hissed.

The sickly greengold hue of the Witch Lord's essence made Tav's stomach twist. They wanted to pull away from her. They wanted to be the sacrifice. They wanted to let her drink them. They wanted to run away. They wanted to join her essence, to lose themselves in her sea.

They were in over their head.

"I am a visitor from another world," they said finally. It was the truth — but the aftertaste of metal and dish soap told them it was only partially the truth.

"You smell delicious," the Witch Lord crooned, her claws tightening on Tav's shoulder, biting skin. Tav clenched their teeth and fought the urge to flinch.

"You smell like the sea," they said.

The cavern remained dark, and in the faint pink light the shadows appeared red and bloody. No longer a ballroom but the site for an execution.

She's like a cat, they thought dimly. *She likes to play with her food.*

They felt the moment a fingernail broke skin, but it wasn't the pain or the blood leaking from their shoulder that Tav needed to worry about. It was the essence that had turned the colour of frostbitten lichen and was inching toward them, calling to something deep inside them. Tav looked down and saw a glow of purple and black flickering in their chest.

"Yes, that's a good boi," the Witch Lord purred. "Come and join me. With me, you will be strong."

A thought broke the surface of the ocean they were drowning in. "Why do we have to be strong?" they murmured. "Why do we need to be stronger? Aren't we strong enough?"

"We need our strength, child." Her was mouth at Tav's ear. The smell of putrid fish was stronger now. Tav's mouth began to water. "We can use our strength to make this world great again. To rescue it from the reckless children. To save the world. To save ourselves. Until we are strong, we will be at risk. Don't you want to be safe?"

Safety. The word rippled the pool of Tav's murky, swampy thoughts. Images, memory, theirs and others', passed down through stories and blood and DNA.

Bodies tossed over the side of the ship.

Cops asking for ID, one hand on a gun.

Hands shoving them into lockers.

"Are we still on the Middle Passage?" they asked, staring past the witch's skin and into the sea of gold and hunger that promised pleasure and pain and, above all, obliteration. Was crossing the stars all that different from crossing the Atlantic?

"I will keep you safe." Damp breath like mist on their neck. In the darkness, the eyes of the other witches burned like embers as Tav spun past them, turning around and around at the whim of the Witch Lord. Dizziness broke over their body likes waves, and they lost all sense of place.

Where were they? Why were they here?

What does it mean, to be safe?

A single thread of greygreen essence touched Tav. Other images flashed across their vision, flooding their senses — a world crumbling into ash, the taste of smoke and sugar on their tongue; the screaming of stone being ground into powder; the lifeless eyes of the daughters and children. Then there was only pain, and they were drowning, lungs collapsing from the pressure of the ocean, their heart ready to burst from adrenalin and fear.

And then everything stopped. Tav's breath came in short bursts. A heartbeat pounding in their head. A migraine squeezing their skull.

Redpink streaks painting the cavern of stone into prison bars of light.

They were alive. They were whole.

What happened?

"You hurt me," said the Witch Lord, shock sparking from her entire being. Tav stared in horror at the single burn mark in the shape of a perfect circle etched below her clavicle.

Tav remembered the dreams of destruction. That wasn't their idea of safety. Someone else's subjugation was no one's freedom.

The Witch Lord's grip tightened on Tav's wrist, manacles clamping down. "If you won't come willingly, you will still come." But Tav heard the underbelly of fear and marvelled at it. When was the last time the Witch Lord felt pain?

Did she enjoy it?

Keep the game interesting. Clytemnestra is coming. They won't leave you here. Eli needs you.

Tav let themselves be drawn closer to the witch. "Have you figured it out yet?" they breathed in her ear, which was lined with black pearls. They tried to wrestle their panicked heart into some kind of rhythm. "Do you know what I am? What I can offer you? Do you know why Clytemnestra sent me?"

The Witch Lord said nothing, just considered the strange human-magic hybrid in her arms. Her essence was now a deep rose with a blueblack shimmer. It matched the room she had made to trap and play with other creatures.

An engine revved from one side of the ballroom, reminding Tav that they weren't alone. So they took another risk, hoping it wouldn't be their last.

"Did you like it, when I touched your essence?"

The Witch Lord drew lines in red on Tav's back, the movement of her fingernails retracing a map of intergenerational trauma and reopening more recent wounds.

The haunted orchestra continued to play, the music reminiscent of a waltz — but it sounded like a symphony on acid overlaid with the sounds of grinding teeth and cicadas.

"We will finish our dance," the Witch Lord said finally. "And you will show me your secrets. Then I will eat you."

Tav didn't need Eli's frost blade to tell them the Witch Lord was speaking the truth.

Tav kept their eyes on the burn mark on her chest, hoping that their body held other secrets that could save them.

THE HEIR

The water was up to her thighs now. The shimmering coils of her skirts floated around her limbs like the stingers of a jellyfish. And still the Coven wept, offering every bit of moisture to Kite's procession.

She was the Witch Lord's weakness. Her betrayal would hurt; and her death, when it came, would scar. After all — Kite's pain was the Witch Lord's pain. They were the same.

She looked down at her pale blue skin and watched the glimmer of whitegold swim across the surface of her left knee. Stolen power. A kind of necromancy.

The Beast had taken the form of a feathered dragonbird and perched on her left shoulder. He nuzzled against her neck. She had told him to stay behind in the Children's

Lair, but he was stubborn. "Try not to die, my sweet," she whispered. He chewed on her hair.

She hoped the children would make a new world worthy of being remembered.

The flow of water around her ankles changed; she turned her head and caught the scent of rosehips and ferocity. The white marks on the made-daughter's brown skin were like drops of bleach. If Kite was stupid, she would reach over and trace a constellation between the pale freckles. But Kite was not stupid.

The assassin. The first one she had found, dismembered, in the depths of the Coven. The one she had put back together. The one who now led the small coalition of daughters who had been recovered through Kite's alchemy or who had fled their mothers and been welcomed in the Children's Lair. The one who would take no name.

The unnamed stared at the Heir, her white eye smooth and clear as cream. The gold power in Kite's body surged toward that eye, the eye that absorbed power and used it to heal. Kite's essence wanted to steal that magic, but she forced the urge down.

"They left their mothers for this fight," the unnamed said. "The daughters that march with us."

"We have that in common," said Kite.

"When this is over, we will be free. We serve no master. Not even you."

"No one will serve me." The truth fell easily from Kite's lips, like water gushing from a fountain.

"We want your promise that you will not interfere with us."

"Do you speak for them?"

"No one speaks for us. I speak only for myself." The words emerged as a canine growl from the back of her throat.

"Then I give you my word." Kite leaned closer, her hair dancing around the coyote-girl's neck. The gold magic urged her to *drink*, but Kite ignored the whispers of a tyrant that sang in her DNA. "And the word is *named*."

The Unnamed's human pupil widened, and a single ripple travelled through the white sucking orb.

"A word and a secret," she purred softly, her voice velvet paws on soft underbrush. "I accept."

What would the unnamed do with this knowledge, that the Heir was not a full witch, that she had lied to her mother, that she truly was one of the children? What would she do with the knowledge that Kite had accepted a name from a part-human daughter, a name Eli had read in the taste of her sea-thick blood?

Kite felt the confession tingle on her tongue and lips like lime and chili juice, but once she had offered it to the coyote-girl she felt steadier, as if her bird-bones were thickening, as if she was growing scales. Becoming more herself.

It was time for secrets to be revealed, for notes crumpled in back pockets to be taken out, smoothed flat, and read.

The time for crawling through filthy tunnels and hiding behind serrated smiles was over.

The time for truth — in all its ugliness and magnificence and violence — was now.

"I hope you survive," Kite told the unnamed.

"Not even death could kill me." A feral smile. It was the curve of a wave the moment its mouth closed around land.

The touch of water on Kite's feet shifted, the only sign that the assassin had fallen back to walk with her sisters. She had been silent as an eclipse.

The Unnamed's smile was contagious, and Kite offered a toothy grin to the darkness.

Bluegreen and goldwhite glowed in her body.

The flood rose.

THE HEART

When the Heart touched the crumbling limestone, she felt like her entire being was strummed by invisible fingers. If she pressed herself into the wall, she could feel the Coven responding to her energy, like hands grasping for something to hold on to.

The Coven guided her back through shifting passages of bone and steel and stone, past stalactites of pale ice encasing fallen stars and stalagmites of marble and beeswax. Phosphorescent moss wrote mathematical equations in blue and indigo and coral light.

The Coven knew where the Heart was needed, and drew her along like a beacon. She didn't need her made-eyes to see the threads of violet and black flame. She knew where she was, and it was not just a reluctant prison. The Coven was older than the Witch Lord, almost as old as the Heart itself.

As she moved through the space, invisible except for the ribbons of shadow and light that wound themselves around her limbs, Eli was no longer a girl with caffeine cravings and a fear of abandonment; no longer a passionate lover or a scared kid. She was something older, deeper, and stranger. She was a spectre of bright and dark, a star, a planet, a breath of air, a sea-changing wind, the roots of a sapling in damp soil, the chlorophyll pigment of the tiniest leaf. An ending and a beginning.

She was the Heart.

The Coven led her to the war room. Once, it had another name. The Heart remembered the silver birch leaves pressed into stone, the fingerprints of children mapping out constellations on the wall. The tide pools of healing and knowledge overflowing with sand and shells and feathers. Once, every part of the Coven had been a library, a sacred place of knowledge. Once, it had been open to the whole world, to every beast and rock and gust of wind that passed through.

But the tide pools were gone, long dried up. The birch leaves had been torn down, the fingerprints burned away. The war room was dressed in pink crystals and wrapped with shadows, a pretty gift that promised faithlessness.

There were many bodies in the room; some visible, others shielded by glamour and wishes. Eli could see the burnt umber colour of their desires, could almost taste the peppermint aftertaste of their dreams in the back of her throat.

Eli loved all these bodies. Every essence, every ankle, every blade and piece of earth. They were hers, and she was their Heart.

From where she stood, Eli could make out the members of the upper rings drifting around the edges of the dance floor like lanterns, only floating heads, their bodies shrouded in light. At the far end of the room was the throne, which reminded her of the junkyard. Objects, piled onto each other, forced together, shattered and broken and beautiful, formed a throne made of sea-glass and sheets of oxidized copper folded into sensuous curves. The spokes of a rusted bicycle stabbed through hundreds of damp plastic bags. A doll's head, the hair matted and dirty, was affixed to the skeleton of a fish. A throne made of flotsam.

Her eyes trailed upward, following the strands of seaweed that were still damp — living and growing from the throne. The crystal chandeliers were trembling.

And then she saw Tav.

Tav blazed into focus, bright and hot and fierce. They were dressed in black and gold, and looked more like a mythical creature than a human with spiky hair. Eli could taste the steel on her tongue, and her human senses came flooding back. She was still invisible, still a ghostly figure of energy and intention. But she was also a lovesick girl missing her broken blade.

Eli had come here to save Tav, but she had been mistaken: Tav did not need saving. They were not the weak one. Proud in their vulnerability, burning with black-and-purple flames, the ghost of feathers following their footsteps, Tav was as terrifying as any of the witches.

What were they?

They were a god.

(Gods were stories humans told each other to make sense of the chaos and beauty that shaped and unravelled their pieces of dirt. Eli was often more human than she liked to admit.)

They opened a hole in you, Eli thought, hand going to her chest. *They reached inside the Heart and survived.*

Tav moved between worlds like it was nothing. They had channelled the power of the Heart. And now they danced with the Witch Lord as an equal. They — not Clytemnestra, not Kite, not Eli — held the power to heal or destroy worlds.

The Heart was drawn to them, to the fine bones of their wrists and the magic essence that was more like wings than honey. The Heart had always been drawn to them, but Eli thought it had been her desire that animated every touch, every look, every press of her skin against Tav's. But maybe the Heart knew that only Tav could free it from its shell, from the broken husk of a weapon that no longer had a purpose.

What did Tav need Eli for? She was only a vessel for the Heart. A thing. No one. Pride struggled with fear as the invisible girl watched a god moving in a dangerous dance, every step an act of war, an elegant pattern of parries and lunges glittering with gold. Without the Heart, Eli would be no one again. A broken tool. A flawed weapon. She would never be powerful enough to be Tav's equal. She needed to keep the Heart to deserve their touch, to be worthy of their love. Eli felt herself begin to fall, again, into to the endless cosmos of the Heart.

She was not a person, not a girl, not someone.

She was the light that the trees drank thirstily. She was the calcium in the stone. She was the decaying bones and flesh of dead animals rotting under the soil. She was —

Tav made a sudden turn, and Eli's eyes fell on the Witch Lord, the rival god, the nameless horror who used made-daughters like windup toys and cast them aside when they were broken. The villain in the fairy tale.

She knew that face.

She had kissed that face.

She loved that face.

Kite.

Eli inhaled sharply, smelling blood and sea salt, and reality came rushing back in. Dizziness overwhelmed her body as she became suddenly and unbearably real.

The room wavered.

Ever-burning essences, floating heads, and thousands of eyes stared at the intruder standing in the centre of a black-and-white checkered floor.

Eli had materialized.

The moment before the witches descended, Eli felt a stab of regret at her mistake, at her arrogance for thinking she could control this body, for thinking that she had become invincible.

She had delivered the Heart right into the hands of the Witch Lord.

THE HEALER

Tav felt Eli's presence a split second before she materialized, her entrance heralded by a memory of crushed petals and honey. Tav saw Eli's reflection in the glossy pearls that served as eyes in the Witch Lord's face, saw the moment the serene mask twisted with hunger.

The Witch Lord was done playing with the mouse; she had a Heart to capture, and this time it would be harder than trapping a firefly in a jar. She let go of Tav and reached for Eli, her silverpinkgoldgreen essence pouring from her mouth like a swarm of silverfish.

Tav had never seen a witch extend their essence from their body; they knew they could shed their skin, but the process was painful and made them vulnerable. But the Witch Lord had magic that no one else did.

Tav did the only thing they could think of — they grabbed the Witch Lord's wrist and pulled her back. The essence split over Tav's body, shuddering away from a stray feather that had fallen from Tav's hair and onto their shoulder.

It was afraid to touch them.

The essence re-entered the bluegreen nymph who still looked so heartbreakingly like Kite that Tav found it unnerving.

"You promised to eat me first," said Tav.

"I'll let you live if you bring her to me," said the Witch Lord.

"No." Tav's grip tightened. They imagined their hand as a door closing shut over flesh and magic, trapping the Witch Lord's body and essence. They imagined their fingers as the gears of a lock intertwining. There was no key. Their magic flared up, fusing to the Witch Lord's, and iron shavings scattered across the floor.

The pearly eyes gleamed in the red light, and the Witch Lord smiled. Her wrist grew spines, and then scales, scratching and piercing Tav's palm. But they held on. They were a closed door. A thousand tiny spiders appeared on the Witch Lord's skin and crawled over Tav's hand and up their arm. Tav held on, staring into the Witch Lord's eyes.

Just a bit longer, they thought. Sweat stained their shirt, and their breathing was ragged. *Just hold on a bit longer.* Their shoulder blades started to itch horribly.

The Witch Lord's hand was a bear paw, and then

a raven's claw, and then a mass of writhing, wriggling earthworms.

Still, Tav held on.

"How are you doing this?" The anger clouded her eyes with silt.

"I make doors," said Tav. "And I close them."

THE HEART

The Witch Lord's servants were everywhere. Eli was surrounded. As she watched the witches close in, her heartbeat returned like a roar, thrumming to the melody of panic that raced through her body. The intense emotion rattled a rosebud in her chest cavity, and she felt it open.

The Coven had found her. She would never escape them. They would force her back into a prison made of paper chains and darkness. They would tear her apart and feed her to the walls.

Not again. Never again.

We are the Heart!

The first witch was foolish, drunk on orchid wine and sugared centipedes, and when she reached for the delicious Heart, the aorta of a star, it burned through her veins and she collapsed onto the floor in a pile of sawdust.

The other witches drew back. A few looked over at the Witch Lord. Only she had the power to overthrow the world. But she was still held in the embrace of something that was not quite human, not quite witch. Something they were starting to think they should be afraid of.

Eli was still an assassin, still a made-thing, and she wasn't ready to give up. She drew two blades — pearl and bone — and turned in a slow, deliberate circle. One eye black, the other yellow.

"The Witch Lord will not save you," she said. Her voice was strange to her — richer and deeper, the sound of wings fluttering and leaves shaking in the wind; the timbre of tree branches cracking and lightning striking. The voice of the Heart.

Punishment or mercy?

"Leave now," she told them. "And we won't kill you."

Mercy, then.

I want to hurt them, Eli thought.

They are my children, the Heart thought back.

The floating lanterns of the first ring were coming nearer, hovering just out of reach.

"Capture her," they told the room. "Capture her and we will never go hungry."

The audience stood, unsure, shards of glass reflecting the pink bordello lighting. Masks of feathers and scales, computer chips and drywall, all turned toward the girl with her blades, the eyes underneath glittering with curiosity.

And then the wall cracked. The great stone slab of the war room that had once been a place of healing broke open. Water leaked from the crack, dripping down the walls. Streaks of salt like lace patterned the grey stone.

First a trickle, and then more. Water gushed through the crumbling stone. Soon the crack was a chasm, the stone falling apart. Pages poured through the gap, forgotten books falling from the sky and climbing out of the bedrock of the Coven. A flood of ink and water and paper.

The Witch Lord's second body climbed through the gap.

THE HEALER

Tav watched the Witch Lord's face as Kite climbed through the jagged crack in the wall, scraps of damp paper stuck in her hair, a starfish clinging to her thigh. There was no emotion, only calculation. There had been much more feeling in the Witch Lord's body when Tav had burned her.

"She can't hurt me. I am her," whispered the Witch Lord. "Our fates are twined together. When I die, so does she. Will your made-thing be happy with you when her playmate is dead?"

Tav's grip slipped for a fraction of a moment — but that was all it took.

"I'll come back for you," breathed the Witch Lord, and then she was gone, and Tav was holding an empty sac of skin and bones. They saw a fiercely glowing light, dark and green as the bottom of the sea, and then her essence was gone.

"Fuck," said Tav. They yanked their mask off and tossed it into the growing puddle on the floor. Then they went looking for their motorcycle.

THE HEIR

A prism of light circling her head.

You will die if I die, it told Kite.

"I know," said Kite.

A pause, and the light circled her body once, as if inspecting it for damage.

I understand. I would have done the same in your place. You have my ambition. But you were only another body for me. Your mistake was thinking you were a person.

"I am a person," said Kite.

The essence of the Witch Lord ignored her daughter, and instead drove another blade into Kite's heart, having discovered in her inspection the only weak spot in an otherwise perfect creation.

Will she still love you now that she knows what you really are?

Kite looked over to where Eli was cornered by the floating heads of the first ring. Fear boiled up in her body, and the water steamed and bubbled around her waist. A piece of sodden paper caught her eye, a fragment of forgotten poetry floating at the surface of the water. Something about love and pain.

"I —" She turned back to the light, but it was gone. The Witch Lord had escaped.

Kite felt guiltily relieved that she was still alive.

THE HEART

Chaos.

The Coven was drowning in ink and salt. Children chewed on the necks of witches, daughters cutting through flesh and magic with weapons cobbled together from junk and desperation.

Some of the witches fled, shedding their skins and retreating farther into the Coven, trying to outrun the bloodlust of the children. Others stayed and fought, using the shattered pieces of their costumes as makeshift weapons, using magic to ensnare and mislead their kin. Glamours of monsters and ghostly sandcastles and silk slips danced with spears and sharpened fingernails, bodies coming together and apart, ebbing and flowing like a tide crashing against a cliff.

Drops of blood were left behind from each encounter on the checkered floor — there a piece of amber, there a fleck of neon paint. Golden dew, cumulonimbus clouds, and mouldy pennies were shed as the magical armies threw themselves against each other again and again.

So much death.

The Heart couldn't watch. It was breaking Eli, the pain of so much suffering blocking out all other thoughts, feelings, desires.

The world was dying, and she had failed to save it.

She forgot who she was, and what she was doing there; she forgot about Tav and Kite and the Witch Lord; she disappeared into shadow, mourning the dead with a light that burned as dim as the stub of a candle.

And then she was gone, falling through time and space, lost in the maze of the Coven, lost in her own nightmares.

THE HEIR

The battle raged around her. Kite stood like a single water lily in the flood. She watched as a made-daughter was torn apart by several older witches. They started chewing on her bones.

The water lapped against her hips as it rushed through the broken wall and poured into the war room. Words in serif typeface and words handwritten in ancient languages brushed against her thighs.

Kite turned her palms and face to the sky, eyes closed, basking in the light and shadow that played across her skin. For a moment everything was still and silent; the sound of breath and sweat muffled by centuries of dust and knowledge. She blocked out the chaos and focused only on the words, only on the feeling of vellum against her cheek.

She knew this place. The Coven was her home. She had grown up with paper cuts and paper airplanes, with notebooks bound in leather that still remembered being animal, with myths and epics scrawled on the backs of receipts and sociology papers.

They had followed her from their prison, slipping through the cracks in walls, wrapping their pages around her hair and fingertips. She was covered in text.

Kite knew that the skeleton of the Coven was made of poetry and feeling.

She pushed away the power to command that danced in her veins, the stolen strength that swam in the marrow of her bones. Her mother's magic.

But Kite was not her mother, even if they shared a face. Even if they shared an essence. They had made different choices. They had fallen in love with different objects.

Please, she asked. *Please fight with us.*

The books came to life.

The papers folded themselves into an army of birds, all shapes borrowed and stolen from the City of Ghosts — cranes and pelicans, crows and ravens, small hummingbirds that moved so quickly they were only a blur; paper and cloth eagles with wingspans longer than a body.

"I love you," whispered Kite, and tears of ink dripped down her face.

She dropped her hands.

Pages ripped themselves from volumes older than planets. The sound of broken spines and damaged bindings filled the room; the carcasses of ruined covers littered the earth.

Kite had declared a side, and the library had declared with her.

The birds fell on the witches, slicing through the flesh and magic essence of the Coven's minions with a thousand paper cuts, each feather lacerating the bodies of her mother's army.

The witches shrieked in pain, the fine cuts welling with black-and-silver blood; some of the cuts smoked or burned or spat hot sparks, catching the wingtip of a peregrine falcon and sending it up in flames, its history lost forever,

Kite wiped her face with the back of one hand, ink mixing with saltwater. Her hands up to her elbows were black and slick, as if dipped in diesel oil.

Clytemnestra fell out of the sky, laughing uncontrollably.

"Burn it down!" she cried as she tumbled through the air, her golden ringlets a tangled nest on her head. Her skin was pink and unblemished as if newborn.

Kite wondered why it had taken her so long to join the battle.

A paper albatross caught the tiny witch midfall, or perhaps midflight, and carried her across the cavernous ballroom. Reaching into her many pockets, Clytemnestra grabbed fistfuls of jacks and iron nails and chips of obsidian, throwing them like confetti over the partygoers.

Kite watched her soar through the crumbling stronghold, envy irritating her vocal cords. The Warlord was ecstatic, caught in the revelry of violence and passion. Clytemnestra's essence pulsed brighter than any other prism of light in the room.

She was a shooting star, a beacon of hope soaked in sandalwood cologne and blood, a float in a parade — the kind with a million balloons that sometimes burst and cause infants to cry.

And Kite was a historian watching what she treasured most sacrifice themselves to fire and water. Watching the ink drain from their wings. Her hair curled into question marks of loss.

An origami periwinkle fell from her hair and Kite caught it in her hand. It unfolded its petals and Kite saw that it was a note Eli had left for her on the island a long time ago. A single word, a simple question, holding within it a universe of meaning, a history of limbs and tongues intertwined, a secret cache of promises and shared dreams.

Tomorrow?

Kite stared at the word for a long moment. Then she curled her fist around the note, and felt her skin absorb the ink, felt the question mark settle into her sternum. Then she opened her hand again and let the blank sheet tumble into the waves.

Kite took a breath, and then launched herself into the battle.

THE HEALER

Ariel purred at their touch, the witch-infused bike recognizing the texture of Tav's palm on its leather seat, responding to the timbre of their voice as they leaned close to the painted mermaid and whispered, "We got this, okay, girl?"

Ariel revved her engine in excitement and emitted a cloud of exhaust.

Tav climbed on, adrenalin shrieking in their tendons and ligaments. Gripped the handlebars. Took a deep breath, letting their rib cage expand. One of the glass buttons on their vest popped off. Tav looked down and realized that the remaining buttons were shaped like the phases of the moons. The one they had lost was the waning gibbous.

It felt like a sign. They were a waxing moon, chasing away the darkness.

They looked out over the sea of bodies — bodies of text, bodies of water, flesh-and-bone bodies, incorporeal beings of heat and magic and comet tails. Looking for a girl who was like a knife. A girl with two hearts.

The Witch Lord wanted the Heart. So Tav had to go after the Witch Lord. No way in hell were they letting Eli get torn apart by some poor-quality photocopy of Kite.

An albatross made out of tissue paper and twine swooped down beside them. Clytemnestra tossed a small package in their direction. It was wrapped in newsprint and tied with black ribbon.

"A gift from the Heir," she said with a wink, her eyelids painted deep plum and gold. "She didn't seem to think she'd be able to deliver it herself."

Tav tore open the paper and the obsidian dagger fell into their hand. Before they could open their mouth to thank her, the girl and bird dove back into the fray, the blue-and-pink wings like the sails of a great ship.

The key turned in the ignition of its own accord. Tav and Ariel took off, weaving through the chaos, leaving the battlefield behind.

Going deeper into the catacombs of the Coven.

They were going on a witch hunt.

THE HEART

So much death.

So much destruction.

Where was she? Who was she? Why was she here?

Everything was dark and cold.

The light of her body moved into the space like a child moving into their bunk at camp, marvelling at the spiders and leaves and the whimpering of small animals at dusk.

Books. Stacks and rows and piles and towers and caverns of books. The light of the Heart kept exploring farther and farther, making visible the gold stitching here, a fragment of prose there — *sunflowers at midnight* and *salt, everywhere, beloved* — until all Eli could see were pages of history and promises of love that had never been fulfilled.

This was Kite's home.

A rustling spilled from above and cascaded down like the rush of a waterfall. The pages were moving; fluttering, shaking. It wasn't a welcoming sound.

Eli remembered this place. She had been a child, with cracks in her stone palms and scratches on her hawthorn knees, heart full of death and lungs full of fear. The place had smelled like witches, and something older and far more powerful. It smelled of empires built and fallen, of sadness sweet as honey and worlds bursting with colour and heat.

This was why Kite left her. This was the place that stood between her and the witch-heir, this room, these living words whispering their secrets in a voice Eli could never understand.

The ink had burned her witch-made body, and Eli had lashed out, thinking to protect herself, but really — she knew, now, and could admit the truth — to destroy the one thing Kite loved more than herself.

Sometimes she still dreamed of paper cuts on her wrists, of the weight of tomes on her chest, and woke up, gasping, reaching for saltwater hair and seaweed-touched hands.

"I remember you," she told the library. The rustling grew louder, a storm of dust and patience turning into momentum and intention.

The library remembered her, too.

A single sparrow of paper spiralled downward toward her. Eli stretched a hand out to meet it, and the bird landed in her open palm. Its edges were singed, the print smudged beyond recognition. And suddenly she understood.

The Coven itself was fighting the Witch Lord. The library was leaving the safe borders of this room, where it had sealed its secrets away from the ambitious and ravenous witch tyrants. Waiting for someone to unlock their magic with love and trust. Someone like Kite.

A wing drooped, the scorch mark spreading like a stain. The rustling continued, a song of mourning and fury. More birds fell, some crumbling to white ash, others ripped and torn and bloody but still struggling to fly. The library was fighting, and the library was dying. For the world. For Kite. For the Heart. For *Eli.*

Eli raised her other hand to her mouth and pressed a yellowed canine to the soft pad of her fingertip. It broke like the skin of an overripe peach and beaded with a substance that was neither wholly human nor witch nor tree, but all together; it was sticky as sap and smelled of lost cardigans and moonlight. *Heartblood.*

Eli sprinkled the blood of the Heart over the paper sparrow. The bird glowed with an inner flame, and then darkness spread across the wings, wet and glossy, and individual feathers were etched onto its surface. It raised its head and chirped. A collective sigh echoed through the space. A drop of Heartblood returning home.

"Thank you for protecting her," said Eli, and she walked into the maelstrom of sharp paper edges and bloody beaks and claws of leather and papyrus and recycled newsprint.

Someone was waiting for her.

For a brief moment, Eli thought it was, impossibly, Kite. She thought somehow the Heartblood and smell of old ink had summoned her, or at least the memory of her, pulled from Eli's mind and dressed in accordion scrolls and embroidery. But as she neared the figure standing in the eye of the paper hurricane, its shape came into the light and Eli recognized it for what it was.

A made-thing.

A daughter.

Someone like Eli.

The girl had eyes like tarnished steel, their surface dull and empty of emotion. She was holding two swords — one was crafted from broken bottles and Phillips-head screws. The glassy brown and green of the smashed bottles glittered dangerously in the soft lighting. The other sword was made from stingers and thousands of dragonfly and wasp wings, shimmering peacock blue and amber and cheery red, cut crystal with dark veins running through the blade like soldered metal framing mosaics of stained glass.

The hunter from her dreams. The assassin who had stood over Eli under a ragged sky, her blade edge aimed at Eli's throat.

"I've been hunting you," she said.

"I know."

Underneath the smell of old paper was the scent of coffee grounds and rust. Eli remembered, then, the deal she had struck with the Hedge-Witch. Three strands of hair and saliva. How had she built a daughter in the City of Ghosts? How long had it taken her to cobble together the materials and magic to make a body strong enough to survive the Vortex?

The assassin had haunted her dreams, had once cornered her in the City of Ghosts. Had followed her across worlds, hidden in the army of daughters in the Labyrinth, and had finally found what she was looking for. Eli should have been impressed at the assassin's ingenuity and tenacity, but instead something closer to pity spilled from the tension in her shoulders.

"You are a good hunter," Eli continued, keeping her voice flat. "That is what you were made for."

"You were hard to track."

"I changed."

"I know."

They stared at each other — the Heart and the hunter. The girl with the empty sheath where a glass dagger once slept, and the brand-new weapon whose sharp edge had not yet tasted death.

Eli tried to imagine herself through the hunter's eyes. A girl with light glowing in her veins and confusion in her eyes. The girl who had no mother, no maker, no one to answer to. The girl who had defied the Coven. What did she look like to this creature — broken, defective, lost?

"You are magnificent," said Eli sadly, letting her eyes trace the black lines of the wingblade, falling to the shadows the screwheads cast over the books lying open between them.

"I am," said the hunter. She took a step forward and her metal eyes caught the glow of the Heart. Eli did not step back, but continued watching the girl's shadow for movement, for the hint of intention. She had not come this far to be killed now. Not like this.

Around them, paper birds tore themselves into confetti and swirled in gusts of knowledge sharp as handfuls of glass. In the eye of the storm, the made-daughters remained untouched.

"She's coming for you," said the hunter. Surprise burst across Eli's eyelids, and spots of light crowded her vision.

"She —?"

"The Witch Lord. She's coming for you. Don't you feel it?" A lizard tongue snaked out of the girl's mouth and smelled the air. "I can smell her."

"The library smells of the Heir," said Eli.

"The one coming smells of revenge as well as the sea."

"How close?"

"Soon."

"Why are you telling me this? Are you afraid she's going to come and steal your quarry from you?"

"Yes." The girl smiled. "And no." She turned her face to the sky for a moment, inhaling tiny pieces of paper, and then turned back to Eli. "I am magnificent, and I'm not going to be used by a witch master. Thank you for slaying my maker. The daughters will be free. The Witch Lord is hunting you, but I am the superior hunter. I came here to watch over you. To fight the Witch Lord if she comes before you finish your task."

Eli swallowed the lump that had formed in her throat. She grasped at words to thank the hunter, her sister, and failed. There was nothing. Instead, Eli closed the space between them and pressed a kiss against the wingblade. The girl allowed it. Eli stepped back.

Calm settled over her body like August dusk.

It was time for the Heart to come home.

THE HEALER

The engine squealed as the bike careened through water, but the magic kept it running. Tav let go of their hold on logic and orienteering (they spent one summer as a preteen at a camp where they learned how to use a map and a compass, but that wouldn't do any good here). They let their intuition guide them. They let the Coven show them the way.

Tav had never realized before how much like the Labyrinth it was — winding passages that changed, walls that lived and breathed and watched. It *was* part of the Labyrinth — or it had been, once, before the Witch Lord had taken a piece of it for herself and kept the rest of the world out with enchantments and violence. Now it was returning to its natural state, the new-built walls of alabaster, bone, and bleach collapsing and leaving smooth earth studded with tiny pink flowers; some passages seemed to be made purely of soapstone etched with drawings made by children long dead, others a tangle of acid-green moss.

The goldpink glow of the Witch Lord's essence wafted through the space. It was easy to follow. Where was she going? What if she got to Eli first? Tav leaned hard on the accelerator and the bike tried to go faster — but even a Kawasaki Vulcan 900 with a drop of witch in it has limits, and bodies can slow us down.

The smell of rotting figs grew stronger.

They were getting closer.

THE HEART

Eli stepped out of the eye and into the storm, her vision immediately obscured by falling paper. The sound of wings flooded her ears. As Eli watched, a few injured paper birds tore at the walls, pecking out the invisible eyes the witches had used to watch them. The eyes had been covered over in papier-mâché, but now they were being torn out by the optic nerves.

"What are you doing?" asked Eli, as soil and rock tumbled down from above. "It will kill you."

The birds rubbed their paper wings together, making a sound like waves moving against the shoreline.

"Stop! I can help you!"

More soil fell, sprinkling Eli's face with dirt. She was sweaty and filthy and her heart was racing in her chest. She had never felt more human.

But her body was still glowing with gold light. Eli drew the pearl blade across her palm, splitting flesh from magic. Golden blood oozed across her hand, and she smeared it roughly across the wall. The blood shimmered for a moment and lit up like a vein of ore before the alabaster and dirt absorbed its power. But the library was still collapsing, even though Eli could see the magic pulsing under the skin.

She turned back to the army of birds. "Take me to the tree," she begged. "I will give the Heart back. The tree can have me. I don't want the Coven to die."

The frost blade trembled at her hip. She had known — had always known — that when the Heart merged with her body that its former host and prison had died.

The tree had never been the Heart's true home. It had never been meant to be trapped in a single body, used as a weapon or a tool.

A small bird landed on her shoulder, folded into the shape of a swallow. Its edges were gold leaf, and it smelled of smoke. It had survived for a very long time. The swallow rubbed its wing against her cheek and then flew to the wall, stabbing at the dirt until its beak was bent and crooked. As the excavation continued, Eli could see flashes of white being exposed to the light.

Under the soil was the spine of the world — the same walls that made up the Labyrinth and the underlabyrinth, the maze of chaos and magic that was alive. It had not been made by the witches, and it did not answer to their rule.

Eli's breath caught in her throat. The birds weren't destroying the Coven, sacrificing their home in order to defeat the Witch Lord — they were taking it back from the witches. They were saving it.

Pearl in one hand, bone in the other. Eli joined them, stabbing at invisible eyes and tearing through spells and enchantments that had made this dark palace a place of power. Setting free the natural magic of the world.

A blur of colour in her peripheral vision, and then the wall shook as another blade pierced the witches' magic. The hunter had joined her, broken bottles and insect wings cutting through malevolent enchantments and cursed thorns.

As more earth was stripped away, pages and letters that had been buried pulled themselves free and joined their kin.

When they were done, the library had been transformed — skeletal and stark, filled with light and colour. It tasted of dead fish and calcified plant life. The magic was not sweet or cloying like the witches' enchantment. It was fresh and alive, deadly and beautiful, pulsing with life and death, love and sorrow.

But the birds were still dying. As Eli watched, a hummingbird trembled midflight and fell to the floor, ink seeping out of its spent body. A hairline crack in the wall was creeping upward. What would happen if the spine itself was destroyed? If the natural magic failed?

Eli was frightened, and this time, she couldn't fight her way out. There was no rush of adrenalin or the power of self-preservation, nothing she could stab or claw or devour with wickedly sharp teeth. She didn't even know how to do it. She felt like a child again, lost in the Labyrinth, not sure what she was running to. Only knowing what she had to leave behind.

A single feather made from the thinnest of sheets of paper, so fine it was translucent, hovered at eye level. Eli held up a hand and it landed on her sticky, bloody palm. A few words were visible, scrawled across the page.

I miss her.

Tears blurred her vision.

The handwriting was Kite's.

Gently, Eli set the feather on the ground, and then knelt down. She pressed her palms against the root of the world and closed her eyes.

She felt the gaze of the hunter on her back. The made-girl was watching over her.

Go home, she told the Heart. *This is where you belong.*

This is where we belong.

We are not a body.

We are many bodies.

We are everywhere.

We are everything.

Eli felt the energy draining from her body, seeping into the walls, the earth, the ink stains. Dissipating into the air. Touching the clouds. Brightening the sky.

In her mind's eye, she saw the leaves of the forest turning bronze and green, shining with new growth. She saw the stones in the wastelands burning with black fire, the rivers spitting sparks and ice onto a desert blooming with sandflowers. The forgotten pit that had been the junkyard was beginning to heal, feeling the rush of remembrance, the nectar of magic, as it, too, was reconnected to the rest of the world.

She saw a glittering, tangled web of connections between everything, saw the lines that had been severed by the witches now begin to be repaired. Everything had a place in the world. Everything belonged.

The Heart tasted the acidic soil of the burned forests and the dry sweetness of sand, felt the pincers of little sea creatures and saw through the eyes of thousands of stones like stars. A sense of rightness filled the Heart as she was finally freed from her cage.

Eli felt the moment her human heart stopped. She heard the silence, the rhythm of breath and blood coming to an end like an orchestra directed to stillness.

She heard the wings of the hunter's blade rubbing against each other, making a rustling sound and then a keening whistle. Her sister was mourning her. Eli wished she had thanked her. She wished a lot of things.

Then there was nothing.

Feathers drifted over her body until Eli was completely buried in a paper tomb.

THE HEALER

The walls trembled.

Snail shells and stray magic fell over Tav and Ariel. Tav wiped sawdust from their face and shook off a scorpion made of glass and aluminum that had fallen on the back of their hand. When they brushed dead leaves off of Ariel, the plants dissolved into sugar and cinnamon.

A thousand insects poured from earth and stone and started waving their antennae and hundred thousand silk-thin legs.

Something had changed.

The goldpink light of the Witch Lord disappeared, overtaken by a kaleidoscope of colours and sensations that flooded Tav's body, the Coven, and maybe the world.

A sense of rightness flared up in every cell. A feeling like being dipped in warm honey coated Tav's body.

Ariel stopped, as if in awe or perhaps in homage to what was happening. The drop of witch essence was glowing like a sun. Tav was bright, too, violet lights dancing along their knuckles and collarbone and the back of their eyelids. They were part of the world. They belonged here. They were home.

A surge of panic flickered through the sticky sweet sensation of connection and belonging.

If the Heart had come home, where was the eggshell of a girl that had kept it safe, had carried it between worlds, and set it free?

What had happened to Eli?

Tav inhaled sharply and turned their intention to Ariel. "We have to find her. Or what's left of her." Their voice shook. "Turn *on*, damn it. We don't have time."

But Ariel was frozen in place, rapturous and dreamy.

Tav jumped off the bike and tried to look through the dancing lights for evidence of Eli — the girl whose ribs they had kissed, whose crocodile teeth they had licked. Eli, with her knives and fists and anger like a beehive.

And then the sky cracked.

Tav stared up into a fractured galaxy. Oxygen stopped. Frost curled over the edges of a cut that had been reopened a thousand times, and now split easily. The fabric of the galaxy had grown thin and fragile.

The transplant of a heart back into its body is no easy thing.

It sent shockwaves across the planet, through its very core, shaking every leaf and stream and gust of air. The power of the Heart infusing the world sent new life into the trees and earthworms and magic creatures hiding under the walls. It pulled on threads that had been left ragged, it made new growth, and sent brush fires racing through the undergrowth of the forests.

It reopened wounds that were still trying to heal.

Tav was pulled into the Vortex, swept away from Ariel, from Eli, from a home they had only just found.

Back to the beginning.

THE HEIR

Kite, one hand wrapped around the neck of a first-ring witch, his lantern-like head flashing like a siren, felt the galaxy crack. The sword trembled of its own accord.

She arched her swanlike neck back, tipping her head to watch the sky open up.

There was no ceiling, no stone, no trees, no clouds. Only empty space, and a few glittering lights — stars or forest fires or birthday candles or the fluorescent lights of a planet that never slept.

Kite let go of the witch. His head floated up, up, up, like a helium balloon, and then vanished, sucked into the vacuum between time and space.

The seam between worlds had come unravelled.

THE HEALER

They were standing on a river of black ice. The river flowed past the outskirts of town, past The Sun, past trees heavy with rich green leaves, their bark dark and glossy as iron.

This was the place where they had first stared into Eli's yellow eyes and felt that kick of desire, that afterbite of guilt, that grassy taste of curiosity.

This was the place they had made their own door, had let the enchanted succulents coax an opening between the City of Ghosts and the City of Eyes. Here the Heart and the boi had broken the laws of physics.

Of course it would take them back here.

Here, to the moment that haunted their dreams.

Just like in the dream, the black sky was slashed with silver and white. The river had frozen over and reflected the sky and the sliver of the moon bearing silent witness. It was night in the City of Ghosts.

There was no logical reason for the ice, but the magic had hardened and turned an August river into a winter nightmare. It was getting easier for Tav to accept these things that defied reason, that broke the rules they had been born into.

In this mirror world it was hard to tell where the City of Ghosts ended and the City of Eyes began. The worlds were coming together at last, a collision more beautiful and destructive than the dying stars who, watching, flickered once, thousands of years away, and went out forever.

Here was the Witch Lord, hiding in the Vortex, in the in-between. Waiting to pick apart a broken boi like an owl with a mouse. The Witch Lord hung suspended between worlds, in a body once more, her essence darting wildly across her finger bones, bluegreen hair spilling out around her head like a halo.

The armies had been scattered like snowflakes: they were stranded on stone and ice, trapped by gravity in the human world, or else watching from the shattered war room as it if were an observatory. Their glimmer and shine made them look like someone had upended a jewelry box onto a length of dark fabric.

The eyes of witches and children and plants and ghosts and objects and humans and assassins glittered like stars, like thousands of fireflies in the night, and Tav couldn't tell ally from enemy. Tav was beginning to suspect that, in the end, there weren't sides, and never had been. Only hope and hurt and longing, and bodies trying to survive in unkind worlds.

Silence, fragile as the mist that wound its way around their feet, pulsed gently in this moment before the end.

There might not be sides, but there was always change; and sometimes there had to be winners and losers; although winning could look an awful lot like losing. Tav knew that. The Witch Lord, raised in the crypt of her own self-importance, taught to treat life like it didn't matter, had tried to make a universe as brutal as her heart and as razor-sharp as her teeth. She did not know that simple truth, had never learned to recognize failure as beauty and power as self-harm. In many ways, she was like a child herself, still waiting for knowledge to deepen into understanding.

Tav stared up at the alien who was also a star who was also family. They knew what they needed to do.

Feeling small, and sad, and human, Tav walked to meet her.

THE HEIR

Kite found herself on a strange shore, the stone rough and quiet under her feet. She looked out over a frozen river that reflected the shattered galaxy overhead, stars like drops of blood on the ice.

There was her mother, the Witch Lord, descending from the heavens like a goddess of vengeance. The moored witches around Kite sighed at her beauty and shrank away from her in fear. They adored and hated her, worshipped and obeyed her. So had Kite, for a long time. But not anymore.

Her eyes slid from the bright star mass that was her mother to the smaller figure on the ice, with torn jeans and messy hair.

Tav.

Kite wasn't the only watcher on the rocky shoreline who saw in the cut of Tav's cheekbones and the fire in their eyes that the human-witch hybrid was just as bright and fierce as the Witch Lord.

THE HEALER

They ran their thumb over the tip of the obsidian dagger. The assassin. Secret death. The black glass that could cut through magic and drain a witch's essence.

Why would a witch give a witch-killer to her made-daughter? Tav hadn't seen any other obsidian weapons in the hands of the daughters in Clytemnestra's makeshift army.

Tav wondered if they should have given Circinae more credit. She really wanted her daughter to survive.

"I challenge you to a duel," said Tav. The words felt right. The only way to dethrone a king was to challenge her in front of her court.

"I accept," said the Witch Lord. She drifted down, landing gently on the ice. Where her feet touched the frosted river, molten gold flowed like cracks, hot and bubbling, and then hardening into thick, shining metallic lines.

Tav felt an itchiness in their shoulder blades. The river was still smooth and clear, but maybe the dream had mixed things up. Maybe the dream offered a shape and missed the details. Time always passed differently in their dreams.

And Eli was gone. Maybe that part of their dream had died with her.

Taking the obsidian blade, Tav reached up and cut two sharp lines in their own shoulder blades.

The pain rocked their body, but it was healing, and felt right. It was the pain of new growth. The pain of necessity. The pain of leaving a childhood friend behind or losing a favourite pair of jeans. It was part of life. It was life.

Two great feathered wings burst from Tav's back. They were black with the oily shine of purple and gold and green. Looking down, Tav saw their reflection in the mirrored surface. Eyes gold and brown with deep shadows underneath. Silver earrings shimmering in the starlight. A mouth set in defiance or grief. Winged like a fallen angel, their feathers catching nightmares and spinning them into strength.

Reaching into their own plumage, Tav plucked a single feather. Its core was steel, and its point sharp as a blade. Dressed in black feathers and buttons shaped like the phases of the moon, holding two knives, Tav faced the Witch Lord.

"What are you?" the Witch Lord asked again, her pupil-less pale eyes shining in the moonlight like lighthouse beacons.

"I don't know," said Tav. But the words felt hollow, like an oak tree sundered by lightning. They were starting to piece together their history and their body and what it all meant.

They had always known they were descended from fighters. Their ancestors had struggled against their captors when they had been forced across a sea of blood and onto a land forged from death, had fought back against the violence they faced in Nova Scotia after slavery was allegedly abolished, had protested the police in Ontario. Tav had been born into struggle, had learned how to resist and survive alongside geometry and the five-part essay. This story was true, and Tav had been telling it their whole life.

The purpleblack smoke that now curled from their nostrils told another story. The story of a witch fleeing the tyranny of the Coven. A witch who fell in love or at least lust with a human. Passion and intimacy breathing dandelion seeds of magic into bile and cartilage.

But that story still didn't explain the wings that now extended from their back. The way doors opened and closed so easily for them, without the kind of sacrifice a witch needed to do her magic.

Tav thought about the ghost who had followed them around, who had treated them as kin.

How had the ghosts come to Earth from the moon?

If any of the moon people had survived, where would they have fled to?

The words rang in Tav's head. *What are you?*

They were histories of forced migration, of leaving homes and making new ones. Of transformation and resilience. They were the harbringers of change.

"No one has ever challenged me before," said the Witch Lord. Curiosity stained her voice. Tav wondered if she got bored in her catacombs of secrecy and surveillance, if a dragon curled up around its hoard of gold ever missed the touch of another creature.

But Tav didn't need answers. They had no more words.

The Witch Lord lunged, drawing Tav into another deadly dance. Tav stepped back, playing defence, avoiding talons and teeth.

The Witch Lord's essence split into a hundred thousand essences, like paint spilling over the ground. It poured from her nostrils and ears and eyes and mouth, gold and silver and copper rivers that reached for Tav, trying to ensnare them in a net of stolen power.

One tendril curled around their ankle and the pain seared like fire. Tav gasped, choking on the panic that took hold of their body. Their wings beat rapidly, pushing back against the Witch Lord. A creature of magic and bone and moonlight struggling against the snares of a predator.

The blades — Tav lashed out at the netting, cutting strips of magic with obsidian and feathered steel. When the net lay scattered in writhing pieces on the ice, Tav turned to the creature before them. Sweat dripped down their face and stained the tattered pieces of their shirt. The tattoos of peonies and roses and chrysanthemums that marked their arm started to move, waving leaves and stamens and petals.

It was time for the game to end.

Another tendril of power wrapped around Tav's waist, and they let it. They breathed through the pain and let the magic drag them closer to the Witch Lord.

"I know what you are," said the Witch Lord, saliva dripping down her chin. "You are nothing."

A small prick. The razor edge of a glossy feather biting into the greenblue essence at the core of the witch. Not the stolen power, not the hues of gold and silver and pink that she had wrenched from other witches. Her own. The essence that matched Kite's.

A look of surprise crossed the Witch Lord's face. They were so unused to pain, to fear, and could not express it. Tav, the greenblue essence pinned in place with a steel feather, raised the obsidian needle and plunged it into the Witch Lord.

A small gasp, like a baby's breath. Kite's eyes stared into Tav's. Tav kept their arms wrapped around the Witch Lord as if in an intimate embrace.

"You smell like peaches," she whispered, eyes bright like moons.

And then the brightness went out.

THE HEIR

Kite watched herself die without emotion, as if she were watching a black-and-white silent film on a screen. She watched as if she were light years away. She watched as if she were already dead.

She was sorry she hadn't gotten to say goodbye to Eli.

The stolen essences in her body shuddered and died, the dead remnants transforming into bits of music. It sounded faintly like Bach. Eli had once brought her a music box that played *Minuet in G* when she turned the handle.

Kite, glad that the dead witches had found peace, felt relief at their absence. Glad that she was free of them. In the end, she would die as herself.

Kite waited for her essence to turn into seashells and sand dollars.

After all, she was only an extra body. Only a part of her mother.

Just a useless clone.

THE HEALER

The Witch Lord's body started to break, a thousand hairline cracks snaking across her body. The china pieces shattered in Tav's arms and turned into dried rosehips, bottle caps, gold dust, and seagull feathers. Her eyes were the last to shatter, the dark orbs smashing on the ice and transforming into a dozen sand bubbler crabs scuttling across the river. Death and life. Endings and beginnings.

Tav hadn't expected to feel this heavy. They picked up a tiny sliver of china that had gotten caught in their hair and contemplated keeping it. Instead, they threw it across the river as if trying to skip a stone.

What happened now?

The constellation of witches and daughters and found things started singing. It was a song of mourning, a way of respecting the dead. But it was also a song of celebration, of newness.

THE HEIR

Kite was alive.

She thought she would die, but she hadn't. Why not? Was it the name she had accepted from a part-human child many years ago? Was it her love for another creature? Was her body truly her own?

The Beast appeared beside her, having chosen to cross the open door to find her. He started licking her face.

"We're free," she told him, wonderingly. She was alive. Her mother was dead. She was no longer the Heir. Joy swam through her bones. When she shook her head in delight, her hair sent pearls and semi-precious gemstones scattering over the rock.

She looked back to the river, where Tav stood over the remains of the Witch Lord. They seemed lost and confused. The children were singing their victory. The victor is rewarded.

Kite and the Beast skipped over the ice to where Tav was waiting.

"You're alive," they said, as Kite approached. Relief and surprise grappling for mastery in their voice. "I thought I killed you."

"She was wrong," said Kite. "I am a person."

"You always were," said Tav. "No one is nothing."

"You won the duel," said Kite, bowing to Tav. The Beast bowed, as well. "I like your wings."

"Thanks." Tav fiddled with the steel-spined feather. "So, what now?" They stared up at the rift in the sky. "What do we do now?"

"I don't know." Kite spun in a circle, leaving seaweed flakes in her wake. "But you might want to greet your people."

"My people?" Tav looked confused. "Which ones?"

Kite laughed. "You defeated the Witch Lord. The throne is yours."

THE WITCH LORD

"What?" Tav's eyes widened.

They turned around and looked at the shoreline dotted with glass and gold and metal and spikes and rust and skin and hair and fur. The remnants of the Witch Lord's court were kneeling, their foreheads pressed to the dirt. Even the floating heads of the first ring of the Coven were bowing to them.

Tav had challenged the Witch Lord and won. The Coven accepted Tav's victory. The only witches not prostrating themselves were the children, who continued to sing and dance.

"I don't want it," they said. "I don't want the throne."

Two figures were walking onto the ice.

"The witches call you their lord," said Clytemnestra.

"We won't answer to you," said the unnamed girl with coyote ears and an eye like a planet.

"I don't want you to," said Tav.

"They would rally around you as a witch king," said Clytemnestra. "They would have you fill the vacuum of power in the City of Eyes. They would have you take control of our world."

Tav turned to address the witches gathered on the shore and raised their voice, wings outstretched to their full length. "The Coven is disbanded. Witches will have to learn to live in the world as equals, not masters. All creatures — made or born — will live free."

Murmurs rose from the shoreline tinged with disbelief and confusion. The children started cheering, and a couple of kids started playing jump rope with the chain of a spiked flail.

A few members of the lower rings rose first, shedding their loyalty to the throne like dead skin. The Witch Lord had not been kind to her own.

Then the upper rings, their numbers diminished from the battle, stood as well. They had been defeated.

"Where will you go?" asked Clytemnestra.

"I'll stay here," said Tav.

"This world is dying," said the unnamed. "You would do better to hide in the forests or open a door to the moon."

"I'm staying here," repeated Tav.

"So am I," said Kite.

"You are no longer the Heir," said the unnamed. "You could return."

Kite reached down and petted the Beast.

"I understand," said the unnamed.

Now that the battle was over, and some had lost, and some had won, and the Heart had been returned, the witches were starting to return to the City of Eyes. In twos and threes, they trickled across the rift like meteorites flashing through the night sky. The unnamed nodded once to Tav, and then left, leading her people back to their home, and to freedom.

"The Children's Lair will be such a mess," said Clytemnestra. "Do you know how hard it is to get tooth marks out of an ivory comb?"

Soon, the sea of glitter and light faded until only Kite and Tav and the Beast remained. Overhead the cracked sky glittered with stars and souls and wishes.

"A Witch Lord in exile." Kite smiled, and brushed a finger along one feather. Tav shivered at her touch. "It suits you."

"Something's missing," they said.

Kite's smile faded. "Eli." She sighed. "I loved her, too."

"Yes. No. Yes." Tav stared up at the rift. "We haven't saved the Earth."

"Not yet," corrected Kite.

"I dreamed —" They cut themselves off, feeling stupid.

"You dreamed?"

"Someone was under the ice."

"Let's look, then."

"It's stupid."

"Is it?" Kite tilted her head, her eyes like two moons. But there was softness in them, and they belonged to only one person. They always had. Kite didn't wait for an answer. She and the Beast started wandering the frozen river, peering through the black glass, looking for any sign of movement.

After a moment, Tav joined them. Something felt unfinished. Something important.

KITE

Kite sensed the wall before she felt it, its soft ridges curving up under the ice.

"What's a piece of the Labyrinth doing in the City of Ghosts?" she asked the Beast, who grew a vestigial wing and started chewing on it.

She called Tav over. "Look," she said, but what she really meant was *feel*.

Tav understood and pressed a hand against the ice. After a moment, Kite placed her palm on top of Tav's and their joint purple-and-green flames lapped at the ice, melting it, making space for the stone and dirt underneath.

The ice cracked, and someone walked out of the river.

THE WITCH LORD

It wasn't like the dream, not exactly. There were no spears of obsidian stabbing the sky; no earthquakes knocking Tav to their knees. The river didn't tear itself in two, although the split sky was reflected in the ice and made it appear just as shattered and broken.

Watching Cam emerge from under the river was like a bird hatching from an egg, the webbing of cracks spreading inch by inch. Cam climbed out of the frozen darkness, emerging from a staircase of limestone and frost. Part of the Labyrinth had crossed between worlds, had wound its way under the river that stretched black and bright under a star-studded sky.

Pieces of ice clung to his hair, which was getting long — *I'll have to cut it for him when this is all over*, Tav thought vaguely. The pair of scissors in the bathroom drawer.

His body was covered in stone, or it *was* stone — gleaming anthracite arched along his cheekbones, mica dust brightening his eyelids. Playful chips of jasper danced against fragments of agate on his wrists. His chest was mottled granite and rhyolite seamlessly embedded in skin and bone. His shirt was gone, shredded by rock, and Tav could make out the curve of his ribs in granite like a fossil. He looked thin. He looked like he belonged in the earth.

In his arms hung a limp figure, her arms and legs hanging at impossible angles. Fragments of quartz glittered where it had broken through skin. Bangs sticking with sweat to a pale forehead. Long arched teeth protruding from a human mouth. Dried blood under her nostrils.

"Give her to me." Tav's voice broke with exhaustion.

They watched the dream unfurl from their memory and onto the ice, the black feathers tipped in red scattered around their feet. The unnatural stillness in the air, the smell of overripe plums. Red and orange streaks like dying fires lighting up the steel-grey storm clouds.

Cam stopped and stared at Tav, at the long wings extending from their shoulder blades. Hawthorn curled from Eli's fingernails and wound around her wrists, torso, ankles, tangled with the stone body that had once been Tav's best and sometimes only friend.

Tav pulled another feather from her wing, its tip sharp as death.

"This ends now," they said. "You can't have her."

The voice of the Labyrinth poured through Cam's body like an echo in a cave deep underground.

"We have waited a long time to be remembered," said the Labyrinth. "The witches forgot our language and kept the sacrifices for themselves. They thought they could chain us, but now we are free."

Tav's grip tightened on the steel feather. The taste of metal in their mouth. "I said, give her to me."

The Labyrinth's human body knelt down, the stones ringing out in a chorus of bells. He gently laid the girl on the ice. His eyes found Tav's, and this time when the creature spoke, they could hear the timbre of Cam's voice tossed with gravel and smooth round stones clattering over a pebbled beach. "Tav, we found her body. We healed her."

Tav hesitated; in the dream, his eyes had burned amber and the ground had shaken under their feet with tremors. Nothing from the City of Eyes could be trusted. Tav wanted to trust him. Tav didn't want to be stupid. Didn't want to hope. Felt hope rising like heat from asphalt.

"We healed her, Tav. We tried. But it wasn't enough."

"You came here to destroy us," they said. "To get revenge for how the witches treated you."

The stones sang in mourning, and a flash of pain flickered across his face. "We don't want revenge. Tav, I've been speaking with the walls, living with the walls, for years."

"And they taught you their anger, and they sent you to kill me." Furious tears burned in their eyes. They could face down the Witch Lord, they could watch themselves and their loved ones bleed and break. But to see Cam turn against them? "We let them take you," they confessed, forcing the words out with a heavy tongue. "It was our fault. It was my fault. I'm sorry. I should have come after you. I should have saved you."

"Thank you," said Cam. "You know I don't love being left behind."

"Cam —"

"It's okay." A wry smile, a spark of light in his eyes. "You can be a dick when you're in love. Work on it, okay?" He nodded at the prone body before him. "Are you going to help her or not? Thought you were the Healer."

"Now they're the Witch Lord," Kite added helpfully.

Suddenly Tav understood. They understood that although trauma was real, it could also lie to you, that fear could colour the edges of your world in darkness. Sometimes nightmares were just nightmares. Sometimes the people who love us don't hurt us. Sometimes our made-families deserve our trust.

Tav realized that they had never admitted how scared they were.

Not when the bottle was smashed over their bike.

Not when the ghost killed the two boys from their school.

Not when they met the gaze of the Witch Lord for the very first time.

But it was okay to be scared. It wasn't a weakness, and Tav let the feeling flow through them and then dissipate into the air, until there was only the stars and the feathers and the familiar face before them.

"I missed you," they said.

"I've been busy," he told them.

"Tell me over drinks sometime."

"I promise."

Kite flowed forward and placed a hand on his torso. "You get more interesting every time I see you," she said.

"I missed you, too, Kite."

Kite glowed.

Dropping the feather dagger, Tav stepped forward and knelt beside the made-girl. "She's breathing," they whispered.

"I told you." Cam gathered his long hair into a pony-tail. "Just because I was pissed at you didn't mean I was going to kill you. The Labyrinth took care of the children for generations. All we wanted was to be heard and loved and remembered."

"The quartz —" Tav traced the lines of new stone that stretched across ribs and calves. They looked up. "You healed her."

"I told you that already." Behind him, the small chasm was slowly closing, the ice moving as if unfrozen, purpleblack glass smoothing out into a perfect mirror.

The obsidian blade trembled in Tav's hand and made a keening sound like the singing stones of Cam's hybrid body.

The body had been healed, but something else was needed to animate the spirit of a girl made from thorns and glass and pearl.

"I don't know what to do," said Tav, frustrated. "She's not injured."

"She needs blood," said Kite. "Lifeblood will wake her."

It was a mark of how strange their life had become that Tav didn't question Kite. And part of them remembered finding Kite pressed into the wall like a fossil — and how Eli had cut her own hand, had fed her own blood to the witch, to wake her and give her strength.

Tav held the blade to their palm and pressed it against the skin, closing their eyes and willing the blade to cut. Blood beaded along a thin red line, and some of it was oxidized red, and other droplets were inky purpleback.

"How do I —?"

Kite flowed forward, resting Eli's head against her distressed skirts. Gently, she coaxed Eli's mouth open.

"That's a good girl," she whispered. "Take your medicine."

Tav held her hand over Eli's open mouth and watched as a single drop of redblack witch-human-lunar blood dripped into her throat. They expected Eli to choke or spit it out, but she only swallowed and then sighed, a sound like a cloud losing itself to snow.

Tav, Eli, and Cam watched the sleeping girl. One, two, three breaths; a gust of summer air ruffled Tav's hair and they felt the ice beginning to melt. The season was reclaiming the land. Soon everything would be brown and dead and dry, and the cicadas would shriek. Already the fireflies were coming back, burning the night like children's sparklers.

Somewhere in the city, people were dancing. Someone was falling in love. Someone was falling out of it. A child pulled a slip from a clothesline and drew it around her shoulders like a cape. Two boys had climbed onto the roof of their school to stargaze but were kissing instead and didn't notice the rift in the sky. A young woman, sitting on a deck that smelled of cigarette smoke and cheap whiskey, looked up into the fractured cosmos and decided to quit law school and become a painter.

An eternity passed in three heartbeats.

Eli's eyes opened.

ELI

She hadn't minded dying.

She hadn't minded being buried. The weight of all those books on her body had been soothing, the pages soft against her skin. Eli had read fragments of diaries and letters as the Heartblood drained from her body, as the light left her veins and returned to the mantle of its origin.

Then there had been only darkness.

But in the darkness the Labyrinth had found her, had repaired her broken body. It had come to her in the fretful dreams of a dying person, and its voice had sounded like Cam's. Its touch felt like a stone dagger returning to its sheath.

Somehow, her mortal body had been revived. She had freed the Heart and survived.

Images slowly came into focus, faces and colours and lights.

Where was she?

Why was Kite crying tears of seaglass over her face?

Why did her tongue taste of blackberries?

The first thing she noticed was that she couldn't see Kite's essence. She switched eyes, letting blackness spill over her irises. Swirls of bluegreen rippled through Kite's body. Then she switched back. It was nice, not having to see and feel everything all the time.

The second thing she noticed was the wound between worlds watching her like a lidless eye.

Eli inhaled sharply, and the ice in the air stabbed at her lungs. Her fingers and toes were thawing out, and the joints ached as they warmed. Her body felt more tangible and heavy and vulnerable since fusing with the Heart.

"You're alive, oh my god, you're alive," someone was repeating over and over like a mantra.

"We have to close it," Eli said. "We can't leave it like this."

Someone kissed her palm. Eli sat up, and a headache split across her forehead. "Fuck."

"You almost died." Tav's tenor captured her attention. "You asshole."

"I guess we're all tougher than we look." Eli twisted to look at Cam. "Welcome back."

"You, too."

"I like what you've done to your face."

"You could use a bit of gardening."

Eli laughed.

The knives at her waist laughed with her.

It was good to be back.

She pulled herself up, Kite and Tav hovering around her in case she might fall. But she was back, and her body was no longer going to vanish or tear itself apart.

"I hear you're the Witch Lord now," she said.

"The walls are a gossip." Tav frowned at Cam, who shrugged.

"Can we stop this?" Kite gestured at the broken sky.

"I don't know. But I'm going to try." Eli pulled the pearl blade from its sheath and tossed it in the air. She caught it by the hilt. It wasn't hard — after all, it was a part of her. She grinned.

"We don't have the Heart," she added, "but we have the wall. A witch. A made-thing. And Tav. That's got to count for something." She offered the hilt to Tav. "Do you want me to swear an oath of fealty?"

"Fuck off." Tav pushed it away.

"Just as well. I don't think I'd be a very good knight." But she didn't sheath it, and instead drew a second blade: the bone blade that remembered her name, dreams, regrets. That remembered the taste of sunlight and honey and burning flesh from its time as the Heart.

The bone blade remembered everything.

THE WITCH LORD

Eli's eyes were bright with excitement, and her movements were filled with energy — almost manic.

"Maybe you should rest," they said.

Eli laughed again. Then she threw her head back and howled at the moon. "Close the door, Tav. Make us a key and turn the lock before the City of Ghosts falls into the sky, before the allium fields are burned with ice, before the moon loses its orbit and is cast out into the void."

"I don't want to risk you," said Tav quietly. "I almost lost you. I can do it on my own." They hoped that was true.

Eli caught their look and held it. "No," she said. "We're not doing that anymore."

"Eli —"

"I love you, and you scare the shit out of me, and I'm not used to relying on other people. But I will if you will. Even baby Witch Lords need help, right?"

Tav's heart shuddered, and an electrical current ran through their entire body, up and down the length of their spine. Dozens of feathers fell from their wings.

"I-I love you, too."

"I'll take that as a yes." Another smile, the curve of a reptilian tooth lengthening from pink gums. God, she was hot.

"Witch Lord in exile," added Kite. Her hair was undulating gently, its shades flowing from pale green to rich turquoise and back again. She didn't seem jealous.

Tav took Eli's hand in theirs, raised it to their lips, and brushed a kiss against her knuckles.

"Okay," they said. "We need to heal the rift. If anyone wants to help, they can, but they don't have to. It's not too late to cross," they added pointedly at Kite. "The City of Eyes is healing."

"This is where my family is," said Kite softly. Cam's stones crooned in harmony with her dulcet tones.

"Me, too," said Cam.

Eli nodded.

Tav looked up at the rift: the frayed edges, the fabric of the universe coming unravelled. The rip slowly spreading like a run in a stocking, until there would be nothing between the Earth and the alien planet that had been feeding on its energy for years. The Witch Lord was gone, but the harm had been done. Momentum carried her project forward, draining the life from a little blue planet.

This was what Tav had promised to do, when they had thirsted for the Heart that burned under Eli's skin. When they were huddled in the dark in the Children's Lair dreaming of power and strength. They had promised to heal the wound.

They looked at their companions. Only Cam had been born here. The other two had chosen to come. All of them had been changed in the past few weeks. They had risked death, and still, they would risk it again. They had saved one home, and now they would save another.

Maybe that's what being born from diaspora meant — having not one home but many, having many places and people to fight for. (It meant other things, too — pain, loss, guilt, and a sense of being unrooted. But now Tav had wings and was a feathered tree.) Maybe it meant understanding that nations and borders and divisions of human/not-human were meaningless. That some lines needed to be crossed. That some lines needed to be eroded by wind and sand and intention.

Healing the wound didn't have to mean locking the door. It didn't have to mean another line they couldn't cross. Doors could open both ways. Healing the rift didn't mean an ending, but a change. It meant a new kind of relationship. Maybe one based on care and love.

Maybe a Witch Lord in exile who was also human and had moonlight in their eyes could bring the worlds together in a way that didn't hurt. After all, worlds can meet like lovers. (Lovers meet like worlds.)

The obsidian blade was warm in their hand. They felt the sharp, sweet burn of Eli's magic whisper through their body. She was with them. She was always with them.

A delicate thread of bluegreen algae inched toward Tav over the ice, hesitating near her feet. Kite was waiting, probably wondering if Tav would flinch away from an essence that had done so much damage. But it felt right that she was here to see this end. Tav pushed her own purpleblack flames toward the algae, and when their essences touched, nothing burned. No one was struck by lightning. There was no pain — only pleasure. Tav wondered if Kite was having the same thoughts they were — if she, too, felt the energy that passed between them. If she, too, longed to feel their bodies pressed together.

The stones began singing, and the Labyrinth joined them. Slowly, Cam drew a circle around them in the ice, etched with a sharp piece of granite. It seemed like he had done it before.

Rituals have power.

Kite joined the song, her voice wavering like a sea wind teasing a sail. She followed the line he had cut in the surface with her sword, a metal monster with elegant curlicues and geometric shapes and gears.

Eli traced the circle with the bone blade.

Now it was their turn. Tav took the obsidian blade in one hand, and a feather in the other. They carved the line deeper with the black glass, and they brushed the soft feather along the smooth cut.

Four bodies stood in the centre of a magical circle.

They were human, witch, moon, animal, and stone. They were made of blood, sediment, glass, sea salt, steel. They were smoke and feathers, hawthorn and ocean, they were hundreds of pasts and even more futures. A small light glowed under the ice, and Tav recognized it as the fire dancing in their eyes.

Hope.

This time, there was no pain. There were no mechanical monsters animated by mutilated witches trying to tear them apart. Tav reached up into the darkness and let their mind and magic touch the ruined edges of the rift, soothing the fever and infection with each touch. A sound joined their chorus, and it came from all around them.

The stars were singing.

As they watched, and whispered to the wound, and drew on the shared power of the circle, the rift began to close. The edges brightened, the frayed tips stretching into tapestries of dark and light, asteroids and comets, and the idea of planets that had not yet been born.

Standing on a river of ice in an August heat wave, ringed by the people they trusted most in the world, Tav healed the wound between worlds. And they didn't just close it; they made it a door that would open both ways, but only when it was asked nicely. Silver and purple glitter fell from the sky like rain, magic dust from another world. Sharing light and heat and enchantment with the blue-and-white planet.

It fell over Tav's upturned face, kissing their cheeks and forehead. It fell over Eli's blades and sparkled along their sharp edges. It fell over Kite and her sword, making them shine like diamonds. It fell over Cam like a hand stroking his hair and shoulders and lower back.

(It fell over the bodies of the two boys kissing on a rooftop, and there would be glitter in their clothes for weeks after, evidence of the perfect night they spent together. It fell over the woman on the deck putting out a cigarette on the plastic siding of the house. She made her hands into cups and reached up to catch the silver as it fell. It fell over the child spinning in dizzying circles, wearing their mother's silk slip as a cape.)

The dust rained down over the world, and for a moment, everything was beautiful.

KITE

Morning sunlight poured from a single, steady star. The river had thawed, and its glassy silverblue water skipped and jumped over driftwood and rusted bicycle frames.

Kite stood on one of the flat rocks by the river and marvelled at the way the sun-warmed stone felt under her bare feet. It was a different kind of magic than the island, but it still felt like magic.

She had escaped.

As children, Kite and Eli had made many plans to escape. They had talked about running away to the City of Ghosts — Grace, Tav had called the human town, although the name didn't fit.

They had planned a life of running and hiding from the Coven.

But now the Coven was destroyed, reclaimed by the twisting maze of ancient rock, its knowledge partially destroyed and the rest freed. The Heart was free. The daughters and discarded objects had come home.

The Witch Lord was dead, and Kite was alive.

She searched through her encyclopaedia of knowledge and history for something that would describe how she was feeling. And there it was, slipped between the pages of a vegan cookbook and a list of fears that had been set adrift in the sea on a paper boat.

Miracle.

It was a miracle.

ELI

The August heat pressed down on Eli and sweat beaded on her forehead and gathered under her breasts. She watched Kite watch the water. The smell of saltwater brushed against her senses and she was taken back to her childhood, to their time on the island together, to the taste of salty blood in her mouth.

Tav and Cam had gone looking for coffee and pastries.

"We're going to have to find a new café," Cam had lamented, after they had told him about the Hedge-Witch.

Kite looked happier than Eli had ever seen her.

Eli's mind flashed to an image of Kite on a throne made of half-rotted fish and wire nets. She flinched and looked away, trying to blot out the memory with something, anything, else. When she turned back, Kite was still standing there, hair and arms limp. She had turned away from the river and was watching Eli.

Eli suddenly wished she could disappear.

But her body couldn't do that anymore.

"I won't touch you," said Kite softly, her voice distorted slightly, vocal cords still swimming in water.

She's more water than flesh, Eli thought.

Kite sighed slightly, and water dribbled out of her mouth. *She could be the river you lie in*, thought Eli. Unbidden, the feeling of branches breaking returned, and she clutched her chest, panicking.

"We're okay," she told herself. "We're okay."

No one answered her.

Being alone in her body again would take some getting used to.

The human heartbeat in her chest reminded her that she was wildly, ridiculously, incredibly alive. The idea that she was safe, that no one was hunting her, was so unfamiliar that laughter bubbled up in her throat like champagne and overflowed.

Kite waited.

She's always waiting for you, Eli thought. *You thought it was* you, *waiting on her — but you left, again and again. And she waited in the library, in the Coven, hoping you would return.*

Did Kite experience worry? Loss? Had she missed her?

"We are the same," said Kite. "Same magic, materials, everything. That's what being trueborn means. She took a piece of her essence to make me."

"You're not the same," said Eli, feeling in her entire body that this was the truth.

"You can't even look at me." Kite's voice was cool and distant. But Eli caught the scent of rotting jetsam and understood that even witches could fear losing someone they loved.

"I've been looking at you since I was made," said Eli quietly.

"But now you see her. You see the Witch Lord."

"She's gone." Eli wanted the truth to heal her, but the wound continued to bleed.

A tremor across Kite's lips, like a bird taking flight from her mouth. Trying to smile, or to hold a smile inside? Eli had no way of knowing. She had been so close to Kite for so long, and then had turned away from her — she had never really seen her for what she was. A girl trying to be free, in her own way.

The silence stretched between them like a shadow, both connecting them and keeping them apart.

Kite swallowed, and Eli was struck by the strangeness of the sound. Witches spat their feelings and words into the world, they didn't hold on to their grief, hurt, fury. But Kite wasn't like the other witches Eli had known. "She's not gone in my dreams," whispered Kite.

Eli suddenly understood. Dreams in the human world wouldn't come to life, wouldn't bury you in sand or tear out your throat. But they still did damage.

She crossed the distance between them in a few steps. She placed a hand on Kite's cold, clammy face. "We'll fight her together, always."

"I smell like her."

Eli kissed her, slipping her tongue into Kite's mouth. Salty and sweet, and something else — something familiar. Something like home.

Eli pulled back and pressed her lips to Kite's ear. "You taste like *you*."

In the distance, she heard car tires on gravel. Tav had been sad that Ariel decided to stay in the City of Ghosts, but Cam had a ride handy as always. The lilting voices of their easy banter washed over Eli as she held Kite close to her body.

A honeybee buzzed around their heads, once, and a handful of purple flower petals swirled around them.

Finally, they were all together, and that made this corner of the universe home.

Epilogue: Homemakers

It was midnight in Grace, Ontario — which Tav would always think of as the City of Ghosts. After the adrenalin and magic of the last few weeks, Tav's body was finally settling back into a circadian rhythm, their humanity welcoming the turning of day into night, the endless dance of the moon and Earth and sun.

The streets were abandoned, and the main square was lit up by only a few flickering streetlights — which was good, since what they were doing was illegal.

As Tav watched, Eli pressed the tip of the blade into the dry soil of an empty flowerbed and waited for the rosebush to bloom, the spiny briars stretching up to the sky. Even magical plants needed to photosynthesize.

When it was done, she sheathed the thorn knife, and reached up to break off a small, delicate rosebud.

She looked up and met Tav's gaze, and a current ran between them. The blade in Tav's palm warmed against their skin. Eli smiled, and her reptilian eyes shone like two suns. She walked over to them and offered the rose.

"For you," she said softly.

"Thank you." They pressed their forehead against Eli's.

"Working hard, I see," said Cam, leaning against a lamppost. He had opted not to wear the glamour Kite had made for him tonight, claiming it was itchy and that no one was going to be around, anyway. He looked rakish and regal under the fluorescent lighting, blue agate shimmering across his shoulder blades.

Eli laughed and shifted slightly to look at him. "Is lookout duty so tiring? Do you need a break?"

"Nah, I'm tough." He tapped his knuckles against a stone torso. "And stylish, of course."

"Very cool," agreed Tav. "You're a punk rocker."

"I live for sex, drugs, and rock 'n' roll."

"One out of three's not too bad."

"Hey, I do just fine with the boys!"

Their laughter intertwined with a lullaby in a minor key, sung by a voice that heralded the arrival of starfish and electric eels. The sounds played across the night air, soothing Tav's anxious body. It would take a long time to learn to unwind the spool of tension in their body. Maybe one day they would untangle those knots. Or they would learn to live with them, and work around them.

"Will you ever go back?" Cam asked Kite. She was drawing intricate designs on the sidewalk with the moon sword. It seemed to have adopted her.

"I don't know," said Kite. "There is so much to learn here." Her gaze flicked to Eli, her smile so bright it could catch fire.

Kite would go where Eli went. They were together now. They always would be.

"I'll teach you how to make the best pour-over coffee in the country," Cam promised.

Kite turned back to him, her expression grave. "Thank you, Cam. I would appreciate that." The Beast wagged his tail, wings folded delicately on his back.

Tav reluctantly disentangled themselves from Eli and made a few more lines with the obsidian blade, following the pattern Kite had taught them. They were learning ritual magic, circles, and other small enchantments.

Cam drummed his fingers against the cement, feigning boredom. "Doesn't the Witch Lord have more important things to do than defacing public property?"

"Witch Lord in exile," Tav corrected him. "And it's an empty title now that the monarchy has been disbanded, the Heart has been freed, and the Coven is empty."

"It's not empty," said Kite dreamily. "The Coven welcomes all who love knowledge." She sighed. "One day we will excavate the library from the soil where it is buried."

"One day," agreed Eli. "I know you miss it."

"There will be trouble." Kite's lilting voice whispered of harmony even as she spoke of unrest. "Not all the witches are pleased that you took the power of the Heart away from them and that their rule has ended. Clytemnestra and the children are reckless. You may be needed to keep the peace. You can't stay here forever."

"I know." Tav extended one arm and gently tugged aside space and time, showing their companions. A glint of bone-white marble peeked through the door. Then Tav closed it, carefully sewing the seams shut.

"Show-off," muttered Cam.

Kite had gone back to crooning as she etched designs onto the ground.

"You think this will really keep the protesters safe?" asked Eli.

"It should." Tav frowned again.

"It will," said Kite. "The magic will hold."

"What if they go outside the lines?"

"We can only do so much." Tav shrugged helplessly. "I was at the meeting. Black Lives Matter is holding a rally here tomorrow afternoon. We don't have the power to cast protective spells over the whole city, so this will have to be enough if the police get involved."

"It's good," said Cam, getting serious. "It will help, Tav."

"And I'll be there, too," they said. "If things get out of hand. I can still heal."

"Yes, we know you're a superstar." Cam rolled his eyes, but couldn't disguise the pride in his voice. "Want to finish this before sunrise? I'd rather not get arrested tonight if it's all the same to you."

Tav's lips twitched into a smile, and they finished the design wordlessly, the only noise the scrape of obsidian on concrete. Then they stepped back to survey their work.

Outside the protective circle, the ghost was watching. It couldn't cross the wards. Tav had seen it approach when they started. No one else had sensed it, not even Eli. Tav wondered if some of Eli's own magic had been lost when she returned the Heart to its home. They hadn't said anything about it. They just enjoyed the feeling of her body against theirs.

Tav raised their head and met the ghost's gaze. They stared at each other for a long time — the monster who had suffered the loss of his home and family and had lived for generations taking revenge on anyone who crossed his path. And another kind of monster, a witch-human hybrid who had finally killed the witch responsible for the ghost's pain. Who still had battles to fight.

Now Tav knew why he had followed them, protected them, fought with them. They were family. For the first time, Tav could see the faint outline of wings extending from his back, a memory of flight. Tav's own wings had moulted a few days after the duel with the Witch Lord, but they could feel them under their skin, ready to be set free again.

Tav nodded, once, acknowledging the ghost's presence. The hint of a smile played at the corners of his mouth, and then he vanished. Tav had a sense that this time, he was gone for good. They hoped he had found peace.

They turned back to their companions, to their best friend with a waxed moustache and a ponytail that suited him really well. To their lover with crocodile eyes who used blades to coax roses out of the earth. Who knew Eli would be such a romantic? The other night she had surprised them with a bouquet of allium flowers and asked if they could go back to the purple fields together. Tav had said yes and tried not to cry.

Their eyes fell on Kite. They knew Eli wanted to take Kite to the fields with them. Tav wanted that, too, but it would take time. They hadn't known Kite as long and were only beginning to learn her silence and song, to speak the language of her hair. So they flirted and brought her zebra mussel shells and handfuls of pink salt, and listened to her tell stories about a civilization on the moon. They were excited to see where that would go. In the meantime, Eli and Kite spent time alone together, climbing buildings to watch the stars and tell each other myths and taste each other. Tav didn't mind. They felt loved.

The apartment was a little crowded, but they were making it work.

Tav turned back to the spells etched into the pavement. Tomorrow was important. They had told their mother about the rally, and she said she was already going. She seemed relieved to have heard from them.

They spun the blade in their hand and grinned.

Tav wasn't done changing the world. They were going to build a new one, brick by brick.

The Feels

Thank you to the Dundurn team, who gave love and attention to this book during an incredibly difficult time. I wrote and edited *The Boi of Feather and Steel* in my pyjamas, often in bed, struggling with depression and anxiety during a global pandemic. I would not have been able to finish Tav and Eli's story without the thoughtful feedback from my editor, Shannon Whibbs. (P.S. I think we can all agree that the cover is gorgeous, and that Sophie Paas-Lang is a genius designer.)

Thank you to my mother for reading to me when I was a kid, for giving me so many stories about girls having magical adventures, and for buying too many copies of my first book.

Thank you to my stepdad, Walt, for helping me pick out Tav's motorcycle and teaching me the difference between a cruiser and a crotch rocket.

Thank you to every person who uses my correct pronouns.

Thank you to Élise Lapalme for answering my panicked questions about hot queer femme sex.

Thank you to my heart and home, Rida Abu Rass. I want to hold your hand forever.

يتايح رون

Thank you to every person who wore a mask, social distanced, and quarantined this year. You saved lives.

The Facts

Black Lives Matter was founded in 2013 by Alicia Garza, Patrisse Cullors, and Opal Tometi in response to the police murder of Trayvon Martin. BLM activists work to dismantle white supremacy through advocacy, action, protest, collective care, and raising awareness of systemic racism. Violence against Black bodies is very real in the United States and Canada. Non-Black queers: we need to stand up and support our Black family. Learn more and donate at blacklivesmatter.com (United States) or blacklivesmatter.ca (Canada). Recommended reading: *The Skin We're In: A Year of Black Resistance and Power* by Desmond Cole and *Policing Black Lives: State Violence in Canada from Slavery to the Present* by Robyn Maynard.

Finally, I want to write a bit about what it means to be a Canadian author living and writing in Canada. I grew up in Kingston, Ontario, on the traditional lands of the Haudenosaunee and Anishinaabe peoples, sixty-five kilometres from Tyendinaga Mohawk Territory. As a Canadian author, it's important to recognize the Indigenous peoples living on the land they have always cared for, and to respect the rights and sovereignty of these nations. I did not write about Indigenous struggles in my book, but I encourage all readers — especially those in Canada — to think and learn more about our relationship to each other and to the land, and to support Indigenous girls, women, and Two-Spirit people. There are so many incredible books written by Indigenous authors telling their stories, so definitely add some to your reading list! Recommended reading: *A Mind Spread Out on the Ground* by Alicia Elliott and *As We Have Always Done: Indigenous Freedom Through Radical Resistance* by Leanne Betasamosake Simpson.

Adan Jerreat-Poole lives with chronic pain, depression, anxiety, and feminism. When they aren't reading or writing, Adan likes to crochet, play video games, and do jigsaw puzzles. They have a Ph.D. in cultural studies and work at the intersections of disability justice and digital media. Adan lives in Kingston, Onatario, with their forever partner, Rida, and their two cats, Dragon and Malfouf.